Lunch with the Do-Nothings at the Tammy Dinette

interlude ✦ press • new york

*Dedicated to Southern women of a certain age,
be you belles in heels or hell on wheels.
I'd name names, but my mama raised me better than that.*

SPECIAL TODAY

Prologue

MARCUS SUMTER HAD ALWAYS BEEN good at reading the signs.

With a mother like his, he'd had no other choice.

For as long as he could remember, usually in early summer, his mother would throw all of their belongings into the bed of her old, red Chevy pickup truck, strap him into the passenger's seat, and give him the usual spiel.

"Baby, it's time to move on."

They would pull into the parking lot of the last diner where she had been waitressing, and Marcus would wait in the truck and reread his book about sailors that he'd stolen from the library in some town he couldn't remember. He liked the stories about life on the high seas and the pictures of the handsome men in tight white pants. While he read, his mother would tell the owner to "shove it" after picking up her last paycheck. She never turned in her uniform or name tag. She'd need those again.

"Now, Mama's going to drive, and you're my co-pilot, my navigator. You have the very important job of reading the signs that tell us where to go. And watch for cops. Lord, the last thing Mama needs is to meet another cop."

"What about a map? In my book, the navigator reads the maps. Or are we going to follow the stars the way pirates did?"

"Oh, sweetie, we don't need a map. All we need is a sense of adventure and a desire to go. And we don't need stars neither. The good people of Georgia done put signs all over the place to tell us how to get there. Now, what'll it be this time? North or south?"

"South, Mama. Let's try south."

First, it was literal signs. *Stop. Speed Limit 65. Rest Area 1 Mile Ahead.* And the most important sign: *Waffle Barn Next Exit.* That sign meant employment for his mother and possibly getting off the road for a year or so for Marcus. Luckily, Georgia seemed to have at least one Waffle Barn at every exit, so opportunities were limitless. It was just a matter of deciding which town to try next.

"Look, Baby! Buena Vista! Ooh, that sounds pretty. Let's try there."

Marcus had quickly learned the towns were never as pretty as their names suggested, but at each city limit sign he would hold his breath. Maybe this would be the town where they would park the truck and finally stop and stay. His mother would find a cheap apartment, get a job at the diner, and register Marcus in the local school. Since tip money didn't allow for after-school babysitters, the diner became Marcus's second home as he sat on a stool at the counter with his heels swinging several inches above the footrest and watched his mother weave her way between the booths and tables with a large tray of waffles and coffee balanced on her shoulder. When they would drag into the apartment after a long shift, his weary mother would slip off her shoes and her smile, collapse in a chair, and talk about what a "sonofabitch" the day had been, but while she was working, his mother seemed to Marcus the picture of grace as she flitted from table to table, flirted with customers, sang along to the jukebox, laughed as she called orders back to the cook, and never once dropped a plate or her smile. He learned all the words and rhythms of the same old songs that played on every jukebox in every joint. Tammy Wynette,

Patsy Cline, and Loretta Lynn became wise older aunts who would give him advice while he did his homework sitting on a stool at the counter or would sing him to sleep as he curled up in a booth in the back corner.

He learned the rhythms of the diner crowds also—old people taking advantage of the early-bird specials in the evening, horny teenagers on cheap dates in the early night, and drunks and cops watching each other warily in the wee hours. As he grew older and his feet no longer dangled above the footrests on the stools, he began to hop from the stool and wander to the grill behind the counter. He learned to make the greasiest of food when a few of the short-order cooks would bring him into the kitchen and teach him their skills in a misguided attempt to impress his mother. By the time he was eighteen, Marcus could flip an omelet as easily as other boys his age could swing a bat. While they learned useless things like algebra and history, Marcus learned the signs of the exact moment to remove bacon from the griddle before it burned or when a steak was in that delicate stage between medium and medium well.

With age, he began to be good at reading his mother's signs too. Just as he knew that Tammy Wynette would stand by her man, he knew his mother would continue her search to find *her* man. First, she would flirt with the policemen who sat at the counter in every town.

"Baby, Mama is going out with that nice officer from the diner tonight."

Marcus never learned their names. He wasn't sure his mother bothered to learn them. When she had worked her way through every unmarried (and a couple married) men on the force, she would move on to whatever greasy man was working the grill during the day shift. "Baby, you're going to stay with the nice old lady next door tonight. Whatshisface from the diner is taking Mama out dancing tonight."

When she grew bored with him or he grew rough with her, her drinking would start again.

"Baby, run down to the jiffy store and get mama some Marlboros and a two-liter of coke. I need something to mix this bourbon with."

A few days later, she'd call weakly to him from her bed.

"Baby, call the nice man up at the diner and tell him your mama ain't feeling too good. I can't be slinging eggs when I'm feeling like this."

Marcus would make the call, bring his mother another drink, and then begin silently packing his things into his duffel bag. He knew what would come in the next few days.

"Baby, it's time to move on."

This pattern continued until the summer after his eighteenth birthday when they had piled into the truck and Marcus had chosen "north." As they sped up Interstate 75 toward Atlanta, exit after exit passed. His mother had been unusually quiet and showed no signs of stopping. With each exit Marcus would point out, she'd just shake her head and grunt, "No, Baby. That town don't sound right."

Halfway through the city of Atlanta, she had pointed out a Waffle Barn sign, flipped the turn signal, and began pulling off at an exit.

"Ooh, Cheshire Bridge Road. That sounds lovely. Kind of queen-of-England sounding, ain't it?"

"Whatever, Mama."

"I'm going to pull into the diner and go see about a job. You run over to that gas station and get Mama some smokes." She shoved a wad of bills into his hand and eased the truck into the parking lot.

Marcus hopped out of the truck and ambled over to the store. After grabbing a pack of Big Red chewing gum for himself and asking the man behind the counter for the pack of cigarettes, he pulled the wad of bills out of his pocket and noticed it was five or six one hundred -dollar bills. "Oh, shit." Leaving the cigarettes and gum behind, he ran back down the sidewalk toward the diner. He stopped abruptly when he noticed his duffel bag sitting discarded on the sidewalk by the diner's front door. His mother's old, red pickup truck was nowhere to be seen.

Yes, other than that one time three years earlier, Marcus had always considered himself good at reading the signs, so he was shocked he had missed the large black and white one that had been staring at him for almost two years from the end of his shady, suburban Atlanta street. As he flipped down the driver-side sunshade to take another look in the mirror at his blackened eye, a glint of sunlight off the sign caught his attention.

Avoid Dead End in Cul-de-sac.

"Now you tell me," Marcus said aloud. With a sharp laugh, he flipped back the visor and rolled down his window. Sticking out his arm, he raised his middle finger at the sign and stepped on the accelerator. As the tires squealed on the pavement, he shot out onto the main road and began speeding toward the interstate. In the rearview mirror, the sign quickly disappeared behind him. He shifted his focus back to his blackened eye and let out a long sigh.

"Baby, it's time to move on."

MARCUS SAT ON THE CURB outside of the emergency room exit and dropped his chin into his hands, not really sure what to do with himself next. For his trip south to have started out so smoothly, things had gone south pretty quick.

The three or so hours he had spent racing down Interstate 75 had gone by with little of note or bother. A stop in a rest area or two to pee and curse his kindergarten kidneys, a brief swing into a Waffle Barn for lunch, and the next thing he knew he was easing the tiny yellow Fiat off the road and under the large green exit sign that stated Marathon/Hwy 134. Marcus was amazed at the beauty of the twenty miles of country highway headed into the town. Though his father had grown up in this part of the state, it was an area Marcus and his mother had never ventured into much in their ramblings. She had claimed the mosquitoes and gnats made it not worth the bother to wander into what she called "the swampy wasteland." But as the countryside whizzed by, Marcus was surprised to see not boggy marshes full of alligators but mile after mile of rolling farmland covered with row after row of tilled soil from the spring planting. Enormous silver sprinkler systems spanned the fields, and twice he had to swerve to the wrong side of the road to avoid getting drenched by an errant spray of water.

He did see an occasional murky pond dotted with lily pads and with cypress trees growing right out of the water, but as a whole it was just pine trees, fields, and a couple of small, white churches with cemeteries beside them.

At the city limit, he was greeted by a large sign with crepe myrtle trees painted along the edges and tall pink lettering that read: "Welcome to Marathon, Georgia! Population 11,502." Underneath, in a fancy, white script, was written, "The name sounds like running away, but we know you'll want to stay!" Marcus had rolled his eyes and drawled, "Don't count on it."

Just past the sign, the highway narrowed from four lanes to two and the roadside became littered with brick ranch houses behind large green lawns dotted with azalea bushes and dogwood trees. A few houses had children playing in the yards, and Marcus slowed his speed to something more appropriate for in-town driving.

"No need to start the day with a speeding ticket," Marcus said aloud to himself. "Shit!" He swerved to avoid a yellow dog that had run out of one of the yards straight for his tires.

Heart racing, he pulled onto the gravel at the edge of the road to calm down and watch the dog trot back into his yard. Marcus brought up the GPS on the screen in his dashboard and began scrolling through the options. He retrieved the law firm's envelope from the passenger seat and entered the street address. "Now how does this thing work?" He pushed the button marked "drive" and waited.

When Robert had bought him the Fiat, Marcus had thought the built-in GPS was an absolute waste of money. In the time before he had the car, he'd used Atlanta's buses and trains to maneuver his way around the city and had learned how to get just about anywhere he needed to go. Also, his time on the road with his mother had given him a natural instinct for navigating the highways and byways. Until this moment, he had never bothered to turn the thing on.

"Proceed one mile and turn left onto Main Street," a soothing woman's voice announced over the car speakers.

"Aye, aye, Captain," Marcus said and lifted his fingers to his brow in a mock salute. He tossed the envelope back onto the passenger's seat and checked his rearview mirror before easing out onto the street. As his car bumped over the edge of the pavement, the envelope slid from the seat onto the floorboard below. "Shit," Marcus muttered as he leaned over to try to reach the paper while keeping an eye on the road ahead. He fumbled blindly with his right hand but couldn't find the envelope. He glanced down and grasped the edge of the paper with his fingertips. As he raised his eyes to the road ahead, he saw a massive, red car heading straight toward him.

The next thing he knew, he was waking, head pounding, on a cot in a sterile-looking white room. He felt a bandage across his forehead and another wound tightly around his wrist. Looking around the room in confusion, he discovered an elderly woman with bluish-tinted hair and a pink-and-white-striped dress sitting in a chair across the room flipping through a magazine. When he cleared his throat to get her attention, she informed him that he was in the Marathon General Hospital Emergency room, that he had been delivered here by ambulance from the accident scene, and that he was not, in fact, dead. After retrieving a doctor to declare him fit to leave, she helped him into a wheelchair, had him sign some papers, and then wheeled him out the exit and to the curb. Marcus turned to inquire about a cab, but the woman scurried back through the automatic doors with the wheelchair and disappeared. Unsure what to do next, Marcus plopped on the curb and pulled out his phone to look up a cab company. When he turned on the phone, he saw the message: *Eight missed calls from Robert.* Then a low-battery warning beeped before the phone shut itself down. He dropped the phone in disgust, rested his elbows on his knees, and propped his chin on his hands. After trying to will away the throbbing in his head, he stood to go back into the hospital and look for a pay phone. Just as he turned to enter, the sound of tires screeching to a halt on the pavement behind him made him spin around.

An older, dark blue Buick idled in the parking lot in front of him. The passenger's side window rolled down.

"Marcus? Marcus Sumter?" a woman's voice called through the open window.

Marcus took a few careful steps forward and peeked inside the window. "Excuse me?"

"Yes," the woman said with a satisfied smile. "You're definitely a Sumter. Spitting image of your daddy. Got that unfortunate red hair all the Sumter men have."

Marcus stared at the woman smiling at him from behind the steering wheel. Silver hair cut in a stylish bob framed the sharp angles of her face, which was mostly hidden behind red sunglasses with rhinestones at the temples. She wore a soft blue button-down blouse with the collar turned up. A tennis bracelet sparkled as she drummed her hand on the steering wheel.

"Um, do I know you?"

"Oh, honey, get in the car and I'll explain everything. The longer I keep this window down, the less my A/C will work. If I let too much humidity into this car, my hair will absolutely deflate, and I don't have time to go to the Cutting Up today to get it fixed. Now hop in, and I will take you where you need to be."

"But, my car and my things…"

"Are probably being towed to Murphy's auto shop. We can deal with that later. But, first things first, I'm going to need you to quit staring at me and get in the durn car."

Marcus looked around the parking lot. "Oh, what the hell," he mumbled as he yanked open the door. He slipped into the passenger seat and pulled the door closed behind him.

"That's better," the woman said and smiled at Marcus as she turned up the air conditioning in the car. "Can you believe this heat this early in June? Course, it's like this all the time down here, so I don't know why I'm surprised. Heck, I was halfway through menopause before I realized I was having hot flashes, and it wasn't just the weather. I can't believe Myrtle made you wait out on the curb. I told her I was on my way. She could've let you sit in the air-conditioned lobby at least." The woman shook her head and drove toward the parking lot exit. "Of course, when you spend all your time being a busybody tending to everyone's business, I guess you don't stop to actually think. I swear that woman—"

"I'm sorry," Marcus interrupted her. "Maybe it's the bump on my head, but I'm confused. Who—"

"Myrtle. Myrtle Hawkins. That woman in the pink-striped dress?" The woman flipped on her turn signal and pulled onto the road. "She's one of the volunteers at the hospital. Pink Ladies, they call them. She says she does it to feel useful, but I think she does it so she can have her nose squarely in everybody's business. Nobody comes or goes in that hospital without her knowing it and telling everybody about it. It's a real pain in the rear when it comes to privacy, but I do admit it makes it convenient for knowing who needs prayers, or a casserole, or when to buy something new to wear for a funeral."

"Yes, but who—"

"Called me? Myrtle called me, silly. Well, not me, my son Raff. Evidently, they found a letter from him in your car and decided to call him when they didn't know who your people might be. He sent me to bring you to the law office. He's busy with a client and, well, he thinks I do nothing all day, which is far from true, but I told him I didn't mind since I was heading out to the Piggly Wiggly anyway. He wasn't expecting you today, but he can squeeze you in. He did adore your grandmother so much, and he and your daddy played ball together. You know, growing up right next door and all."

"Ma'am—"

"Oh, where is my head. I totally forgot to offer you my condolences for your—"

"Ma'am!" Marcus yelled.

"Good Lord, child," the woman said with a gasp as she slammed on the brakes and squealed to a halt. "No need to yell. I'm right beside you."

"Yes, ma'am, but who *are* you?"

The woman stared at him, then threw her head back and laughed. "Where is my head? Just rattling off at you like this. I'm sorry. My name is Helen Warner." The woman stretched her left hand between her body and the steering wheel toward Marcus. "Pleased to meet you."

Marcus took her hand and shook it slightly. "Hello."

"I'm going to blame that breach of etiquette on Myrtle too. I swear that woman just burns my butter, and off I go. Sometimes my mouth gets ahead of my brain." Helen stepped on the gas pedal and zoomed along the street, making Marcus fumble for the handle over his head.

"I gathered. And you're picking me up because…"

"Like I said, my son, Raffield Junior, is a lawyer. He's handling your grandmother's estate. He and my late husband, Raffield Senior, own the most respected law firm in town, Warner, Warner, and Thompson. Thompson was my daddy. Anyway, your grandmother was my next-door neighbor and one of my dearest friends in the world. We knew each other since Jesus was a child. Her passing was one of the saddest days of my life. I'm so sorry you lost her, honey."

"Well, I never really met her."

"Oh, yes. That's even sadder. Your grandmother was the kindest woman in town. Everybody loved her."

Marcus shifted his eyes from Helen to the roadside. As the car rolled past a softball field and the empty playground of a school, the light flashing between the trees made his head throb. He patted his chest pocket searching for his sunglasses before realizing they were probably in his car, wherever it was. He closed his eyes and rested his head against the cool glass of the window. Hoping more conversation would distract him from the headache, he opened his eyes and asked, "And you knew my father?"

"Sure did." Helen glanced over at Marcus and smiled before turning her attention back to the road. "I was the first person your grandmother met when she and your granddaddy moved to Marathon. They barely had the moving van half-unpacked before the other girls and I were over there with casseroles. Your granddaddy was going to be the new city manager, so it was important we made a good impression." She slowed the car before skidding to the right around a corner. Marcus braced himself again using the handle over the window. Helen continued her chatter with no notice of her squealing tires. "This was years before he became the mayor. I ran his campaign. Well, Inez Coffee and I did. Once the two of us got on board, his election was sealed. If anybody had not voted for the candidate Inez and I picked, they knew they would've been ruined in this town. His campaign slogan was… wait. What was I talking about?"

"My father?"

"Oh, yes. I remember Raff came with me and soon he and Nat were running around in the yard together as if they'd known each other for years." Helen giggled. "I haven't thought about this in years. I remember I told my friend Priss, Priscilla Ellington, you'll meet her later, and, when you do, try not to stare at her awful hairdo. I've told her time and again to quit going to Maureen at the Beauty Spot and go to Tanya at the Cutting Up, but she won't listen. Try not to cuss when you see it. She's the preacher's wife and doesn't take kindly to cussing."

"Yes, ma'am." Marcus shook his head and chuckled. "I'll keep that in mind."

"Anyway," Helen continued, "I was walking her back to her car—this was back when she still lived over by the Baptist church, mind you, before she moved in on the other side of your grandmother's house, but I said to her that your daddy was one of the ugliest children I had ever seen in my life. Bless his heart, he was awkward. All orange hair and freckles and the knobbiest knees I'd ever seen. Who'd have guessed he'd grow up to be so handsome?"

Intrigued by information from someone who had known his father, Marcus lost interest in the shops and businesses and the small dogwood trees that were lined up along the sidewalks. He took a deep breath and asked, "My dad was handsome?"

Helen nodded and said, "Indeed. He had all the local girls after him all the time, but your daddy didn't care. He and my Raff didn't have time for girls. They were both in love with sports, playing football, baseball, basketball, anything. Those boys were inseparable growing up and they went off to UGA together. They shared a room in the dorm. Well, until your daddy met your mama in that diner and ran off in the middle of the night. Can't say I blame a girl for wanting to run off with your daddy." Helen pulled the car over to the curb in front of a large brick building and put the car in park. "But that's enough about that. Here we are. Let's go get you the keys to your house, neighbor!" Helen swung her door open and stepped out of the car. Her khaki skirt flitted around her knees as she stalked up the sidewalk toward the door.

Marcus hopped out of the car and ran after Helen. "House? What do you mean house?"

Helen stopped and shook her head. "I've already said too much. Raff will explain it all. It's all in the will."

"You know what's in my grandmother's will?" Marcus slowed his gait when he reached her. "Isn't that some kind of ethical breach or something?"

"Oh, sweetie, I'm in that will too." Helen waved away his words and concern. "As I said, I was your grandmother's best friend. Also, Raff thought it might be nice if I helped you get settled in and welcomed you to town. After all, manners will always trump ethics. Now, come on." Helen pushed the door open with her hip. She slid the sunglasses to the top of her head as she stepped into the cold air of the lobby. "Raff? Sweetheart? Oh, hello, Diane," she said to the teen-aged girl sitting behind the reception desk in the small front room. "Is that son of mine around here somewhere? I picked up the package he asked me to retrieve." Helen jerked her thumb over her shoulder at Marcus.

"Just one minute, Mrs. Warner," the girl said and smiled over the older woman's shoulder at Marcus. She pushed a button on a speaker phone on her desk and said, "Mr. Warner? Your mother is out here with some man."

"Oh, this is silly," Helen said as she scooted past the desk and into the hallway. "Raff, honey? Where are you? I've got the Sumter boy. He's a little banged up, but I got him here in one piece."

A man stepped out of a conference room to the right of the hall. Raffield Warner stood barely over five feet tall and was nearly that wide. The white dress shirt he wore was rumpled and only halfway tucked into his blue suit pants. The tail of his crooked necktie extended below the wider front part of the tie. He had a fringe of dark hair around his temples, but was completely bald above that. He sighed and stood with his hands on his hips. "Mama, I have asked you a million times to please not barge in on me. You can wait in the lobby until I come get you. I could be with an important client."

"Foot," Helen said and scoffed. "Need I remind you it was my daddy's and my husband's money that built this building and I'll come in here any time I want?" She swatted him on the shoulder and walked past him into the conference room. "Now let's get this unpleasant business over with."

"Raffield Warner, Junior." Raffield stuck out his hand to Marcus. "But everybody calls me Raff. And you have to be Marcus Sumter. I swear, you look just like your daddy. Looking at you, it's like time stood still for him and just walked all over me. It's mighty fine to finally meet you. I was beginning to think you were never going to respond to my letters. I must've sent at least five letters to that address I found on the Internet before you responded."

"Yeah." Marcus shrugged and looked away. "Not the best neighborhood. Mail goes missing sometimes."

"No. These were sent certified. Somebody had to sign—"

"Well, I don't know what to tell you. I never got them until the last one. That's when I called you. Didn't you say there was something I needed to sign?"

"Ah, I see." Raffield stared at Marcus before clearing his throat and gesturing down the hall. "We can take care of that down here. Boy, that's some bandage you got on your head there. What the hell happened?"

"Delores Richards happened!" Helen called from the conference room.

"Oh, good heavens. You're lucky to have stepped away with just a goose egg if you ran into Delores Richards."

"Well, he's practically a resident now that she ran into him."

"Yeah. I guess that is kind of a rite of passage around here," Raffield said as he led Marcus into the conference room. "Miss Richards has a hard time staying on her side of the road. She ran into me once coming down Elm Street. She walloped me good. I instantly jumped out and told her it was all my fault. 'But I ran into you!' she said. I said 'Yes, ma'am. But I saw you coming three blocks away and I could've turned off when I had the chance. So this is clearly my fault.'"

"Oh, Raff. You tell that story all the time."

"Well, it's true, Mama. Honestly, I don't know why the police haven't taken her keys away yet."

"Because that would just be rude. There is no need to bring the police into such matters. We always settle up with her on the side. Plus, Hank over at Murphy's just takes care of everything and sends the bill to Miss Richards's sister. And lord knows, the Richards have more money than sense."

"Mama," Raffield chastised her.

"Well, it's true."

"So, did the fine doctors at Marathon General get you all patched up? You going to live?" Raff asked with a chuckle. He picked a glass from a table along the wall, filled it with water from a pitcher, and handed it to Marcus.

"Yeah. Got a splitting headache, and the doctor says I'll never skate in the Olympics now."

"You skate?"

"I'm kidding." Marcus took a sip of the water and looked around the room at the pictures of bulldogs in red and black sweaters hanging on each wall.

"Oh. Heh." Raff chuckled politely. "Well, your daddy was such a good football player. I was too, though you can't tell it now." Raff smacked his hand on the belly protruding over his belt. "I played at UGA when I was there. You play sports, Marcus?"

"No, sir. Sports aren't really my thing."

"Well, that's too bad. My son isn't really into sports either. He wants to be an actor or some such nonsense. Guess it takes all kinds. I can't believe Nat Sumter's boy isn't a sports nut. Your daddy was crazy about anything that involved balls."

"Well, we have that in common, I guess," Marcus mumbled, quickly taking another sip of the water to hide the blush rushing into his cheeks. Hoping to change the subject, he said, "Um, I never really knew my daddy."

"Oh, um, yeah. I guess after the accident..." Raff stammered and glanced at the floor awkwardly. "Well, let me see if Diane has some aspirin for that headache. Won't you sit down?" Raff gestured toward the large table in the conference room where papers lay spread out.

Marcus stepped to the table and perched in one of the oversized leather chairs surrounding it; his head pounded with each beat of his heart.

Raff shuffled a few of the papers and said, "Boy, looks like you got a good deal of money coming to you…"

"Oh, Raff," Helen said and clucked her tongue, "don't talk about money. It's tacky. Honey, I'm going to go find you a headache powder while you men handle all this paperwork business."

"Now sign here." Raff pointed out a line at the bottom of a paper. "Then initial here."

Marcus scribbled his name where instructed, then set the pen gently on the table. He read the final paragraph of the will to himself one more time. *To my grandson Marcus, I leave all my other worldly possessions, my assets and most importantly, my house, so that maybe, just once in his life, that poor boy can have a real home.*

"So, it's all mine?"

"Well, it has to go through probate and such, but yes. Basically, it's all yours."

"And I have to live in the house? I mean, she says she wants it to be my home."

"Oh, good lord, boy," Helen said and laughed. "Your grandmother was a former mayor's wife, not the queen of England. It's a will, not a proclamation."

"My mother is correct. You can do with the assets as you see fit, once her few debts are paid off."

"So I could sell it?"

"If that's what you desire. As a matter of fact, my wife, Katie Nell, is one of the most successful realtors in Marathon. I'm sure she could sell it for you in a heartbeat if you want."

"Raff, you quit trying to drum up business for that nitwit wife of yours." Helen picked up the pen from the table and inspected it before opening her purse and dropping it in. "Marcus, you don't have to decide anything right now. Why don't you spend a little time here and see

17

what you want to do with it? How soon do you have to be back where you came from? Back in…?"

"Um, Atlanta." Marcus let his eyes wander off from Helen to the photographs on the wall behind her. "No rush. Nothing important waiting on me there."

"Then it's settled. You stay here for a few weeks at least and see what you want to do. The other Do-Nothings and I have already gone through your grandmother's house and got it nice and clean for you. Of course, there's no real food in there, but we'll get you settled, and I'll bring over something for you to eat tonight. Tomorrow, we will run you up to the Piggly Wiggly and stock you up."

"Well, I guess I can stay until the house sells at least." Marcus looked at the table as Raff slid a manila envelope across the table to him.

"Here are your copies of all the paperwork. There are a bunch of things in there. Here are the keys to the house." Raff pushed a key ring across the table. "And I wrote Katie Nell's number on the front of the envelope so when you get ready to sell—"

"*If* you sell it," Helen interrupted her son. "You never know, little man, we might just charm you into staying." Helen grinned at Marcus and then turned to her son. "Now, Raff, I'll run him on home and please tell your wife I really need her to bring back my punch bowl that she borrowed months ago." Helen stood and took her purse out of the chair beside her. "Come along, Marcus. Bye, Baby." Helen kissed her son on his bald spot.

"Mama, I'm fifty-four years old. Don't call me Baby."

Helen rolled her eyes at Marcus and grinned. "Let's scoot. I need to get you home."

"Helen, what are Do-Nothings?" Marcus asked as he stared out the car window while the houses along the street rolled by. He rubbed the single key on the key ring between his fingers and glanced at the shiny brass letter E that dangled off the ring beside the key.

"What, honey?"

"Do-Nothings," Marcus said, still staring at the key ring. "Back there, you said you and the Do-Nothings had cleaned my grandmother's house."

"Did I say that? Well, it's true. Not that there was much to do. Eloise Sumter was an immaculate housekeeper, even at the end, when she was so sick she could barely get out of the bed. Mainly we just got rid of all the medical equipment. Figured you didn't need to see all of that. Also, I hope you don't mind, but we each took some of her clothes and donated some to Brother Marty's. It's a local place that sells used stuff and uses the money to run a soup kitchen for the needy."

Marcus shrugged. "That's fine. But the Do-Nothings?"

"Oh, that's just a bunch of old women. We were all your grandmother's friends. Have been for years and years."

"So you're a bridge club or something?"

"No. It's just what the name says. We do nothing."

"I don't understand."

"You see, your grandmother actually came up with the idea. Being the mayor's wife, she had to take part in every last blasted thing that went on in this town: garden club; quilting circle; Junior Ladies Club, which is full of women who are hardly junior or ladies, I might add. All kinds of nonsense that she was always dragging me along to. All of that on top of raising a family and keeping up a house, it was plain exhausting. So, one day, we were riding back from a PTA meeting, I think it was, and she said to me, 'wouldn't it be heaven to do absolutely nothing?' And that was when we decided to create the Do-Nothing club. Once a week, we would get together and do nothing. No refreshments. No flower arranging. No bible study. No card playing. Just sit around and talk and enjoy a whole hour of doing nothing. Now that most of us are widows and don't have jobs and families, we spend most of our days doing nothing, but we've had the club for over forty years. Seemed silly to quit. We also meet more than once a week now."

"You don't do anything? Isn't that boring?"

"No, child. It's marvelous. And we don't just sit and stare at each other. We gossip, tell stories about the old days, and talk about our grandchildren. Catch up on the latest news. Inez goes to New York to see a musical a couple of times a year, so she will tell us about that. Sometimes we swap recipes we cut out of the *Southern Living*. Francine tells us what is happening at the diner and about her daughters and their love lives. I'll catch the girls up on *Days of Our Lives*. Just whatever we feel like that day. You know, chatter. When Priss isn't there, we might have some wine. You know those Baptists and their thing with alcohol. Don't tell her that part when you meet her."

"Your secret's safe with me." Marcus grinned and looked back out the window. As the car slowed, he noticed a small brick sign that read "Crepe Myrtle Manor" sitting in the middle of an island that divided the street. Yellow, purple, and pink pansies bloomed around the base of the sign, and a few red cardinals sat on the top. He braced against the door to keep from falling over as Helen whipped a sharp right turn into the entrance to the subdivision.

"Welcome to our little neighborhood. It's supposed to only be for people over the age of fifty, but if you decide to stay here, I'm sure we can bend that little rule." At the first intersection, Helen jerked the wheel again, and the car skidded into a small cul-de-sac. "This here is our street. Pecan Circle. Though I don't know why we called it that, because it doesn't really circle back to anything."

"Great. Another dead end," Marcus mumbled and braced himself again.

As Helen eased the car into the driveway of a house, Marcus looked at the neighborhood. Several small brick houses surrounded the paved circle of road with its small central circle of grass. Robins and blue jays fluttered about the limbs of the old oak trees that grew between several of the houses. Their imposing branches draped with Spanish moss stretched over the black-shingled roofs of the houses. Circling behind the houses were row upon row of leafy pecan trees.

Helen turned off the car and pulled the keys out of the ignition. "Well, this is me. Your house is right over there between Inez Coffee's and Cookie Ginsburg's. It's nothing fancy, but it's a wonderful little neighborhood. This all used to be nothing but a big old pecan orchard, but my husband, Raffield Senior, bought this land many years ago for almost nothing. He was a whiz with real estate. He and I convinced the girls to invest in this place as somewhere we could live out our days in peace without a bunch of screaming kids running around. You know, after you've raised your own children, it's nice to know you don't have to worry about anyone else's."

The houses were all of a similar construction, squat red brick one-story bungalows with only the color of the front door and its placement vis-à-vis a bay window flip-flopping from house to house. Though the neighborhood reminded Marcus of the bland, suburban conformity where he lived with Robert in Atlanta, the personality of each home's resident was clearly visible in the landscaping and decorations that were lovingly placed in front of each. One house had concrete statues of a doe and a buck staring blankly from a flower bed toward the street. Another had birdhouses and hummingbird feeders hanging from several rafters and a birdhouse built to look like a grand southern plantation house atop a tall wooden pole. Another had a small statue of a child kneeling in prayer next to a battered wooden cross. Robert had praised the rules forbidding such things in their neighborhood, stating that it kept people from "putting their trashy on display." Seeing the care his grandmother's neighbors put into making each cookie-cutter house seem individual, Marcus found the "trashy on display" to be charming and inviting.

"So, here we are! Crepe Myrtle Manor. South Georgia's finest community for the over-fifty set. Welcome home, honey. It's going to be so nice having a youngster in the neighborhood."

"Helen, thanks for the ride, but I really doubt I'll be staying here. I'm just going to settle the estate and—"

"We'll see. We'll see. Now you go on in there and get yourself settled. I'll be over in a bit to bring you some dinner. You aren't allergic to cream of mushroom soup, are you? Not sure why, but every casserole I make seems to have it in there."

"That's fine, but you don't have to do that."

"Yes, I do. Marcus, I'm an old, southern woman. We bring people food. It's in the state constitution or something. Now scoot." Helen patted him on his knee and opened her car door. "Your house is number five, the one with the green shutters. Go on."

Marcus stepped out of the car, crossed the street, and stood at the end of the driveway to look at the house. The mailbox next to him had a number five stenciled in white on the front flap and the name "Sumter" painted in a playful cursive script along the side. Hanging baskets of ferns swayed lazily in the afternoon breeze at the corners of the empty carport. Faux stone pots spilling over with bright red begonias sat on either side of the front stoop, and a wreath of silk daisies and sunflowers hung on the dark green front door. Twirling the key ring on his finger, he walked to the front door, unsure why his stomach was full of knots. Near the front door, nestled in one of the pots of begonias, sat a small hand-painted sign that read "There's no place like home." Marcus rolled his eyes as he yanked the sign out of the dirt. He pulled the screen door open and slipped the key into the lock. He held his breath and turned the key. *Here goes nothing.*

Marcus pushed the front door ajar, unsure of what he expected to find or how it should make him feel. He knew that legally this was all his now, but it still seemed as if he was breaking into a stranger's home, as if at any minute someone could come along, say "just kidding!" and haul him away as a petty crook. He pulled the key out of the lock, let go of the front door, and let it swing open into the house. He stepped inside and fought the urge to wipe his feet and call out to see if anyone was home. The screen door slammed behind him, making him jump and then laugh at his nerves.

All of the blinds were drawn, and Marcus couldn't adjust to the darkness in the room. Fumbling at the wall beside the door, he found a series of switches and flipped the first one. The porch light came on, casting his shadow along the floor in front of him. *Not that one.* He flipped the next switch and a rush of air brushed across his face as a ceiling fan whirred to life. *Not that one, but it sure helps.* When he flipped the farthest switch, a pendant lamp hanging to his left came on over a round table covered with a blue gingham tablecloth with four ladder-back wooden chairs around it. *Where the hell is the light switch?*

Marcus slipped over to the table and dropped the sign from the flower pot, the envelope of papers from the attorney's office, and the keys onto the table. The table sat in an alcove with a bay window whose closed wooden blinds faced the street. Marcus grabbed the string beside one of the blinds and flipped them open. In front of him was an open kitchen: a wall of counters and plain white cabinets that ended in a corner with a stainless steel refrigerator.

Marcus wandered into the living room and noticed another panel of light switches on the wall over an upright piano next to a hallway leading into the back of the house. He flipped the switches, causing the hall light to turn on beside him and the fan overhead to turn off. Down the hall, he could see three doorways; the one at the far end led into a bathroom. The living room remained dark, with only a few streaks of sunlight cutting through the blinds on the windows. Marcus shrugged and flipped the switches to turn the fan back on.

Marcus wandered the room trying to gather clues about the woman who had lived here and who was willing to leave all of it to a stranger. In the dim light from the hall, he could see a blue and white plaid sofa sitting in front of a glass-topped coffee table with a few magazines scattered across the top. He picked one magazine off the table, *Southern Living*, and read the mailing label at the bottom. *Eloise Sumter.*

Well, that much I knew.

Marcus sat in one of two green slipper chairs under the front windows, a small cocktail table between them with a brass lamp sitting on top sat between them. His leg bumped a basket full of balls of yarn, knitting needles, and a swatch of a half-finished project. *So she knitted. I know that at least.* Marcus sat staring at the room, unsure what to do next. *The house is yours. Do whatever you want.* He sat and stared at the room's beige walls.

He walked back to the piano and ran his finger along the keys; the plinking notes broke the silence of the room. He caught his reflection in a mirror over the piano and grimaced at the bruised and bandaged face that stared back at him. He squinted as he inspected his black eye and touched the bandage on his forehead. A clump of blood had dried in his bangs and plastered them to his forehead. As he tried to bend closer to the mirror, he placed his hands on the back of the piano and knocked over several framed photos scattered there.

"I'm sorry," Marcus said as he attempted to set the frames upright again and knocked a few more over in the process. "Jeez, Marcus, clumsy much?" he muttered before pausing over one photo of himself as a young child sitting on the back of a horse. "Where did this come from?" Marcus held the frame closer to his face as he tried to make out the image in the dim light. A loud rapping on the door behind him startled him and made Marcus drop the picture back onto the piano. He scrambled to put all of the pictures where they had been.

"Come in," Marcus said over his shoulder.

"Hello?" a woman's voice called through the cracked front door. "I hope you ain't naked, because I'm coming in."

Marcus turned around to find an elderly woman shoving the front door open with her foot. She had jet-black hair floating around her head in a tall bouffant and bright red lipstick smeared across her lips. A chunky gold necklace hanging across her large bosom glittered as she stepped into the room. She carried a plastic jug filled with an amber liquid.

"No, ma'am. Fully clothed."

"Well, shit. Thought I might get me a free peek. Why are you standing in the dark?" The woman set the jug on the kitchen counter, raised her hands, and clapped twice. Three small lamps scattered about the room lit, casting a warm light over the room. "That's better." She thrust the plastic jug at Marcus. "I thought you might be thirsty, so I brought you some sweet tea."

In the light, Marcus could see the woman had dark skin, tanned and freckled by many hours in the sun. She wore a dirty old Atlanta Braves T-shirt, and the knees of her capri pants were stained with muddy patches. A pair of gardening gloves was tucked into the waistband of her burgundy fanny pack, and a gardening trowel poked out of her pocket.

"Hello, darling, my name is Inez Coffee. I live right next door. The house with the deer in front?" Her voice had the sandpaper rasp that came from years of smoking. "Excuse my appearance. I was working in my flower beds when I saw you and Helen pull in and thought I'd just come on over and introduce myself." Inez thrust her hand out to Marcus and smiled; the many bangles on her wrist clinked. "Only stopped to slap on some lipstick, because, well, I wasn't raised in a barn."

"Hi. Marcus. Um…Sumter." Marcus gave her hand a weak shake. "But I guess you knew the last part."

"Good lord, yes. I'd know that strawberry hair from across a football stadium. You can't deny your roots. Now my roots," she turned to the mirror hanging over the sofa and fluffed her hair, "well, that's between me and my hairdresser."

"Well, a person's got to have some secrets."

"Oh, Marcus, do you have secrets?" She spun to face him with her eyes opened wide. "Thank god. That's something we need on this street, some new secrets. I've heard everybody else's. I was just telling Helen the other day that if something interesting didn't happen in this town soon, I might have to run naked down Main Street just to give us something different to talk about. But now that you are bringing some new, younger life to the street, well, we should have a whole lot to talk about."

"Oh, I'm not staying on the street." Marcus crossed his arms over his chest. "I'm just here to tie things up with my grandmother's estate and then I'll be moving on. Did you need something?"

"Hello? Marcus?" Helen's voice called through the screen door. "Inez Coffee! What are you doing over here? This boy's barely had time to kick off his shoes, and you're already over here getting all up in his business. Now you shoo." Helen flung the screen door open and stepped into the house with a glass casserole dish covered in aluminum foil.

"The hell I will. I'm saving this boy's life. Marcus, whatever you do, do not put a drop of that," she gestured to the container in Helen's hands, "in your mouth. Helen here is a whiz at many things, but how she raised a family without killing them all at the dinner table is a mystery to me."

"Inez, shut up." Helen stuck her tongue out at Inez.

"What is that?" Inez tipped her head back and stared down her nose at the dish.

"It's a broccoli chicken casserole, and I used your recipe from the church cookbook. So if he dies, it's on your head."

"I'm sure it will be fine," Marcus said as he took the container from Helen and set it on the counter. "I'm not very hungry right now anyway."

"Well, you just stick that in the fridge. When you're hungry, take off the aluminum foil and throw the casserole in the microwave for a few minutes and it'll be just fine. You can just give me my dish back when you're done. My name's on some tape right there on the bottom." She turned back to the other woman. "Now, Inez, I'm serious. You've introduced yourself. Now run along and leave this boy alone. He's had a hard day, tangling up with Delores Richards and signing all that paperwork for the will. The last thing he needs is to try to be sociable."

"I'm not just here on a social visit." Inez turned to Marcus and shook her finger at him. "Young man, I have a bone to pick with you. You went and blew it for us all."

"Inez, what are you babbling about?" Helen asked as she slid one of the barstools out from the island and sat.

"Delores Richards. That's what. Evidently, this fella came rolling into town in a car so little that, when she hit him, the police and ambulance had to come." Inez glared at Marcus. "Why on earth would you drive a car that little?"

"It was a gift?" Marcus replied and shrugged.

"You won't see anything that little in this town. Hell, I couldn't get my hair in something *that* little."

"Inez, lay off the boy. It's not like he hit her on purpose."

"No," Marcus said and shook his head. "But it was *my* fault. I wasn't looking where I was going."

"Honey, even if you'd had both your eyes on the road and a lookout riding shotgun, you were doomed the minute she turned on her ignition." Inez shooed the thought away with her hand and frowned. She pulled the other barstool out from the island and hopped onto it, letting her lime green sandals drop to the floor below her dangling feet. "But that's not my point. When the police got there, they asked her for her license."

"Oh no." Helen gasped and covered her mouth. "You mean—"

"Yes." Inez looked at Marcus and shook her head in disbelief. "She promptly turned to Spud Stewart, he's our local sheriff, and said 'License? What the *hell* is a license?'"

"You don't mean?" Marcus asked.

"Yes." Inez threw her hands up and rolled her eyes. "That woman has been driving for fifty years without a damn license. All the rest of us were smart enough to keep the police out of it. But now they know and they took her keys away, so all of us are going to have to spend our days driving that bag of bones all over town. It was all well and good, but you done ruined it. Personally, I think it should be your job to be her chauffeur."

"Well, I would but, as I said, I don't plan on staying very long and also I don't know where my car is."

"Shoot!" Helen snapped her fingers. "I forgot. Raffield told me that Hank Hudson hauled it down to his garage. I'll take you there tomorrow morning to get your things and see how bad the car is." As Marcus grimaced, she assured him, "I'm sure Hank can fix it, no matter how bad it is. He's a miracle worker with a car."

"And easy on the eyes, too," Inez leered and elbowed Helen in the side. "Good lord, that is a sexy young man!"

"Inez Coffee! First of all, he is young enough to be your grandson. And secondly, you're a married woman."

"Married, not dead! I can still appreciate a good-looking man when I see one. It's not like I'm going to chase him down and jump him."

"You couldn't catch him if you tried. At least, not without breaking a hip."

"Don't I know it?" Inez threw her head back and laughed. "But as I always say, it don't matter what cranks the mower as long as you stay on the right lawn."

"Inez, the last thing this young man wants to hear about is the fantasies of an old woman."

"True. Marcus, I'm sure you prefer your women a little younger than me and old Helen here."

"Well..." Marcus looked at his feet.

"A fine-looking young man like you, I bet you have to beat them big city girls off with a stick."

"Not exactly."

"Oh?" Inez leaned forward onto her elbows on the counter. "You have a girlfriend? Steady lady? Wife?"

"No, ma'am," Marcus said with a chuckle. "No girlfriend."

"Well, you're young. Time for all that foolishness later. You should be out there sowing your oats while you can. Lord knows, if I had it to do over again, I'd've kicked a few more tires before I settled down with Elbert. No, you take your time, sweetheart, and find the right girl."

"I don't think that'll happen."

"Oh, now come on." Inez clucked her tongue. "She might even be right here in this town. You never know—"

"Inez, hush." Helen slapped the back of Inez's hand. "You're making a fool of yourself. I think Marcus is trying to tell you politely that he is a confirmed bachelor."

"A what?"

"You know. Good to his mama?"

"Helen, what are you babbling about?"

"For someone who loves New York City theater so much, you sure don't know much. A homosexual, darling."

Inez turned to Marcus and stared. Marcus grinned and nodded his head.

"Oh! Helen!" Inez kicked her feet against the counter and clapped her hands, making her bracelets clatter. "How exciting! A real-life, confirmed homosexual right here on our street! It feels so modern! Wait 'til I tell Francine!"

"Now, Inez, don't you go blabbing that all over town. That's not really your business to tell."

Marcus shrugged and took Inez's jug of tea from the counter. He opened the refrigerator and stuck it inside. "I don't care. It's not as though I know anybody in this town. And it's not really something I hide. I'm not ashamed of it."

"Nor should you be," Helen said and shook her finger at Marcus. "You be proud of who you are. You should make every day of your life one of those pride parades."

"Well, listen to miss modern Gloria Steinem over here," Inez said with a grunt. "Like you know anything about a gay pride parade."

"First of all, I watch the Netflix. I know things. And you know good and well my grandson Skeet is a gay. He's told me all about this stuff." Helen opened her eyes wide. "Oh! I'll have to introduce you two!"

"Good lord, Marcus. Now you've done it. Nothing in the world makes Helen Warner happier than getting in someone's business and trying to play matchmaker."

"Well, if that isn't the pot calling the kettle black."

"You take that back," Inez shot back at her. "I just want to *know* everybody's business. I don't feel the need to go messing in it."

Marcus leaned his hip against the counter and crossed his arms. "Helen, I appreciate the offer, but I don't really need anybody to play matchmaker for me, okay? I'm not planning on staying here long enough for that. And just because we're both gay doesn't mean we'll have anything else in common."

"I didn't mean for you to date him. Good grief. He's barely eighteen. And he's leaving town in the fall to go to college. No, I just thought you might like to have a friend in town that has something in common with you."

"Well, I appreciate that but—"

"No arguing." Helen raised her hand to silence Marcus. "It's settled. Tomorrow after the Do-Nothings meeting at Francine's, I'll drive you to Hank's to get your car and I'll get Skeet to meet us."

"Oh, shit. I forgot to tell you."

"Inez, language, please. Tell me what?"

"Francine's done lost another cook. She's going to have to work the grill tomorrow so she can't be at the meeting. And Priss has a doctor's appointment in the morning so she and I thought maybe we could all meet at the Tammy tomorrow instead of riding together."

"Actually, that's perfect. The Tammy is right around the corner from Hank's. I can drop Marcus there and I'll just have Skeet meet us."

"Good. I'll call the girls and tell them to meet there tomorrow. Ten-thirty?"

"Like always."

"Well, I better skedaddle back home." Inez pushed the stool away from the counter and slid off to her feet. "I need to finish planting that border grass and Elbert will be wanting his dinner. It was wonderful to meet you, Marcus." Inez rubbed Marcus's upper arm as she cocked her head to one side. "And I'm really sorry about your grandmother. I swear, I think about Eloise every day. Lord, I miss that woman." Inez sighed and frowned. "Now I better go before I start bawling. Anyway, see you at the Tammy tomorrow." Inez bustled out of the house. After the screen door had slammed behind her, she stopped and turned around. "I want that milk jug back." She turned again and disappeared down the sidewalk.

"Well, that was…um…interesting." Marcus said and chuckled.

"Marcus, honey, don't let Inez get under your skin. She means well, but all those trips to New York have given her a filthy mind and a filthy mouth."

"No. It's fine. She's funny." Marcus climbed onto the barstool beside Helen. "But what the hell is the Tammy?"

"Oh, that's the local diner that our friend Francine Jones owns. The Tammy Dinette. We all just call it the Tammy."

"Tammy Dinette? Like Tammy Wynette?"

"Yes. Francine is obsessed with her. Uses that woman as a guide for living, which I don't understand at all. I mean, it made a wonderful TV movie but… well, that's neither here nor there. I thought we were going to have to bury Francine the day Tammy died. Of course, you're way too young to know much about Tammy Wynette."

"Oh, no." Marcus shook his head. "I know Tammy. 'Stand by Your Man.' 'D-I-V-O-R-C-E.' 'Golden Ring.' I know them all. But I've always been more of a Patsy Cline guy myself."

"I'm a Loretta Lynn girl."

"Did my grandmother enjoy music?"

"Your grandmother loved music. She played that piano over there all the time. Mostly classical. Beethoven. Bach. But when she was with the rest of us girls, all she wanted to hear was stuff from the fifties. You know, doo-wop?"

"Bomp-shoo-bomp and that kind of thing?"

"Yes!" Helen began to giggle. "I shouldn't tell you this, but who's going to hear?" Helen looked around as if checking for an eavesdropper and then whispered to Marcus. "Her favorite thing in the world was to make the lyrics dirty."

"What?" Marcus said and began to laugh.

"Yes. There's a song called 'Sh-Boom.' Well, she always changed the lyrics from 'hey nonny ding dong' to 'how long's your ding dong?'"

Helen threw her head back and laughed. "We felt so naughty singing that! Of course, compared to the things in music today..."

"Yeah. Kind of tame, but still funny." Marcus walked to the piano. He chose a picture of his grandmother. In the photograph, his grandmother wore a flamboyantly patterned pantsuit in neon colors that clashed with her red hair. She was standing with a group of men in front of a grocery store holding a pair of oversized scissors over a red ribbon. "I wish I'd known her."

"She would've spoiled you rotten."

Marcus returned the photograph to the piano back and pointed at another. "Where did she get these pictures of me? Like this one. I don't remember this."

Helen walked behind Marcus and peered over his shoulder. "First of all, *that* picture," Helen pointed at a black and white photo of a young man riding a horse, "is not you. That's your daddy. But the other ones were sent by your mama. She would never bring you down here to see your grandmother and, frankly, I think that's a crime. But every now and then, your grandmother would get a letter from your mama with a picture included. Eloise would bring the picture to the next Do-Nothing meeting and brag about what a cute baby you were, though I never thought so. She said she could just tell you were smart, too. She'd say your mama promised to come to town to see her if she would send her some money to help with the gas. We knew good and well all she wanted was the money, but your grandmother would just know she was going to show up this time. And she'd put the money in an envelope and send it off."

"If she had an address to send the money, why didn't she try to find us?"

"Oh, she did. One time she convinced me to drive all the way over to Eganville to look for you." Helen tucked her hair behind her ear and frowned. "But when we got there, the landlord said your mama had packed up and left town in the middle of the night. Your grandmother felt so bad, she paid him the rent your mama had forgotten to pay."

"Yeah, that sounds like my mama." Marcus lifted another picture of himself. His much-younger face smiled out from the picture. In the photo, he wore tattered overalls and a plaid shirt and stood holding a balloon in front of a bronze statue of a gorilla. Marcus had no memory of the statue or the picture, though the overalls seemed familiar. He set it back carefully.

"Between you, me, and the fencepost, I don't think Eloise cared much for your mama. I mean she took her son away from her and then kept you from her, too."

Marcus plucked up a picture of his father in a football uniform, kneeling and holding a football on his knee, and stared at it. He looked at his reflection in the mirror over the piano and then back at the photo. Other than differences in hairstyles, his father's plethora of freckles, and the presence of sports equipment, Marcus could've sworn it was a picture of him. "I do look a lot like him, I guess."

"Spitting image," Helen said and placed her hand on Marcus's shoulder. Making eye contact with his reflection, she added, "Well, except for that shiner you got there."

Marcus shrugged her hand off his shoulder and put the photo back on the piano. "Yeah, must be from the wreck."

"Honey, the wreck was today. That black eye is at least two days old."

"No." Marcus broke eye contact with Helen's reflection and stepped away from her. "It must be from the wreck."

"Marcus, sweetie, you don't have to tell me what happened, but I'm not an old fool. Francine, that owns the diner, her second husband… well… when he had a few beers, he liked to get to swinging. Francine put up with it for God knows what reason, and, I'm ashamed to say, most of us just kept our mouths shut about it. She'd claim it was an accident, but we all knew." Helen leaned closer and looked Marcus in the eye. "Finally, Inez had enough and she took one of Elbert's shotguns over to Francine's house. She told that good for nothing that if he touched Francine one more time, she'd shoot his thingy off. Then she turned around and shot the flag off their mailbox just to prove she could do it. Inez grew up hunting squirrels with her daddy since she never had any brothers. Of course, it didn't really matter because he upped and had a heart attack about a week later. Which, thank God for small favors."

"Helen, a man died. That isn't a favor. God or no God."

Helen dismissed him with a wave of her hand. "Don't be trying to change the subject on me. We aren't talking about religion. We're talking about that eye of yours."

"No. We aren't."

"Fine. But let me just say that I hope whoever gave you that eye doesn't feel the need to come around here."

"He doesn't know where I am."

"Ah-ha! It *is* a he! I knew it."

"Yes. It's a he. But I don't want to talk about it, okay?"

"Fine. But if he shows up here trying to hurt anyone—"

"You don't have to worry about him coming here and hurting anyone. He won't."

Helen stared at Marcus, as if waiting for him to continue. When he remained silent, she cleared her throat and glanced at her watch. "Well, it's getting late. You better get some rest so we can get up and go see about your car tomorrow morning. Don't forget to put that casserole in the fridge." Helen crossed to the door and paused with her hand on the handle. "Oh, Marcus? I'm not worried about the person that gave you that shiner. Well, not worried for us. More for him. You are Eloise's grandson, so you are an honorary Do-Nothing. We protect our own, and, frankly, I think Inez is still a little pissed off she didn't get to shoot someone the last time."

MARCUS WOKE WITH A START, sitting straight up in bed and looking about the room in confusion. After taking a deep breath, he flopped back on to the pillow and groaned at the stiffness in his neck and the throb of pain from the cut on his forehead. He swatted over toward the bedside table to hit the alarm clock and stop the music that had awakened him. As he fumbled around on the nightstand, he realized there was no clock. He sat up and looked around, trying to figure out where he was.

"My grandmother," he mumbled and dropped back onto the pillow, which he discovered was damp with sweat. He lay staring at the ceiling and let the music wash over him as the fog of sleep drifted away. The ceiling fan sat still and, as Marcus pulled his sweaty T-shirt away from his chest, he wished he had thought to turn it on before tumbling onto the bed. By the time Helen and Inez had left him alone, he'd quickly realized just how exhausted he was. He had not bothered to eat anything or to clean himself up or to remove his bloody clothes. He had clapped twice to turn out the lights, wandered down the hallway to the bedroom, and dropped onto the bed. Sleep had tackled him almost as soon as his head touched the pillow. Now he regretted that decision, as his clothes had practically fused themselves with his skin. He was hot and uncomfortable, and his stomach grumbled loudly with hunger. Also, he seemed to be hallucinating a piano concerto.

Can a head wound make you hear music? Marcus swung his feet over the edge of the bed and onto the floor. His head spun at the sudden movement. He braced himself against the mattress, and the music stopped. He squinted his eyes and concentrated to see if that could make the music start again. A scale of notes made a flourish as if in response. *God, what is this music?* He looked around the bedroom again and realized the sound was coming from the living room. He stood, pulled the pink bedspread around his shoulders, and stumbled toward the sound of the piano.

He found an old woman sitting on the piano bench and playing. Her eyes were closed, and she rocked back and forth in time with the jaunty song she was banging out. The bench creaked slightly under her weight. Her long white hair, pulled back on her head and held behind her by a wide, zebra-print headband, swayed with each shift of her body.

"Um, hello?"

The old woman opened her eyes and looked over at him. She smiled broadly, nodded her head, and kept playing. Her bright white tennis shoes danced on the damper pedals in time with the music.

"Can I, um, help you?"

The woman just smiled again and kept banging away on the keys. Marcus listened. It would be rude to interrupt her, but then again, maybe he should call the police. As she ended the song with a run up the keyboard, she closed her eyes and took a deep breath. When she stood, Marcus noticed her rainbow-striped T-shirt was inside-out. She closed the cover over the piano keys and turned to Marcus to smile again. Behind her thick, pink-framed glasses, her eyes shone like the eyeglass chain that dropped from her temples. She lifted a shaky hand

and patted him on the cheek. Then she crossed to the front door and walked out of the house; the screen door slammed shut behind her.

Marcus stood with his mouth agape and watched her walk down the sidewalk until all he could make out was her bright fuchsia jumper. When she turned to the left on the road and disappeared from sight, he rubbed the heel of his hand in his eye and pulled the bedspread tighter around his shoulders. "What the hell was that?"

He stood staring out the open door until an urgent need to pee brought him back to the world. As he turned to go into the bathroom, he heard a voice call through the open door.

"Yoo-hoo!"

"God! I should install a revolving door."

A pudgy woman stood in the doorway on the other side of the screen. She cupped one hand over her eyes as she attempted to peer through the screen and held a brown paper grocery sack by her side in the other. Though she stood barely five feet tall, her hair, white with a bluish tint, floated so far above her head in a frizzy puff it nearly doubled her height.

"Can I help you?" Marcus asked as he crossed toward her.

"Marcus?" the woman asked as she pulled the screen door open and stepped into the room. The heavy-looking pewter cross on a chain bounced against the chest of her simple dress with each movement. "You must be. You look just—"

"Like my father. Yes. We've covered that."

The woman looked him up and down and frowned. "Is that what you are wearing to the diner? It looks like you slept in them."

Marcus spread the blanket open and looked at his wrinkled, bloody clothes. "Well, I did."

"Goodness, they're all bloody. Well, that'll never do. I know it's just the diner, but you really don't want everyone's first impression of you to be what mine is. You look like a hobo, bless your heart."

"Well, I don't have much choice. My clothes are all still in my car, I hope. Also, I was exhausted last night, you know, what with being in a wreck and all."

"Young man, there is no need to get huffy. I'm simply suggesting that you might want to get cleaned up before we head to the Tammy. Here." She thrust the paper bag toward him. "I brought you some old things out of the church's clothing donation bin. Helen said you might need some clothes. And please hurry. Helen gets so uppity if we're late."

Marcus took the sack from the woman and glanced inside. He could see a brightly patterned Hawaiian shirt and some plaid pants. He grimaced at the clash of patterns and colors. He looked back at the frowning woman. "I'm sorry. I'm not trying to be rude, but I just woke up and I'm a little confused. Also, my head is pounding and I really need to pee."

The woman crossed her arms and glared at him. She looked at the kitchen counter and gasped. Her chubby cheeks, swathed in bright pink blush, wobbled as she shook her head. "Did you leave that casserole sitting out all night?"

"Guess I did." Marcus shrugged and shifted from foot to foot. The pressure in his bladder was increasing.

"Good heavens. Are you trying to get the ptomaine or something?" She crossed to the counter and read the name scrawled on a piece of masking tape stuck to the bottom of the dish. Her eyebrows, already painted on in an arch of permanent surprise, shot farther up toward her bouffant. "Helen Warner made this? Well, it is God's grace you didn't eat it. It might've killed you even without sitting out all night." She removed the foil from the dish, stepped over to the trash can beside the island, and dumped the contents out of the dish. "Well, why are you just standing there staring at me like a scarecrow? We need to get a move on."

"Look, I walked in here to find some strange woman—I have no idea how she got in my house—sitting there playing god knows what on the piano. Then she just smiled and walked out. Never said a word. And now another strange woman is standing in my house insulting my clothes."

"Oh, honey, I wasn't trying to insult you. I just thought you might want—"

"Ma'am, who the hell are you?"

"Well, there is no need for such language. Your grandmother never would have stood for that kind of language in her house. Not even from Inez." The woman pursed her lips and glared at Marcus. Slowly she stuck out her hand and said, "My name is Priscilla Ellington. Helen asked me to come get you. She had to pick up Delores Richards and take her on some errands, thanks to your little tangle-up yesterday."

"Yeah. Miss Inez already got on to me about that. Could you just hang on for one second?" Marcus dropped the sack onto the piano bench and hurried into the bathroom. Closing the door behind him, he rushed to lift the toilet lid and pee. After finishing up, he stared at the bandage on his forehead while he washed his hands. He called out through the closed door, "You're the preacher's wife, right? Mrs. Ellington?"

"Yes, but you can call me Priss. Everyone does. I take it my reputation proceeds me?"

Marcus stepped back into the room, regret over his foul language making him blush. "Helen and Inez mentioned you last night."

"Really? Well, don't believe a word they said. Inez Coffee lets her mouth get going and lord knows what will come out. I try to get her to quit gossiping and clean up her language, but you know those Methodists." Priscilla threw up her hands and shrugged her shoulders. "I even made her a lovely needlepoint with James three verse six on it. Do you know that one? 'And the tongue *is* a fire, a world of iniquity.' But do you think that did any good? Shoot. I saw that very same gift at Brother Marty's in the discount bin not two weeks later. And that thing took me at least a week to stitch."

"I'm sure she didn't mean to offend—"

"Pfft." Priscilla waved his words away. "I've forgiven and forgotten. Anyway. As for your other mysteries, the woman playing your piano was Annie Gordon. You don't need to worry about her. She's harmless, really. She only plays good church music. She used to be the organist at the Methodist Church, but she has a little blood flow problem now," Priscilla pointed at her temple and winked her eye. "So they replaced her with that prissy Martin Prescott." Priscilla crossed to the piano and bent toward the book of music resting there, then slid her glasses down her nose so that she could read the title. "The song she was playing was apparently 'In the Garden,' which is such a lovely hymn. I think it was your grandmother's favorite. We don't sing it at the Baptist church, but that's neither here nor there. Any song about Jesus is a good song, don't you think?"

"Um, I don't really have an opinion on that."

"You're not one of those big-city atheists, are you?" She looked at him with a skeptical squint.

"No, ma'am. But I didn't really grow up going to church. The only gospel music I heard was on the radio in the car sometimes. My mama always had to work on Sundays so—"

"Well, that'll never do." Priscilla clicked her tongue and shook her head. "You should come to church with me. Our new preacher isn't as good as my husband was, but ever since he had his stroke, Frank can't really preach as good of a sermon as he used to in the old days."

"We'll see." Marcus snatched the sack from the piano bench and pulled the clothes out. "I don't really plan on being in town very long. I'm going to go put these on, okay?"

Priscilla nodded and sat on the piano bench. Marcus went into the bedroom and removed his blood-stained clothes. As he stepped into the bright plaid pants, he called out, "I still don't understand why this Annie person was in here playing my grandmother's piano. And how did she get in? I swear I locked that door last night." He buttoned the

41

pants, which hung loosely around his narrow hips. He picked up the vibrant floral shirt and winced as he slipped it over his tender arms.

"Oh, she does that to everyone. Well, not everyone. If she thinks your house is dirty she won't come in. Cleanliness next to godliness and all that."

"And everyone just lets her?" Marcus asked as he poked his head out of the bedroom doorway.

"Of course. Would you want everyone in town to think your house was so dirty she wouldn't come in? Shoot, even Cookie Ginsberg lets her come in and play hymns." Priscilla raised her hand to shield her mouth and whispered, "She's Jewish!" She prattled on, "One time, Cookie's husband, Samuel, came home from work and found Annie sitting at the piano and teaching his daughters to sing 'Jesus Loves Me.' He was livid. He stormed into the kitchen and said to Cookie, 'Do you hear what that woman is teaching your daughters? Jesus loves me!' Cookie was so worried that people would think she had a dirty house if Annie didn't come in, she just turned to him and said 'Samuel, maybe he does!'"

"Oh my god! That is hysterical." Marcus turned back into the bedroom and glanced at himself in the full-length mirror in the corner. His close-cropped red hair was mussed, and his blue eyes were bloodshot from his fitful sleep. He couldn't decide if it was the clashing colors or the cut over his brow that was making his eyes water. *I look like I escaped from a loony bin.* As he buttoned the shirt, the fading bruise around his eye caught his attention. *Guess I did in a way.*

He turned to one side and inspected himself in the mirror. The clothes hung from his trim frame and made him seem thinner than he was. Marcus frowned. Besides the garish patterns, he hated the bagginess, preferring to show off the lean body he had worked so hard to maintain despite Robert's insistence that they eat incredibly fattening food. Robert had liked him in the tight clothes too; he considered

Marcus's lithe, young frame a trophy to be displayed. After shaking his head to clear the thought of Robert, Marcus snagged a corner of the tape that held the bandage on his forehead. The tape yanked at his skin as he tried to pull it off. "Ouch!"

"You okay in there?"

"Yes." Marcus dropped his arms to his side. As he looked around the floor for his shoes and belt, he mumbled, "My bandage."

"I can say a prayer on that if you want."

"That's okay." He stepped back into the other room to find Priscilla staring at a framed photograph she had retrieved from the back of the piano. "You know, Miss Annie played real good but she didn't say a word to me."

With her eyes locked on the photograph, Priscilla replied, "She never does. Well, not for nearly forty years. Oh, that is a sad, sad tale." Priscilla closed her eyes and thought. "I probably shouldn't…well, I guess it isn't gossip if it's the truth. See, Annie and her little sister used to run around with all of us girls, even though her family was much poorer than ours. But we didn't care about that. While the rest of us got married and had families, Annie and her sister were poised to be old maids. But the railroad transferred this young fella here, and he took a shine to Annie. I was shocked because her sister was really the pretty one. But he up and asked Annie to marry him. The Do-Nothings helped her plan the ceremony, though we weren't the Do-Nothings back then, just a bunch of silly girls. We wanted to make the day special for her, so I helped with the flowers. Inez made the cake, and Helen planned all the songs. Your grandmother, she had just moved here and barely knew Annie, but she made the prettiest dresses for her and her sister. Your grandmother was always doing kind things like that. Look," Priscilla said as she handed the photograph to Marcus. "Inez took that picture the morning of the wedding."

In the picture, several young women in frilly dresses posed with their arms around each other's waists. Marcus could barely make the young grinning faces in the faded picture favor the older women he had met. His grandmother, apparently determined to remain a mystery to him even in photographs, had her head lowered, and her hair fell across her face so that he could barely make out her features. He traced the outline of her face with his finger and smiled.

"Anyway, the day of the wedding came, and the whole town was at the church. But that young man and the sister never showed up. Turns out, they'd done run off together. We were all in a state of shock, I tell you." Priscilla took a deep breath and sighed. "Poor Annie was so heartbroken, she walked over to the piano at the front of the church, sat, and started to cry. We all rushed over to comfort her, but she just pushed us away. She threw her shoulders back, wiped away the tears, and started playing the piano. Well, since then she hasn't said a word to a soul. All she does is wander around town and play people's pianos." Priscilla heaved another deep sigh. She stepped to Marcus's side and looked over his shoulder at the picture. "It's all sad but, you know, all those years of playing really did improve her piano skills."

"Is that you?" Marcus pointed at a pregnant woman in the picture.

"Used to be." Priscilla chuckled. "Look how happy Annie looks there. Marcus, don't ever break some girl's heart like that."

"You don't have to worry about that."

"Look at how pretty your grandmother was," Priscilla said in barely a whisper as she pointed at the picture. "Lord, I miss her. She was so pretty right up to the end. We made sure she looked real pretty in her casket." Priscilla stroked Marcus's arm. "Her illness made her lose a lot of weight, but, you know, when people die, they sometimes swell up a little, and it really made her look more like her old self."

With a small gasp, Marcus jerked his head to stare at Priscilla.

Priscilla didn't move her gaze from the photo. "I could take you out to her grave sometime if you want."

"Ooo-kay." Marcus screwed up his face and gestured toward the front door with his shoulder. "So maybe we should get going? I'm supposed to go to see about my car and my duffel bag. I think it's at some garage?"

"I know. Helen told me. I'm supposed to drop you off there." She took the photograph from Marcus and sat it back on the piano. "Let's go. I better not be late. The last thing I need today is Helen Warner giving me grief." She turned from the photograph and looked Marcus up and down again. "You look real handsome in the Reverend's old clothes."

"So that's the historic district. The town council decided to call it that, and now you have to get their approval on paint colors or anything else you want to do with your house."

Priscilla gestured wildly with one hand and held the steering wheel in a death grip with the other. With each motion of her free hand, her other hand jerked the wheel and made the car swerve slightly to the left or right. During the five-mile drive into the town, Marcus was beginning to feel seasick from the wild rocking of the car. He had been a bit concerned for his safety when he first saw Priscilla's car, which had several large dents scattered along the passenger side, but she had assured him those were from a previous run-in with Delores Richards. His fears were not eased, however, when he climbed inside and realized that Priss sat on two thick Sears catalogs to help her see over the steering wheel.

"They really are beautiful homes," Marcus agreed as he turned away from the woman and closed his eyes tight.

"Inez and her husband used to live down there but she didn't take too kindly to being told that she had to get rid of the cement deer she had in her front yard, so she moved out to the houses near Eloise and Helen, which I will never understand. It was such a lovely old house that had been in her family for years. Also, those deer are just plain tacky. I'd have given anything to live in one of those old houses, but we always lived in that gloomy little rectory that the church provides. We didn't move out to Crepe Myrtle Manor until just a year or two ago, after Frank's stroke. Anyway, we are entering downtown now."

Marcus watched the town roll by, reminded of every other small town he and his mother had passed through. The usual tree-lined streets of cracker-box homes gave way eventually to a quaint downtown. Without looking closely, he could guess the businesses he would find. He knew there would be a pharmacy, a jewelry store, and a dress shop with a name intended to sound classy and possibly French, probably next to a hardware store with a family's name painted across the windows. However, Priss parked before they had driven far enough into downtown for him to see much.

"So, here you go. Hank Hudson's garage." Priss gestured out the window.

Marcus looked at the building and knitted his eyebrows in confusion. "The sign says Murphy's?"

"Well, it used to be Jessie Murphy's, but he retired and sold it to Hank Hudson."

"So, I should ask for Hank?"

"Honey, it's a one-man shop. You can ask, but you'll be asking him. Now, Helen said to remind you to come on over to the Tammy when you get things settled here. It's just a couple of blocks that way, so you can find it again, right? It's just past The Chic Petite dress shop and Dobbins Feed Store. It's got a big old neon sign, so you can't miss it."

"Yes, ma'am. I should be fine. Thanks again for the ride." Marcus hopped out of the car onto the sidewalk and shut the car door. He patted the roof of the car and bent over to wave to the woman inside. He stood with his hand still poised in the air as Priscilla's Buick swerved its way down the road before making a U-turn in the middle of the next intersection and speeding past him toward the diner. Marcus sighed in relief to feel the solid ground of the sidewalk beneath his feet. His stomach rumbled as he thought about the food that would be available at the diner. "No," he chastised himself, "take care of the car and get some decent clothes. Then you can eat."

Marcus turned to face the two-story building behind him. To the left of the building, a chain-link fence blocked off a parking lot with several old cars scattered about, some missing doors and tires or with crinkled bumpers. Just inside the fence sat a lawn chair. A piece of cardboard with the words "Skeet's Carwash. Skeet'll be back later." scrawled on it in black marker sat in the chair.

The left side of the building was dominated by two plate glass windows with the words Murphy's Auto and Body. Est: 1957 painted on them in red, white, and blue lettering. Under these words, in what appeared to be a fresher coat of paint, someone had added, Yes, I can fix it. To the right of the windows, a glass and metal door led into the room beyond. A sign listing the hours of business hung on the inside of the door below another that stated, "In God We Trust. All others pay up front."

Marcus cupped his hands around his eyes and peered through the window. He could see mismatched chairs lining the walls of a waiting area around a coffee table covered with magazines. The red and white reflection of a soda machine in the corner flickered across the gray tile floor and cast a murky hue across the room. Marcus looked to the right of the door. Two large garage doors stood open and the sounds of loud music and someone banging on metal clanged out into the street. The back end of a massive, red Ford LTD poked out of the farthest garage door and blocked part of the sidewalk.

Marcus pulled the door open, stepped into the waiting area, and crossed to the counter. He noticed a sign next to a beat up, old cash register that read: "You can have it done quick or you can have it done right. Your choice." He snickered and hit the silvery bell next to the sign. The ding of the bell echoed off the bare walls and tile floor of the room and made Marcus tense at the harsh sound. Marcus drummed his fingers on the counter and waited. He glanced up at a black and white television that was suspended over the counter and flickered and rolled with a pattern of static and the occasional flash of an image from a television show.

"Hello?" He leaned over the counter to try to see into the small rear office. He could see a metal desk covered with catalogs, papers, and, sitting on an old newspaper, a greasy car part. Behind the desk, an archway revealed the first few steps of a staircase leading to the floor above. "Anybody?"

With a frustrated grunt, he wandered back to the sidewalk and walked to the tall garage doors. As he stepped into the garage, the smell of motor oil and gasoline made his nose crinkle and his empty stomach churn. The music he had heard on the street grew louder and made his ears ring. To his right, he could see the crumpled front bumper of the red Ford. He stared at it, trying to place why it looked familiar. *Oh my god, that's the car that hit me.* He took a step closer to look at the minor damage on the front end of the car, but his attention was grabbed by a loud clang of metal followed by a string of curse words from under the hood of a green car that sat in front of him.

"Come off of there, you little sonofagun."

Marcus saw a man bent over the car with his head under the hood. His dark blue work-shirt rode up in the back, exposing a swath of tan skin above a thick leather belt. His faded jeans fit snuggly over his well-formed backside; the lighter patches of fabric worn by years of wear defined his ass and thigh muscles and the white outline of a wallet on the right back pocket. A clip of keys dangling from a belt loop on his left side clanged against the metal of the car as he moved. He wore heavy leather work boots, and his heels rose slightly from the floor as he strained to reach into the chassis of the car. Marcus

49

watched the man's back muscles flex as he wrestled with something under the hood. Only a glimpse of his hairy forearm appeared for a second as he worked his arm back and forth. "Well, God bless Levi Strauss," Marcus whispered before raising his voice and calling out, "Excuse me?"

The man took no notice of Marcus's call but let out another string of foul language.

Marcus tapped the man on his shoulder.

The man jolted up and hit his head on the hood of the car overhead. "Goddangit," he yelled and rubbed the top of his head. He staggered and then turned to face Marcus with a look of confusion. He ran his greasy fingers through his sandy brown hair, which was parted to one side, and then slid his hand across his cheek to scratch his full but neatly trimmed beard. A long trail of grime streaked from his left ear across his cheek and nose. His broad shoulders flexed under his shirt as he rubbed his head, and Marcus could just barely make out the faded name *Hank* embroidered over the right pocket of the shirt. The top few buttons of his shirt were open, and thick, brown chest hair glistened with sweat underneath. In his other, grimy hand he held a wrench. Marcus stepped back, fearing the man might swing the wrench at him. The edges of the man's brown eyes crinkled as he began to laugh. "Christ, you scared the crap out of me."

"Um, I'm looking for Hank." *It's right there on his shirt, idiot. No, don't point at it.* "And the name on your shirt," Marcus added as he jabbed his finger into the other man's chest, "leads me to believe I have found him." *Put your hand down.*

The man stared at Marcus before dropping the wrench onto the car and wiping his hand down the side of his shirt. He stuck his hand out. "Indeed you have. Or I think you have. Kind of hard to think with as hard as I just hit my head. You got to give a fella some warning when he's elbow deep in a Chevrolet."

"Sorry about that." Marcus dropped his chin and gestured over his shoulder toward the waiting area. "I tried ringing the bell in there but I guess you couldn't—"

"It's the music. I ought not to play it so loud, but I can't stand it when it's too quiet. Plus it gets a little lonely in here all by myself once Skeet goes running off. I don't know why I let that kid…aw, never mind."

Marcus listened to the music pouring from the radio on a shelf in the corner. A high soprano voice pierced the silence between the men as it ran up and down a scale. "Is that opera?"

"Yeah." Hank grinned as he walked over to the radio and turned the volume down. "The public radio station plays it. It's about all I can pick up in here but, luckily, I love it."

"Really? All those women screeching in a foreign language? I never could understand it." *Shut up, Marcus.*

"Well, I happen to like the way those screechy women sound and, as a matter of fact, I speak Italian so…"

"Eh. Give me a good old country tune any day," Marcus said, causing Hank to frown slightly, shift his eyes, and fold his arms across his chest. "Opera's not really my thing but, hey, whatever revs your engine." *Why did you say that?* Marcus blushed and he instantly regretted his clumsy attempt at a pun.

"Rev an engine. Heh. Funny." Hank's face softened, and he dropped his arms again.

"I *am* sorry I startled you."

"Like I said, serves me right. So…" The man stared, his eyes scanning Marcus up and down.

"Sorry?" Marcus asked, unsure what the man was seeking. *God, his eyes are gorgeous.*

"So did you just come in here to give me a concussion and insult my music or was there something I can do for you… mister?"

"Oh, yeah. Sorry." *Jesus. Quit apologizing.* "Sumter. I'm Marcus Sumter. I was told my car might be here?"

"Maybe. What model car?"

"A yellow Fiat?"

"Oh!" Hank's eyes widened, and his eyebrows shot toward his hairline. "You're the one Miss Richards walloped!"

"Guilty."

"Whoo, boy. Yeah, your car is here. Well, what's left of it. Afraid in a battle between that little European thing and Miss Richards's Ford LTD over there, you didn't stand much of a chance." Hank pointed toward the red car on the other side of the garage. "Barely made a dent in her car, but your sardine can? Well…"

"Is it bad?" Marcus cocked his head and chewed on his lip.

"Well, you won't be driving it out of here today."

"Shit," Marcus spat out and dropped his head. "I was really hoping to get back on the road pretty soon."

"Not going to happen."

"Well, your sign out front says, Yes. I can fix it."

"Oh, that?" Hank chuckled and reclined, bracing himself against the fender and lifting one leg to rest against the tire. He picked up the wrench and flipped it around. "When I took over the place from old man Murphy, most of the people here didn't know me or trust me. They'd all come in wanting him to work on their cars instead of me. I got sick of them always asking me 'Are you sure you can fix it?' so I added that to the sign."

"So, can you? Fix it?"

"Eventually," Hank drawled out the word. "You must not have seen your car after the wreck?"

"No. I barely remember it happening. I woke up in the hospital with this stupid thing," Marcus pointed at the bandage on his forehead. "Everything's been a little foggy since then."

"Including your fashion sense?"

"What?" Marcus asked and then glanced at the clothes he was wearing. "Oh, god. I forgot. These are *not* my clothes."

52

"I was going to ask you how many batteries that shirt took." Hank laughed and pushed off the car. "I figured, with the Fulton county tag on the car, maybe those clothes are some Atlanta thing."

"God, no. My normal clothes were messed up in the wreck, and this old woman gave me…" Marcus tugged on the hem of the shirt, trying to cover as much of the loud plaid pants as possible. "Did you find a duffel bag in the car?"

"Oh, I didn't go into the car. Just towed it back here." Hank placed his hand on the small of Marcus's back and steered him toward the garage doors open at the back of the room. "Let's go take a look. It's out back." Hank's hand on Marcus's back made a tingle run up his spine.

Marcus walked into the lot behind the garage and groaned when he saw the twisted metal that had been his car. "Good lord!" The front end sat completely off kilter and the headlights were shattered like empty eye sockets. The hood stood open like a casket lid with pieces of the engine jagging into the open space. The front left tire was flat. The windshield and driver's side window were milky from shattered glass, and the door sat slightly ajar, apparently unable to close correctly over the warped frame. He stared at the car, and his head begin to spin, and a bead of sweat formed on his brow. "Holy shit."

"Yeah. Looking at it, I can't believe all you got was that scratch on your head and a black eye."

Marcus reflexively patted his eye. He spread his legs wider to steady himself as the ground beneath his feet seemed to shift. Tears began to sting the corners of his eyes, and he bit his lip to stop it from trembling.

Swinging the wrench beside him, Hank walked over to the car and peered through the back window. "Yep. There is a duffel bag back here. But I'll probably have to get a crowbar to get this—"

Marcus crossed to the back of the car, took the wrench from Hank, and smashed the back window. Angrily swinging the wrench around in the opening to knock the pieces of glass loose, Marcus turned his head to the side to avoid the flying shards. When the opening was clear, he stuck his arm in and grabbed the strap of the duffel bag and pulled it out. He flung it over his shoulder and dropped the wrench onto the pavement. He spun on his heels and began storming back into the garage.

"Or you could do that," Hank mumbled behind him as he stooped to pick up the wrench.

Marcus took a few more steps toward the garage and stopped. His eyes flashed with each beat of his heart, and rivers of cold sweat ran down his temples and between his shoulder blades. "Um…I suddenly don't feel so good. Could you…" Marcus dropped the duffel and tried to steady himself. He saw the sky above him spinning as he began to fall backward. Marcus braced himself for impact until Hank's arms wrapped around his chest from behind.

"Easy there. Why don't we sit you down?" Hank pulled Marcus into the garage and sat him in a chair. He knelt and looked into his eyes. Marcus's stomach flipped again; he was unsure if it was from the panic attack or the intent stare that Hank gave him. "You going to be all right? Let me get you some water."

"No. No. It's fine. I just. Oh, god." Marcus dropped his head into his hands and tried to slow his breathing.

"Are you sure?"

"Please, just let me sit here for a second." The paved floor of the garage between his feet and the tips of Hank's work boots blurred in and out of focus. *Oh god. What have I done?*

"I'm getting you some water."

Hank's boots disappeared as he hurried into the waiting room. As soon as the coast was clear, Marcus hopped from the chair and bounded to his discarded duffel bag. *You idiot.* He snatched the bag from the ground and slung the strap over his shoulder. He hurried across the garage as quietly as he could. Just as he reached the doorway, he heard Hank's voice calling from behind him.

"Dude? Where are you…"

Marcus lowered his head and stormed down the street away from the garage with the weight of the duffel bag banging against the backs of his thighs. *Keep walking. Keep walking. Don't look back.* He stopped to look at the street sign on the corner and his knees grew weak again. The letters on the sign blurred behind the tears in his eyes, and he staggered around the corner. *Just keep walking.*

MARCUS SCURRIED AROUND THE TWO-STORY brick building on the corner without a passing glance behind him. His pulse thumped in his ears, and sweat ran from his temples and hairline, stinging at the cut on his forehead. He steadied himself against the side of the building, leaned back, and tilted his head toward the bright blue morning sky. He dropped his duffel bag at his feet. The building's red brick, which had been heated by the morning sun, sent soothing warmth through his back and shoulders. He bent and placed his hands on his knees, trying to slow his breathing and the pounding of his heart.

As the spinning sensation began to die down, he stood and took a few more deep breaths before looking around to orient himself. *Where the hell is that diner?* Marcus scanned the buildings across the street, but the flashing in his eyes made it hard to focus. *You just need some food. Food will help.* He took a few more breaths and swallowed the lump in the back of his throat. *God, you idiot. How could you make such a fool of yourself in front of a complete stranger? And a hot stranger at that.* Marcus closed his eyes and placed his hand on the bricks. He felt a sharp tap on his shoulder. *Don't be him. Don't be him.*

"Excuse me." A high-pitched voice interrupted his thoughts.

Marcus opened his eyes and focused on the face in front of him. A young man stood staring at him with blue eyes wide open and expectant. His mouth was twisted to one side in a look of concern. His brown hair was buzzed close over his ears but was longer on top and swept into a pompadour. *Oh, thank god. It isn't him.*

"Are you okay?" The boy angled his eyebrows toward his nose.

"Um…yes. I just feel a little…dizzy?" Marcus fumbled out his words between gasps of air. "And I'm lost."

"Ha!" the boy laughed loudly and dropped his hand from Marcus's shoulder. "How could you get lost in this Podunk town? There are only four streets in the whole downtown."

"Well, as I said, I'm a little dizzy and I couldn't read the signs."

The boy crossed his arms over his chest, covering the words *Guys and Dolls* printed on his T-shirt. "Are you Marcus?" the boy asked.

"Yes."

"Oh, good. Come on." The boy held out his hand and jerked his head to motion down the street. "I figured you were him. Or some homeless person. God, those clothes! Did you dig them out of a ditch? But we don't often have homeless people here, so I figured you must be him. Let's go."

"What?"

"Nonnie told me to come find you. I'm supposed to bring you to the Tammy."

"Oh. Yeah. Okay. That's what I was looking for."

"Well, we haven't got all day." The boy shook his hand toward Marcus and looked at him with an impatient smirk.

Marcus took the boy's hand and stumbled slightly as the young man jerked him toward the street.

"You think it's from the wreck?"

"What?"

"The dizziness. Frankie said Miss Myrtle was in the diner this morning and said some redhead was in the hospital yesterday because

Miss Richards rammed the bejeezus out of him. Well, I saw the red hair and that big old bandage on your head, and just figured—"

"Yes. That was me. But can we talk about something else."

"Okay. Like what?"

"Like who are you?"

"Oh, yeah." The boy stopped abruptly, dropped Marcus's hand, and turned to face him. "I forget everyone don't know me yet. But they will someday. I'm going to be a big star on Broadway. Then I'm going to do TV and movies. Me and Frankie got it all planned out. Once we save enough money to get to New York. And then, bam! My name in bright lights all over Times Square."

"And what name are we going to see?" Marcus couldn't follow the boy's words, which seemed to bounce from thought to thought just as he bounced down the sidewalk, jumping over cracks on his way. Despite the clunky workman's boots he wore, the boy was surprisingly light on his feet.

"Raffield Warner the third!" The boy puffed out his chest and hooked his thumbs in his belt loops. "Ain't it classy?"

"Oh, you're Helen's grandson."

"That's me! Pleased to meet me!" The boy bowed slightly.

"I thought Miss Helen said your name was Skeet."

"Well, everyone here calls me that, thanks to my granddaddy." The boy wrinkled his nose before turning to amble down the street as Marcus shuffled along beside him. "On account of me being a third, my mama wanted to call me Trey, can you imagine? Like a cafeteria tray? Ugh. But, when I was little, my granddaddy said I was always buzzing around bugging everybody like a mosquito. Skeeter. Which became Skeet. It stuck. But I don't think Skeeter will look very good on a marquee."

"No. Probably not." Marcus chuckled. The boy's excited babbling should have set Marcus's nerves on edge, but after the mad rush of the panic attack in the garage, he found the boy's twangy voice oddly soothing. Skeet's voice grew louder as he nattered on about the plays he was going to do someday. The boy never turned to look back to see if Marcus was still following him, but skipped on ahead with his hands gesticulating wildly with every word. By the time they stopped walking, Marcus's heartbeat had returned to a normal pace and the spinning in his head was nearly gone.

"Here we are. The finest little diner in all of Marathon, which, conveniently, is also the *only* diner in all of Marathon." Skeet swept his arms out and gestured at the building they faced.

The diner took up a quarter of the city block; its silvery siding glimmered in the morning sun. A metal bracket jutted over the diner door and held a bright neon sign that flashed "The Tammy Dinette: Stand by Your Ham and Eggs." Below the sign, two tall and wide single-paned windows showed the bustle of the crowd inside. Marcus could see that most of the booths along the windows were occupied, and a tall redheaded waitress stood next to one of the booths furiously scribbling on a pad and nodding her head.

"Let's go," Skeet said as he hopped to the door and yanked it open. He swept his arm across his body and said in a terrible British accent, "After you, my good sir."

Marcus grinned at the boy and stepped into the diner. The sudden rush of country music mixed with the murmur of the restaurant crowd, the smell of greasy food and coffee, and the glare of fluorescent lights from the Formica tables and countertops flooded Marcus with a sense of relief and comfort. He could feel the last bits of tension slip from his shoulders as he watched the two waitresses in pink uniform tops and skirts scurry from table to table as different patrons raised their hands to get each woman's attention.

"Georgette?" Skeet called to the redheaded waitress. "Georgette!"

"Skeet, what do you want? I'm so in the weeds here I need a lawn mower."

59

"Will you tell Frankie I'm back? I'm going to take Marcus here to sit with Nonnie, but I'll wait for Frankie at the counter."

"She's five feet in front of you at the register. Tell her yourself," the woman said as she shooed the two men away with her order pad. "Paulette? Did you get table four?"

"That's Georgette. Her mama, Miss Francine, owns this place. She's probably back in the kitchen. That other waitress with the black hair?" Skeet pointed across the room. "That's her other daughter Paulette. And then Frankie over there with the blond hair is the youngest. She's my best friend."

"Georgette, Paulette, and Frankie? Why not another 'ette?"

"Her real name is Frankette, but that's just awful. We're going to have to change it in New York."

"Ooh. Yeah." Marcus winced. "Why not Yvette or something?"

"Oh, each girl is named after her daddy. So it had to be Frankette. Miss Francine is our own Liz Taylor. She's had three husbands. George, Paul, and Frank." Skeet shrugged and waved his fingers toward Frankie at the cash register.

Marcus twisted his head to take in all the sights around the diner as he followed Skeet through the occupied tables scattered around the center of the room. The pink walls were plastered with posters of Tammy Wynette and various country singers, some of whom he recognized but most of whom he did not. Old album covers and records, the occasional mirror, and clusters of photographs of people eating in the diner filled the few empty spots between the posters of women with big smiles and bigger hair.

"Wow, it's crowded," Marcus said as he stepped around a table and followed the long counter that ran most of the length of the room. All but a few of the aqua stools were taken. "The Waffle Barn was never this busy."

Marcus was so caught up in watching the frenzy of the staff that he didn't notice Skeet had stopped walking until he had bumped into him from behind.

"I know I've got a cute ass, but you could buy me dinner first?" Skeet drawled over his shoulder as he ticked his right eyebrow upward.

"Um…" Marcus shot Skeet a confused look.

"Relax. I'm kidding."

"Marcus, darling!" Inez's loud voice shot over the din of the room and brought Marcus's attention to the turquoise banquette in the corner. Helen, Inez, and Priscilla sat in the booth with steaming cups of coffee and a few half-empty plates scattered on the table in front of them. "We were beginning to think you'd been abducted by aliens or something! What in God's name are you wearing?"

"Skeet, honey, thank you for delivering him in one piece." Helen smiled at her grandson. "Now go find somewhere to sit and let the grown-ups talk."

"I'm eighteen, Nonnie. I'm a grown-up."

"Fine. But you skedaddle. The Do-Nothings and I need to have a little chat with Mr. Sumter here." She fanned the boy away from the table. "Go on."

"Fine," Skeet groused and stuck his bottom lip out. He turned and flounced toward the cash register. "Rather talk to Frankie anyway."

"Marcus, sweetie," Helen said, "you look a little pale. Are you feeling all right?"

"I just got a little lightheaded at the garage. Maybe it was the fumes?"

"You ate some of that godawful casserole that Helen brought over, didn't you?" Inez shook her head in dismay. She pulled her burgundy fanny pack from around her waist and dropped it on the table. "I think I've got some antacid in here somewhere."

"Inez, will you lay off my cooking?" Helen swatted Inez on the shoulder as the women all laughed.

"No, ma'am. I was so tired, I went straight to bed. I actually didn't eat anything."

"Well," Priscilla said, "that's probably what's wrong. We need to get some food into you. Inez, scoot over and let the man have a seat."

As Inez shuffled over, she waved toward the waitress. "Georgette! Georgette! Could you bring Marcus a menu?"

"Just a second," Georgette sang as she scampered past the table with several plates of food on her arms.

"Is it always this busy?" Marcus asked as he glanced around. From the booth, he could see behind the counter where a cutout in the wall showed a slice of the kitchen that lay beyond. An older woman, her salt-and-pepper hair bound in a hair net, flung a plate onto the pass-through and rang a bell that sat there. The dark-haired waitress burst through the swinging door that led into the kitchen, bumped Frankie in the back, and hustled to the shelf to snatch the plate of food. Frankie shouted something at her sister before she turned back to hand money to a short, skinny man in a policeman's uniform. The cop hiked up his pants by his gun belt with one hand as he took the cash with the other.

"Only for the breakfast crowd," Helen said as she stretched over the back of the booth and snagged a menu from the dirty table behind her. She handed it to Marcus and continued, "Lunch is a little calmer, and then she closes at three. Closed on Sundays too. Francine always says someone else can take care of dinner and God can take care of Sunday. Plus, she doesn't want to miss *Wheel of Fortune* at night. Normally, Francine would sit with us, but like Inez said last night, one of her cooks up and quit on her yesterday, and now she's in a bit of a bind."

"Why did that boy run off like that?" Priscilla asked, putting down her coffee cup, its rim marked with several dark streaks of lipstick. "I swear that's the fifth cook she has lost this year."

"He probably got tired of Francine hitting on him." Inez rolled her eyes.

"Inez, that's a terrible thing to say," Priscilla chastised her.

"Oh, please. You know Francine hires men she thinks can handle a sausage, if you get my drift."

"Inez Coffee, I'm not going to sit here and listen to you talk dirty." Priscilla wadded her napkin and tossed it across the table at Inez. "You might offend Marcus."

"Oh, Priss, relax. I'm just joking. See, he's laughing. Not all of us have our girdles pulled as tight as you."

Paulette approached the table, set a plate in front of Helen, and handed a menu to Marcus. "Here you go, Miss Helen. I hope I got it right this time."

"Paulette, is that a ham and cheese omelet?"

"Um…" the dark-haired girl stammered as she looked at the plate. "I think so?"

"Sweetheart, you know I don't eat dairy. Get that mess away from me. It is supposed to be a vegetarian omelet with *no* cheese."

"Oh, shoot. I think this is for table six. I'm so sorry." The girl scooped up the plate and hurried off to another table.

"She is playing fast and loose with her tip," Helen muttered and tucked her hair behind her ear.

"Excuse me," the redheaded waitress interrupted as she set a menu on the table in front of Marcus. "Here is that menu you asked…oh. I see you already got one. Can I get you something to drink while you look?"

"Sweet tea, please," Marcus answered as he looked over the selection of breakfast foods on the menu.

"Hello there, Georgette," Helen said as she smiled at the waitress. "I noticed Sheriff Stewart at the counter earlier watching every move you made. You convince him to make an honest woman of you yet?"

"Miss Helen, you know he asks me to marry him every Saturday night, like clockwork. But I can't get married to such a tough old thing as a policeman. I need a man who is a little more cultured and in touch with his feminine side." The ding of the bell on the counter made Georgette turn her head. "I better go see if that's for me. I'll be back to get your order, mister." The woman walked away from the table.

"Tough old thing, my foot," Inez said to Marcus. "Sheriff Stewart is one of the scrawniest, wimpiest men I have ever met. Hell, he is half her height. She could throw him across this room if she wanted. But he is crazy about her. I don't know why she won't just give in and marry him. She's almost thirty. Not like she's got a lot of options."

"Not like her sister Paulette," Priscilla added. "That girl has half the men in town after her. And she runs just slow enough to let most of them catch her. Though I never thought she was that pretty. Frankie's the pretty one."

"Pretty, yes," Helen nodded her head, "but, bless her heart, her head doesn't cast a shadow."

The women paused in the chatter as Paulette walked back to the table with another plate balanced on her arm. She slid the plate in front of Helen and turned to hurry away. Marcus glanced at the plate to see two sunny-side up eggs, a bowl of lumpy grits, and three slices of bacon.

"Paulette, dadgummit!" Inez hollered across the diner as she looked at the plate. "This is still not right!"

"I'll take that one," Marcus said as he used his fingertips to slide the plate across the table. He glanced around for some utensils. "But it appears I will have to eat it with my fingers."

"Here's your tea," Georgette said as she approached the table and set the glass of iced tea in front of Marcus. "Did you know what you want to…oh…you already got food. Did Paulette take your order? She knows this is my table. If she is trying to take my tips I swear I will snatch her bald."

64

"Can you just find me some silverware?"

"Hold on," Georgette said and blew a quick puff of air to move her strawberry bangs off her forehead. She turned and hurried back toward the counter.

"So, Marcus," Helen said as she turned to face him, "you went to the garage and met Mr. Hudson, I assume."

"Yeah."

"And?"

"And he's nice, I guess." Marcus turned away from the women to look around the diner, hoping to hide the embarrassment that he could feel creeping across his face.

"No, darling, the car."

"Oh." Marcus dropped his chin and stared at his eggs. "Can we not talk about that?"

"Honey, what's the matter?" Inez asked.

"Well, to be honest, I think the car is really what made me feel so bad. When he took me out back to see it, I couldn't believe how smashed up it was. And even more, I couldn't believe that I was able to walk away from it."

"Was it really that bad?" Priscilla asked, her eyes widening behind her glasses.

"The front bumper is practically the back bumper now. Seeing it all crushed like that, I just realized that I could've died in that thing and I freaked out." Marcus nabbed a piece of bacon, shoved it into his mouth, and bit off the end. "I guess you'd call it a panic attack."

"Oh, you poor thing." Priscilla titled her head.

"And I made a complete idiot of myself in front of Hank." Marcus tossed the bacon back onto the plate. "Y'all, I nearly fainted!"

"No," Helen said with a small gasp.

"As if I was some southern belle in a bad romance novel. God! I feel like an idiot. He actually had to catch me to keep me from falling out right there."

"I'm sure he understands," Inez said, trying to sound as soothing as possible. "I mean it was such a shock seeing your car all smashed up. Did you explain it to him?"

"Well, no. He went to get me some water, and I slipped out. I was too embarrassed to talk to him and I needed some air. That's when Skeet found me and brought me here. Hank probably thinks I'm a moron."

"Oh, who cares what he thinks?" Inez brushed his comments away with a wave of her hand.

"No. I guess not. But the worst thing is now I don't know what I am going to do about a car. Until the money from the will or the house comes through, I can't afford to have that one fixed or buy a new one." Marcus could feel his heart rate picking up and sweat forming on his brow. "And I really want to get back on the road soon."

"Sweetie, you're getting yourself all worked up over nothing. It'll all work out in the end." Helen placed her hand on his.

"Your grandmother used to get all in a dither when she was hungry, too. Drink some of your tea and calm down." Inez craned her neck to look out into the restaurant and yelled, "Paulette, where is that damned silverware?"

"Marcus, God will provide," Priscilla added as she reached across the back of the booth and snagged a set of silverware from the table behind her. She unrolled the napkin and handed the fork to Marcus. "And clearly Jesus has a plan for you. He and his angels were in that car and protected you from dying, after all. I bet there is something really special just over the horizon that you can't see yet. Maybe some girl out there you're meant for."

"Priscilla, I told you Marcus is gay." Inez tossed the wadded napkin back at Priscilla. "Why would you go and say such a thing?"

"I was trying to comfort him, Inez. And you know I'm not really comfortable with that whole gay thing."

"This isn't about your comfort. This is his life. You can't sit over there and—"

66

"Girls! You are upsetting Marcus," Helen interrupted the squabbling women. "He's had a bad enough few days without you two fighting like cats."

The group sat in uncomfortable silence until Paulette approached the table and slid a plate in front of Helen.

"Here you go, Miss Helen, I think I finally got it right."

The four figures at the table leaned over to look at the plate.

"Paulette, you nitwit. This is French toast."

"That's it," Marcus spat out as he slid to the edge of the booth and stood. "I'm putting an end to this nonsense."

"Marcus, honey, where are you going?"

"To get Miss Helen her damned vegetarian omelet." Marcus stormed away from the table and around behind the counter.

"Excuse me, sir," Frankie called as he rushed past. "You can't go back there. Um, mister?"

Marcus stalked over to the kitchen door and shoved it open.

"Can I help you?" Francine Jones demanded as she looked up from the grill.

"No, ma'am, I think it's the other way around." Marcus grabbed an apron from a hook on the wall and tied it around his waist. "Now where do you keep the damned eggs?"

MARCUS UNTIED THE APRON, SLIPPED it over his head, and flung it over his shoulder. His feet ached from standing behind the grill for a few hours, but he had to admit the hustle and bustle of the kitchen had invigorated him. He had finally eaten something while he worked, and the orders coming fast and furious through the pass-through had kept his mind off his foolish behavior in the garage. His mind clear and his heart light, he jogged out of the kitchen to the table where the Do-Nothings sat chatting. He pulled a chair from the nearest table to the edge of the booth, turned it backward, and sat on it with arms draped across the back. He lifted his feet when Georgette came by with a mop and swished it under his chair.

Francine flipped over the sign hanging on the front door so that the word *Closed* was facing outside and waddled over to the table. Though Marcus suspected she was old enough to be his grandmother, Francine's slim figure and girlish face made her appear nearly as young as her three daughters. She wore the same pink uniform top and skirt her daughters wore and white tennis shoes and ankle socks over a pair of support hose. She let out a long whistle as she dropped into the booth beside Helen. "Marcus, you saved this old lady's backside today."

"Yes, Marcus," Helen said, "you never told me you were a chef! Your cooking was simply marvelous!"

"I'm a cook. Not a chef. No fancy white hats on this head. Just a paper hat or a hairnet."

"No, you were good," Francine said as she slid her shoes from her feet. "Paulette told me that Old Man Rumson said the hash browns hadn't been that good in years."

Marcus ducked his chin and blushed. "I grew up behind a grill."

"You ain't looking for a job, are you?"

"No, ma'am. I mean, thank you, but I'm not really planning on staying in town long enough to need a job."

"No! This is perfect!" Helen began to wave her hands. "You've got to stay here for a while to settle your grandmother's affairs. Why not work here at the diner while you do? You can put the money toward fixing your car. Then when it is all settled you can move on to wherever it is you're headed."

"Oh, yes," Francine pleaded. "That would be a lifesaver. Please say you will. I only need you three or four days a week. You'd have plenty of time to do other things."

"I don't know. As I said, I really want to get on the road as soon as I figure out the car—"

"Girls!" Helen interrupted Marcus. "I've just had a brilliant idea!"

Everyone at the table turned to listen to her.

"Can you cook anything besides breakfast?" she asked.

"Some," Marcus said and shrugged.

"Why don't we get Marcus to make the food for the dance?"

"Oh!" Priscilla exclaimed. "That is a wonderful idea!"

"Yes! Then I could finally enjoy one of the dances." Francine looked at her grease-spattered uniform and added, "I could wear a pretty dress without fear of ruining it with food!"

"Ladies, I'm a short-order guy. I can do omelets and chili and that kind of thing, but canapes and crudités aren't really my thing."

Helen sniffed and pushed her shoulders back. "Well, then it is a wonderful stroke of luck that I *just* decided the theme for this year's dance will be "Hoedown for Health!" You can make chili and other cowboy foods!"

"Oh, Helen. That is a wonderful idea!" Priscilla piped in. "Plus, it will give me an excuse to pull out my old square-dancing skirt!"

"No." Helen shifted her eyes to the side at Priscilla and grimaced. "We can still dress like civilized people. Honestly, Priss."

"We can decorate with hay bales and gingham tablecloths and ooh! Mason jars! Lots of mason jars!" Inez suggested. Her glasses slid down her nose with the animated bob of her head.

"Then it is settled." Helen pounded her hand on the table as a makeshift gavel. "Marcus, you are hereby hired to be the chef for our hoedown and you will work at the diner until then."

"But, Miss Helen, I don't—"

"Shush," Inez said and waved her hand at Marcus. "No sense in arguing with Helen Warner once she has her mind set on something. Just do yourself a favor. Nod your head yes and smile. Trust me. It will save you a hell of a lot of headaches and heartaches."

"You know, Helen." Priscilla leaned closer to Helen, "I have all of that blue speckled enamelware left over from when little Shel was in Boy Scouts. That looks very cowboy, don't you think?"

Inez pulled the order pad and pen out of Francine's chest pocket and began making a to-do list. "And I can talk to Golly Dorney about some western-looking flowers and Larry out at the feed supply about getting the hay bales."

"I doubt they will let us drag all that into the armory building," Priss said.

"Why don't we close off the town square and have it out there?" Francine asked. "Oh, think of it! White lights strung up everywhere. And people can dance right there in the middle of the street. We can let Martin Prescott play DJ in the gazebo!"

Marcus tuned the women out as they prattled on with their plans. He sank farther into the padding of the chair and let the stress of the day seep from his bones. Glancing over at the counter, he noticed Skeet and Frankie sitting on stools and hunched over something laid out between them. Their legs kicked freely under their stools, and occasionally Skeet would toss his head back and laugh. Paulette and Georgette whisked around the room cleaning tables and mopping the floors. Marcus walked to the jukebox in the corner and scanned the listings of songs. A hand tapping on his shoulder interrupted his thoughts.

"If you push B-17 and B-19 at the same time, it will give you five free songs," Paulette said with a wink as she leaned against the glass of the machine. "Don't tell anybody that. It's just a little secret I tell to the cuter customers."

Marcus pushed the two buttons, and the digital number flipped from zero to five. "Well, look at that!" Marcus began punching in the combinations for several songs.

"Oh, look at you, picking Loretta Lynn songs. Why don't you play something slow and give a girl a little dance."

"Paulette! Back away from the new meat!" Skeet's voice came ringing from across the room. "Marcus you better play 'You Ain't Woman Enough to Take My Man.'"

"Oh, Skeet, he ain't your man."

"No, but trust me, he won't be yours either. He doesn't play for your team."

Paulette looked at Marcus with an anxious grin. "So, I'm barking up the wrong tree?"

"Ma'am, I'm afraid you're in the wrong forest," Marcus said with a laugh and a wink back at her.

"Marcus, honey!" Helen called to him from the booth. "Why don't you get Skeet to run you back home? I'm sure you must be worn out after running around that kitchen all afternoon. The girls and I have a lot of details to work out about this hoedown. No need for you to sit here waiting on me."

"And you're going to need your rest tonight so you can be back here in the morning," Francine added. "We open at seven, so you should probably be here at six to help me get everything prepped."

"Miss Francine," Marcus said as he walked back to the booth. "I don't remember saying I would accept the job."

"I don't rightly remember asking you."

"Well, how am I supposed to get here with no—"

"I'll pick you up," Paulette said from the jukebox. "I'll probably be over there anyway, because I got a date with Jerry Dobbins tonight. He lives over that way and, well, you know—"

"Paulette, we don't need to know all the details," Francine said and frowned. "I suwanee, young lady, in my day, a little discretion was the least you could offer the world."

"I just don't know if I want to—"

"Marcus," Helen interrupted him, "I saw you in that kitchen, and honestly it is the first real smile I have seen from you since you got here. Now hush and admit defeat."

Marcus looked back and forth between the women as he thought about the job. He had to admit it had been invigorating to be back in the hustle and bustle of a diner kitchen, almost like returning home.

For the first time in months, he had actually been productive, and the ache in his feet made him feel rooted to the ground. If nothing else, he would at least have some money to tide him over until he was able to settle the estate and sell his grandmother's house.

"All right. All right. I surrender." Marcus threw up his hands. "But I'm not wearing one of those pink uniforms."

"Aw, come on, Shoe Button," Francine drawled. "You'd look adorable in a little pink skirt."

"Paulette, I will see you in the morning." Marcus turned to face the counter. "Skeet? Think you can run me home now?"

"Sure. I was supposed to go back to the car wash, but I guess it's a little late for that now." The boy pushed off the counter to spin his stool and drop dramatically to the floor. "But don't you want to listen to the rest of your songs?"

"Nah. I'll be sick of them in a few days, I'm sure."

"Bye, Franks." Skeet kissed Frankie's cheek. "Come over tonight and we can finish casting our dream revival of *Mame*."

"Bye, Skeet. And you think about what I said about Patti Lupone. She'd make a great Auntie Mame."

"Whatever. You know it's Streisand or no one." Skeet shook his head and rolled his eyes at Marcus. "Come on. I'm parked over by the courthouse."

As he and Skeet strolled toward the door, Marcus heard a sudden uproar of laughter from the women in the corner. He glanced back to see their four heads hunched together conspiratorially over the table.

"That's a wonderful idea, Helen. Eloise would be so happy if we could do that."

"Now you each know your jobs, right?"

"I really don't think I can take part in this with the church and all. I'll have to beg off on this one, girls."

"Oh, Priss, you're such a pain in my ass."

"Inez! Language!"

OVER THE COURSE OF THE next month, Marcus fell easily into the rhythm of his new life in the diner. The black ring around his eye faded, and thoughts of Robert and his mangled car began to fade as well. Francine and he perfected their frenzied dance around each other behind the grill when the diner was filled to capacity. As he worked, the familiar tools of spatula, whisk, and knife once again became extensions of his hand, and the smells of bacon frying and eggs cooking made his appetite for food and life return. The silly names the sisters invented for customers made Marcus belly-laugh, the sensation of it bubbling up in his chest an almost-forgotten pleasure. With each passing day, it grew easier to rise early in the morning and catch a ride to the diner with Francine or one of the girls.

The only part of the day he dreaded was life outside the diner and returning to a too-quiet house filled with photographs of people who shared his face and name, but who were complete strangers. The house was in theory his home, but it still seemed as if he was intruding on someone else's space. He hadn't bothered to unpack the few clothes left in his duffel bag or put away the clean clothes from the laundry basket on the bedroom floor. In the silence of his grandmother's house, he would hear the ringing of Robert's plaintive texts, the nagging thoughts about what to do with his wrecked car, and the haunting words of his mother, "Baby, it's time to move on."

More and more, he lingered well past the end of his shift at the diner to avoid going to the house. Usually he would end his day by wandering over to the Do-Nothings' corner booth to check on the latest town gossip or to see how preparations for the hoedown were going. Marcus would shuffle his way into the booth and tuck himself between Helen and Inez so that the women could explain to him who each person they gossiped about was. Most of the names meant nothing to him until he began to connect them with their usual orders, just as he had at the Waffle Barn. The more stories the Do-Nothings told about the customers who hurried in and out of the diner daily, the more the citizens of Marathon seemed like friends. He would sit happily silent and let the women's laughter and rapid-fire words sooth his work-weary muscles as he sank into the padding of the booth.

But not today.

He had finished cleaning the cooking area, flung his apron onto its hook, and headed into the dining room. He was tired but, for the first time since Robert had pressured him to quit working at the Waffle Barn in Atlanta, he'd felt useful again. As he reached the kitchen door, he'd caught a glimpse of himself in the mirror. Despite the hard work and grueling heat of the kitchen, he'd seen that he wore a pleased smile, a smile he wasn't sure he had worn since the days after his mother and before Robert. He'd straightened his back and nodded at himself in the mirror. *Hello, stranger. Where've you been?* With the smile lingering on his lips, he had glanced through the porthole window in the swinging door and seen Hank Hudson standing at the counter.

The sudden reminder of his foolish behavior the day he met Hank and of the heap of metal that sat at Hank's garage had knocked the smile from Marcus's face. His heart had begun to race as he'd ducked down below the window. He had successfully avoided dealing with

Hank or the car and had no intention of changing that. He'd placed his hands over his ears and tried to calm his breathing. He'd hidden in the kitchen until the blinds were drawn, the door was locked, and the Do-Nothings and Hank were long gone.

Once the coast was clear, Marcus crept out of the kitchen and sat at the diner counter to wait for Skeet to show up and drive him home. He silently helped Georgette and Paulette refill the sugar dispensers and ketchup bottles while he listened to their mindless prattle about their love lives. He was so distracted by the ups and downs of Paulette's busy dating schedule or the ridiculous displays of affection that Sheriff Stewart poured out toward Georgette, he had almost pushed thoughts of the crushed Fiat out of his mind.

"I told Jerry, 'I'm sorry, sugar.' He knows Tuesday nights are reserved for Andy. He will just have to wait for Thursday." Paulette punctuated her story by banging a sugar dispenser on the counter. "I told him it's just like the menu says. No substitutions."

Marcus laughed with her until a loud rapping on the diner door made his neck muscles tense. He looked at the door, dreading that Hank had returned. Outside, Skeet stood with his face pressed against the glass, his features mashed out of proportion, and his eyes crossed. "Look at that idiot," Marcus said and chuckled.

Marcus looked forward to his little chatterbox taxi arriving each afternoon. Seeing the naive joy of the boy as he flounced into the diner made him giggle. Skeet's optimism and hope were as nourishing for him as anything he cooked on the grill. Just the sound of the boy drawling "Hey, y'all," as he swung through the diner door made Marcus happy. He knew the ride home from the diner would be filled with some amusing chatter, off-key singing, and Skeet's meaningless flirtation. He hopped off the counter stool and rushed outside.

"You and Frankie are really good friends, huh?" Marcus asked as he and Skeet shuffled down the sidewalk toward the car. "You're lucky to have that."

"Oh, my god! I shudder to think of my life without her. For the longest time, I think everyone just assumed we would grow up and get married one day. I think she might have thought it too. Well, until she caught me making out under the bleachers with that exchange student from Austria we had junior year. His name was Franz. Turns out he had been under there just the day before with Frankie. One of them bisexuals, you know. Well, that just about put an end to our friendship."

"Because she found out you're gay?"

"Oh, hell, Marcus, everyone always knew I was gay. I ain't exactly like all the other boys in town. My mama always said when I told her that I liked boys, she wanted to say 'and water is wet.' No, Frankie was just pissed because she thought Franz was her ticket out of here. She started out mad at me because she thought I stole him. Which is stupid. Not like she had branded her name on his ass."

"Yeah, but I can still see where that could make some troubles."

"Well, it turned out the laugh was on both of us. Just a few days later we caught him making out in the school parking lot with Evie Dupont, the captain of the cheerleaders. I knocked on the window and told him he should've gone to France since he was clearly more interested in learning about French kissing than he was about English talking."

Marcus laughed. "You didn't."

"I did. And what really burns my butt is he wasn't even that cute. It was just that durn accent. God, it just made my knees get all wobbly. He could really kiss, too. But I can tell you one thing, I'm done with Europeans."

"Well, I can't imagine he represents the whole continent."

"I guess not, but still. So what about you? You got a boyfriend? Any funny-talking fellas in your past?"

"Not anymore."

"Oh? Do tell."

"Skeet, I'd rather not go into…shoot, there goes my phone." Relieved at the interruption, Marcus fished his phone out of his pocket and glanced at the number on the screen. "I have no idea who that is. I don't even know that area code."

Skeet peeked over his shoulder at the screen. "Oh, that's Nonnie's number. You better answer that."

"Hello?"

"Marcus?"

"Yes, ma'am."

"Oh, good. It's Helen. Helen Warner. Look, I just wanted to call and ask you to please come back to the diner tonight around seven. We want to meet with you to go over some specifics for the hoedown. We've got some of the other gentlemen who are helping out coming over and thought it might be easier if we could just plan everything all at once."

"Sure. I can do that."

"Oh, good. I will see you at seven. And Marcus?"

"Yes, ma'am?"

"Wear something nice. Bye!"

The phone went silent, then beeped as she hung up.

"What was that all about?" Skeet asked.

"Miss Helen wants me to come to a Do-Nothing meeting."

"That's weird. They never let men come to those meetings."

"Well, your Nonnie has decided I'm an honorary Do-Nothing."

"Look at you, Mister Trendsetter. The first male Do-Nothing. Breaking boundaries and you've only been here a few weeks."

"Hardly. Plus, she said some other men who are helping with the dance would be there."

"That's strange."

"And she told me to wear something nice."

Skeet stopped walking and folded his arms across his chest. "What are those old busybodies up to now?"

"It's just a meeting."

"Marcus, I think I better come to that meeting with you."

"Oh, Skeet, it's just going to be a bunch of women talking about flower arrangements."

"Trust me. When a bunch of old southern women are together talking, flowers aren't the only thing they're arranging. I'm coming with you."

"Suit yourself. You want to hang out at my place until time for the meeting?"

"That's cool. Mama asked me to put that in your yard anyway." Skeet pointed at a rectangular metal sign in the back seat.

For Sale was printed across the top of the sign in bold black lettering. Underneath was a picture of a woman who looked like Skeet but with overdone makeup, overdone hair, and an overdone smile. Below that, written in an almost indecipherable font, were the words "If you lived here, you'd be home!" followed by Katie Nell Warner and a phone number. The borders of the sign were wrapped in gaudy, gold Christmas tree garland.

"Huh," Marcus said. "I was wondering when she would get around to doing that. I talked to your mother about selling the house weeks ago in the diner. I thought maybe she forgot about me. What's with the gold stuff on the edges?"

"Mama calls it pizazz." Skeet shrugged and opened his car door. "Hey, do you care if I call Frankie and get her to come over, too? We can hang out and play cards or something. Ooh, I know! We will show you our routine we worked up for the senior recital. It brought the house down. Do you know if your grandmother had any hats? It really works better if we have hats."

MARCUS STOOD IN FRONT OF the full-length mirror in the corner of his grandmother's bedroom and looked himself up and down one last time. He had left most of his clothing at Robert's house, trying to take nothing with him that he didn't own when he had first moved in. He had done so partly out of a sense of not wanting to leave Robert any claim over him, but also because he had learned early on from his mother how much easier it is to leave in a hurry if you don't have much to take with you. He had dug his old duffel bag out of the back of a closet, shoved some clothes in it, and hit the road. He would've left the car as well since Robert had bought it for him, but that was the one area where he didn't have much choice. "Well, Miss Richards took care of that last lingering detail," he said to his reflection and shrugged. He smoothed the front of the white Oxford shirt and then pushed the shirttail a little farther into the waistband of his darkest pair of jeans.

"Marcus?" he heard Skeet call from the other room. "Are you almost done? My grandmother will be so pissed if you're late."

Marcus turned from the mirror and stepped out of the bedroom into the living room. "So, do you think this is good enough?" He pivoted in front of the two young people. "I didn't expect to need anything dressy, so I didn't bring a whole lot with me."

"It's a little wrinkly," Frankie said as she glanced from the couch. She sat playing solitaire on the coffee table with the cards they had used to play a game the pair had taught him earlier. It was a complicated game with strange wild cards and two hands for each player that Marcus still wasn't quite sure he understood how to play, though he had apparently won one round. He hadn't actually cared that it made no sense, because he had to admit it had been fun to spend an afternoon laughing, talking, and goofing off with people closer to his own age. "Surely Miss Eloise had an iron."

"Well, it was shoved in my duffel so it didn't really travel well." Marcus tried to smooth the front of the shirt with the side of his hand. "Does it look too bad?"

"It's fine," Skeet said as he walked to Marcus and picked a loose thread from the shirt. He patted Marcus on the shoulder then scanned down his body. "And those jeans do you all kinds of favors."

"Skeet…"

Skeet laughed and shook his head. "Trust me. Those women have already decided what they think of you, and no shirt is going to make a difference."

"Is that supposed to be comforting?"

"It is what it is." Skeet grinned and crossed to the sofa. He flopped beside Frankie and dropped his head onto her shoulder. "So Franks, think our little boy looks good for his first date with the Do-Nothing club?"

"Little boy? He's older than us."

"Never mind, sweetie." Skeet patted her hand and pecked her cheek. "It's a good thing you're pretty."

Marcus chuckled as Frankie swatted Skeet away. "I appreciate you guys entertaining me this afternoon. It was fun to hang out like this."

"Well, I'm sure it's nowhere near as fun as all the stuff there is to do in Atlanta," Frankie said as she scooped the cards into a pile. "I mean museums, plays, and the aquarium. Fancy restaurants. Opera and ballet. You must've been out on the town all the time."

"I didn't have a lot of friends in Atlanta. Me and Rob…um…I kept to myself. Plus I worked all the time. And a lot of that fancy stuff is really overrated. Just a bunch of uppity old people trying to impress each other with how much money they have or the eye candy on their arm."

"But still, it's culture." Frankie shuffled the cards and dealt another hand of solitaire. "It beats lunch at the Tammy and going to the movies. This town is *so* boring. When me and Skeet move to New York, we are going to do that fancy stuff all of the time."

"Well, we better find us a couple of sugar daddies if we're going to do that stuff. It ain't cheap. Right, Marcus?"

Marcus blushed and slipped into the kitchen. He opened the refrigerator and pretended to look for something.

"Ugh, a sugar daddy?" Francie asked. "How can anyone do that?"

"Lots of people marry for money. Hell, Franks, your mama did it."

"That is not true. Her first husband didn't have two cents to his name. She married him because his name was George Jones."

Marcus stood and spun around to face the couch. "What?"

"Don't you know? Frankie's mama is our version of Liz Taylor. Well, Liz had eight husbands and Miss Francine only had three, but she's got getting married down to an art."

"Skeet, that's my mama you're talking about."

"But did you say she married a man because his name was George Jones?"

"Yeah. That's my sister Georgette's daddy. You know Tammy Wynette was married to George Jones, right? Well, when Mama met her George Jones at a bar, she thought it was a sign. So she married him and named my sister after him and Tammy Wynette. But he left her about a year later, which Mama was okay with because it let her sing that Tammy song about divorce more often."

"Then she married Paulette's daddy."

"Right, Paul. But he wasn't for the money, either. She married him because his last name was Jones and she didn't want to have to change her license."

"Yeah, Miss Helen told me about him. He died?"

"Right. Then she married my daddy, Frank Jones. That's why I'm Frankette. Which I hate. I'm changing it when we move to New York."

"And she married him for the Jones name too? Or was he the money?"

"No. The name was a happy coincidence. She says she married my daddy because he was so good-looking."

Skeet looked at Marcus and rolled his eyes. "He was thirty years older than Miss Francine. He got better looking when she found out he had money. Men usually do."

Marcus laughed. "This is like a soap opera."

"Look, my mama was a single woman with two daughters to raise and no money. My daddy was from New York City. He had run a diner up there in some place galled Astoria. Anyway, he said he got sick of the winters and moved down here to open a new diner. Mama needed a job, and he hired her."

"And love blossomed right there over a big old pot of grits."

"Frankie," Marcus said with a gasp and dropped his jaw in mock shock, "you're half-Yankee?"

"Shh. We don't talk about that part. It was a mixed marriage."

"Oh, shoot, Marcus, look at the time. We better get over to the Tammy or Nonnie will skin our hides."

"Are you coming too, Frankie?"

"Please. Like I want to go hang out with a bunch of old women. I'd sooner die. No, I'm going home. Y'all can handle that without me."

Marcus stepped to the piano and checked his reflection in the mirror over it. "Are you sure I look okay?"

Skeet stepped behind him and hooked his chin over Marcus's shoulder, making eye contact with his reflection. "Not as pretty as me, but it'll do."

Marcus shifted his shoulder to knock Skeet off. "Whatever, goofball."

"All right, let's go feed you to the lions."

As soon as Marcus walked into the diner, Inez zeroed in on him and dragged him over to the spread of refreshments along the counter. He noticed that the jukebox was playing but that the volume was turned down. The shades on the windows were all drawn low and the lights were dimmed. The tables around the room had lit votive candles, and a few men sat at each table talking. Inez hugged him, shoved a plate into his hand, and began shoveling food on it while she flagged someone down over his shoulder. Skeet grabbed a handful of peanuts from a dish and scampered to a booth in the corner.

Marcus stood with a plateful of food he had no desire to eat being introduced to a man he had no desire to meet. "Nice to meet you." Marcus shifted the small plate of cheese and crackers from his left hand to his right so he could shake the hand of the man standing in front of him. The man looked to be in his early sixties and wore a powder blue jacket over a powder blue shirt that stretched across his ample belly. His thinning hair, dyed a shade of blond that would never exist in nature, was swept across his head in a tragic comb-over.

"Marcus, this is Martin Prescott." Inez introduced the man. "He's the choir director over at the church. He's a musical genius."

"Oh, Inez." The man tittered and ducked his head. "You exaggerate. It's the talent of you girls in the choir that make me look good." He raised his head and grinned at Marcus. "So, Inez tells me these girls convinced you to cook up some food for the hoedown?"

"Yeah. Still not really sure how that happened. What are they talking you into doing?"

"Music, of course," Inez answered for Martin. "Can't have a dance without music. Marcus, you enjoy music, right?"

"As much as anyone does, I guess."

"Good. You two can talk about that. I need to go check on the punch bowl. Excuse me." She flittered away, leaving the two men standing in silence.

The man stood staring at Marcus and smiling. Marcus looked at a booth across the room where Skeet sat watching him. Marcus shrugged at him and turned back to the silent man, "So…"

"Marcus, do you like big organs?"

"Excuse me?"

"Maybe I could show you my organ sometime."

"Um…"

"It's a little old, I guess, but it brings everyone so much pleasure that I just can't give up using it."

"I just met you."

"Why should that matter…oh! Oh, my!" The man's face turned bright red, making his hair look brassier in contrast. "No, silly, I didn't mean…." Martin giggled uncomfortably. "A musical organ. At the church. It's an antique with big old pipes. Maybe you could come by the church and let me play you something."

"Um, I guess I could—"

"Marcus," Helen interrupted as she walked up escorting another man on her arm. "So glad you could make it."

"Perfect timing," Marcus said as he looked at Helen in relief. "And I wasn't really given a choice about coming."

"Well, you look nice," Helen said as she looked him up and down. "So glad you dressed up a bit."

"And you look as stylish as always, Miss Helen," Martin said through a toothy grin.

"Oh, Helen Warner is dressed to the nines every day," the man next to Helen drawled. "Like she's got a job to go to or something. Don't see why. All she does is flit around all day being seen."

"Golly, being seen around town is my job. And I believe you should dress for success." Helen turned to Martin and smiled. "Pardon me for interrupting, Martin, I wanted to introduce Marcus to Golly." Helen gestured at the splinter-thin man standing beside her. "Marcus, this is Golly Dorney. Golly, this is Marcus Sumter, Eloise's grandson."

"Golly? That's an interesting name." Marcus stuck out his hand to the man, who looked at it with a slight sneer before looking at Marcus and raising an eyebrow. The man wore a tight black polo shirt that had Flowers, by Golly embroidered over the chest pocket in bright pink stitching. His long black hair was pulled back in a tight ponytail, and he wore a thin mustache over his lip that looked as if he had drawn it on with an eyebrow pencil. He appeared to be in his late fifties.

"It's a family name." The man sniffed and turned up his nose before turning to Helen with a glare. "He's a redhead."

"Yes, Golly. All the Sumters are redheads. You know that."

"Well, you know how I feel about—"

"Marcus," Helen continued, ignoring the man's comments, "Golly is going to help us with the flowers for the dance. I thought maybe you had seen something fancy up in Atlanta that you could tell him about."

"Helen, I have been arranging flowers in this town for thirty years and have never needed some city boy to tell me how—"

"Now, don't get upset, Golly. I was just trying to—"

"Shoe Button!" Francine swept up to the assembled group, dragging a man behind her with each hand. Both men wore plaid shirts and camouflage trucker caps. The two men favored one another, but one had a thick beard. "Helen, you're hogging the new boy. I haven't had a chance to introduce him to anyone at all. Why don't you go help Inez with the punch bowl?" Francine gently shoved Helen and Golly to the side. "Marcus, this is Jerry Dobbins and his brother, Larry. They run the feed store and are going to give us some hay bales to use for decorations. Boys, tell Marcus about your little store while I go fetch Jim and Dale from the butcher shop and bring them over. Or maybe Randall?"

Francine hurried across the room to a group of four men gathered around the punch bowl, some of whom Marcus recognized as regulars from the diner. She snatched a crystal cup from the table and began ladling the bright pink punch into it before handing it to one of the men and pointing toward Marcus. She put her hand on the man's back and shoved him. The dumpy young man in a police uniform stumbled as he lurched toward Marcus and spilled the punch onto the floor. Helen gasped and hurried over to the man.

"Randall, dear, you've made a little mess here, haven't you?"

"Sorry, Miss Helen," the cop said as he dropped to his knees and began mopping at the spilled punch with the napkin he held. "I was just trying to bring the redheaded guy some punch like Miss Francine asked me to."

"Oh, jeez," Marcus muttered. He turned back to the men standing around him and cleared his throat. "Gentlemen, I'm a little thirsty and I think he just spilled my punch all over the floor. If you'll excuse me." Marcus stepped away from the men and waved his hand at Skeet to call him over. The boy bounded out of the booth and skipped over to Marcus's side with a smirk.

"This is the weirdest freaking night," Marcus whispered to Skeet. "Come with me to get some punch." Marcus walked toward the table with the punch bowl until Skeet caught his elbow and stopped him.

"You really don't know what's going on here?" Skeet asked.

"What are you talking about? We're supposed to be planning the hoedown, but at the rate we're going it'll be midnight before we start planning anything. These women seem to prefer socializing to actually planning anything. And I need to go to bed early if I'm going to be back here to make breakfast tomorrow morning. I mean it's nice they want me to meet the other men that are helping—"

"Jeezumpete, you're dense."

Marcus tilted his head to one side and looked at Skeet with his eyebrows up. "What?"

"These women are trying to set you up with these men."

"Oh, come on. They are not."

"Marcus, every man in this town who is possibly gay, including me and you, are currently in this room." Skeet scanned the room and laughed. "Well, there are a few here that clearly aren't gay, but I'm not sure what that is about."

Marcus looked around the room at the men gathered in small groups chatting. In each group, he noticed at least one man glancing at him and smiling. "Why do I suddenly feel as though this is a museum and I'm the statue of David?"

"Don't flatter yourself. But, yeah, you're definitely the center of attention for a few of these guys."

"Okay, but that's just a coincidence. I mean, they wouldn't actually be trying to—"

"Shoe Button," Francine interrupted him as she walked up with another older man in tow, "this is Mickey Fletcher. He owns the antique store, and I ran into him at the liquor store. I was picking up a little something to slip into the punch since Priss isn't going to be here, and I just thought it might be nice for him to meet you. Why don't you two run out to the kitchen, fetch us some more ice for the punch bowl, and get a little better acquainted?"

Marcus's chin dropped, and his eyes widened as he turned to Skeet. "Oh. My. God."

"Told you."

Marcus's face grew hot, and his eyes flashed as his heartbeat grew faster. "That's enough of this." Marcus raised his voice, causing Francine to step back. "Excuse me, gentlemen. Can I have your attention?"

The men in the room all turned to face Marcus.

"Marcus, honey, what are you doing?" Helen rushed to his side, her face darkened.

"Guys, I'm afraid we're going to have to cut this meeting a little short. I don't think you're all aware of exactly why you were asked here. While the ladies and I appreciate your willingness to help with the hoedown, I think we can all coordinate on our own between now and then. Sorry you had to give up your evening for no reason, but I'm going to need you all to please leave."

"Excuse me, you aren't the hostess here. I will be the one to decide when we are—"

"Helen, hush," Inez chastised her. "He's on to us."

"Gentlemen, thank you for your time, but I think you all need to be going along." Marcus put his hands on Martin's back and pointed him toward the front door. "I need to speak with the ladies privately, so if you could all just go." He took the young policeman by the wrist and handed his arm over to Skeet. "Could you please take Officer Randall out with you?" As he turned back to the women in the room, he added, "I don't need him here to witness when I murder three old women."

"GOD, I HAVE NEVER BEEN so humiliated in my life," Marcus shouted as he dropped onto a stool at the counter and buried his face in his hands.

"Well, imagine how I feel!" Helen said as she crossed her arms and pouted. "I have a reputation in this town that you have seriously damaged. That was just rude to run everyone off."

"Really, Helen? You want to make this about you? For god's sake, I felt like I was being auctioned off tonight! What in the hell were you women thinking?"

"Shoe Button," Francine said, "we just wanted to introduce you to some people you might have something in common with to make your life here a little more enjoyable."

"How many times do I have to tell you this? I'm not going to have a life here! As soon as I get all of this settled, I *am* moving on. Okay? There is nothing for me in this little Podunk town."

"Well, there is no need to insult our town, darling." Inez placed her hand on her chest in offense.

"Not the point, Inez. I just don't want you meddling in my personal life. Did those men all know why you brought them here?"

"Well, Martin knew," Inez said and stared at her shoes. "He's a really nice man, Marcus. Couldn't you at least try—"

"Inez, Martin Prescott is old enough to be his grandfather." Helen clucked her tongue and shook her head. "And that comb-over. I mean, honestly."

"Well, he is better than Golly Dorney. That man is just a b-i-t-c- you know what."

"Inez, you take that back. Golly is a perfectly nice—"

"Oh, Helen, give it up. She's just mad that Marcus clearly preferred my choice of Mickey." Francine looked over at the frowning Inez. "Inez, don't frown. You'll get more wrinkles. Smile! It will improve your face value."

"Francine, shut up! It will improve your life expectancy."

"Girls, girls!" Helen pleaded as she stepped between Inez and Francine.

"Inez," Francine said and walked away from the other women, "there is no need to get ugly about this. If anyone should be mad it's me. I didn't get to introduce him to half of my choices."

"Yes, Francine, what was the deal with that?" Inez's eyes flashed as she spun to face the other woman. "We agreed we would each bring one suitable person for Marcus to meet. Why in the heck did you bring ten? And most of them were straight. Those Dobbins boys both run around with Paulette all the time."

"Well, what do I know from gay? I've always heard that one in ten men is gay so I figured if I just brought ten single men, then by the law of averages—"

"Ladies!" Marcus yelled to silence the bickering women. "This is all beside the point! I don't want you trying to set me up with *anyone*, okay? I mean, what made you think you had the right to go behind my back and do that?"

"As I said," Helen said meekly, "we were just trying to help. I didn't expect you to pitch a fit and fall in it."

"Help? I don't need your help. I'm fine on my own!"

"Helen, tell him the truth." Francine backed away from the group and sat at a table.

"Now is not the time."

"Yes, it is. Just tell him," Francine encouraged.

"Tell me what?"

"No," Helen said, "you're clearly upset. I think it would be best if everyone just went home and—"

"Spill it, old lady." Marcus glared at Helen and crossed his arms over his chest.

"Fine. But I still think it would be better if you were calmer when I told you this."

Marcus took a deep breath and closed his eyes. "Helen, this is as calm as I'm going to get tonight."

"Fine. Let's sit down." The group meandered to a table and each took a seat. "It's about your grandmother."

"What does she have to do with any of this?" Marcus asked.

"Well, at the end she was really struggling at the hospital. The doctors told her there wasn't much else they could do for her. She called me that night and told me if she was going to die, she was going to do it in her home." Helen lowered her head and took a deep breath. "I called the girls and the next day we went to her house and got it all set up for her."

"We each took shifts staying with her," Francine explained, her voice low and quiet.

"I was with her on her last day and I could just tell it wouldn't be long," Inez said and began to sniffle. "Your grandmother had been just lying there quiet for days. She finally looked over at me and said 'call a meeting.'"

"We were all there when she…" Francine's words faded as tears began to stream down her cheeks.

"She gave us a little task before she left us," Helen said.

Marcus leaned forward in his chair. "Go on."

"Marcus, your grandmother meant the world to all of us," Helen said, struggling to keep her emotions under control. "She was really the glue that held this group together. Anything she would've asked us to do we would do, but especially we had to fulfill her dying wishes."

"You see, darling," Francine offered, "your grandmother wanted us to find *you*."

"And to make sure you were happy," Inez added.

"And this I will never forget as long as I live," Helen said with her lip quivering. "She looked me right in the eye and said 'Make sure that boy has a home. The way his mother dragged him around…' Her voice faded out there. Then she took one last breath and said 'That boy needs love.'"

Marcus stared at the women, unable to formulate anything that seemed an appropriate response. He considered what they were saying. Yet again, it seemed that the grandmother he had never met cared more about his happiness than those closest to him ever had. He rested his elbows on the table. As he slid his hands up his face and smoothed his hair, he let out a long slow breath.

Francine dabbed at her eyes with a napkin. Inez turned her face away, but he could see her neck was flushed. Helen rested her forehead on her hand. She mumbled, "What were we supposed to do? Ignore her wishes? When Raff called and told me you were in town, I knew we had to do whatever we could to fulfill her wishes."

"Yes, but…"

"Of course, we didn't have any idea you were gay." Francine looked at Marcus and forced a half-hearted smile. "What do we know about playing matchmaker for a gay person?"

"But that first day you were here in the diner," Helen explained, "we all discussed it and decided this was the best thing to do."

"And where is Priss?" Marcus asked.

"Well, she…you know…with the preacher's wife thing and all. She didn't think it would be appropriate to…it doesn't matter."

"Ladies, I really appreciate you trying to fulfill my grandmother's wishes but I really don't want to stay here. And I really don't want to get into a relationship with anyone. Can you please just let me—" Marcus's phone began to ring in his pocket. "What now?" he mumbled as he fished the phone out and glanced at the screen to see Robert's name. "Oh, that's just perfect." He quickly hit the reject call button and tossed the phone onto the table.

"But, sweetie, everyone wants to find love. Why don't you let us—"

"You know what Helen? That is the last thing I need right now. And this is why." He snatched the phone from the table and showed them the screen. "I just…" Marcus's eyes stung with tears. He tilted his head back to stop himself from crying. He willed his mind and body to calm down and prevent another panic attack. The women all began to question him at once, their words tumbling over each other.

"Oh, darling, what is going on?"

"Is that who gave you the eye?"

"That's not from the wreck?"

"Oh, come on, Inez. You know as well as I do where that kind of thing comes from."

"Sweetie, tell us."

The jarring barrage of questions made the muscles in his neck and his shoulders tense. "Can we just drop it and move on?" Marcus could feel his chest tightening and taste the vomit at the back of his throat. "I don't need you all meddling in my life. Okay?" He pushed against the table and slid his chair back in frustration.

"'Cause you are clearly doing such a great job by yourself." Inez huffed out a disgusted breath and leaned back in her chair with her arms folded.

"Inez," Francine chided, "That wasn't very nice to say."

"This is really none of your business." Marcus lolled his head back in frustration and stared at the tiles in the ceiling.

"The hell it isn't," Inez spat out. "Is some violent man going to show up on our street?"

"He doesn't know where I am." Marcus folded his arms on the table and dropped his head on them to stop the spinning of the room. Through his arms, he mumbled, "And he's not really violent. Could we please change the subject?"

"That black eye says you're lying."

"Girls," Francine said, "drop it. It's his business to tell or not. We gave it our best shot and now we have to admit defeat. Also, I need all you old biddies to go home so I can close up shop. Marcus and I have an early day tomorrow."

"I still don't see why—"

Marcus jerked his head toward Inez with anger flashing in his eyes. "Miss Inez, drop it."

The women and Marcus sat in uncomfortable silence. Inez crossed her arms and frowned at the other women. Helen looked at the table and shredded a napkin into tiny pieces. Marcus looked at Francine to see her staring at him with a concerned look. Marcus blinked the tears away from his eyes and tried to force a smile at his employer. Francine smiled back and nodded her head knowingly. The bell over the diner door cut through the silence as Skeet bustled through from the street.

"Well, I finally got all those very confused men into their cars and on their way," Skeet said as he strolled into the room and flopped on a chair at a nearby table. "I think a couple of them figured out what game y'all were playing but… Wow! You could cut diamonds with the silence in here."

"Marcus was just making it clear that he didn't appreciate our very kind act of trying to find him some friends." Inez threw up her hands.

"Kind?" Marcus scrunched up his face and frowned. "I'd call it more meddlesome than—"

"Moving on," Skeet interrupted him. "I take it no love connections were made here tonight. Go figure. Honestly, Nonnie, was that the best y'all could come up with? Golly Dorney? Martin Prescott?"

"It appears that none of our choices were Marcus's type," Inez said. "Though I thought they were all perfectly nice gentlemen." She stood and snatched her purse from the counter. "Francine, I'm leaving. I don't think I need to stay around here where I'm not appreciated."

"Aw, Miss Inez, don't be that way." Marcus leaned toward the departing woman and tried to grab her hand. She snatched it away and stormed toward the door.

"Sweetie," Helen whispered in his ear, "you just got to let that one stew in her juices until she's done. Trust me, by tomorrow she'll have found someone else to be mad at, and this will all be forgotten."

Francine untied the apron from around her waist and waved it toward the other women. She turned to Marcus and said, "Punkin', why don't you head on home and I'll close up. You've had a rough night." She kissed Marcus on the cheek. As she pulled away, she added quietly, "If you ever want to talk about *anything*, I might understand better than you would think." She turned toward the kitchen and called back over her shoulder, "Now y'all get the hell out of my diner."

"That's perfect," Helen said as she rose from the table and held her hand out to Marcus. "Marcus and Skeet can escort me to my car."

Marcus stood and took Helen's hand. "Fine, but I'm going to let Skeet drive me home."

The threesome stepped out into the night air, and Helen hooked each of her arms through one of the young men's arms. "Sweetheart, you'll have to forgive us old ladies. Really, it was my idea and I talked the other girls into it, so don't be mad at them. My mind just gets to going sometimes, and I forget to think it all the way through. But we really didn't mean any harm."

"I'm sorry I lost my temper, too. I just felt ambushed and… well… I don't know." Marcus shrugged.

"So, Marcus, you have disappointed all the women of the Do-Nothing club," Skeet said. "I guess I'm going to have to take you to The Woodshed."

"I beg your pardon?" Marcus stopped and scowled at Skeet. "I'd like to see you try, you little squirt."

"No, I don't mean beat you. Good lord, I ain't into that. It's a bar. A gay bar."

"In this little town?"

"Marcus, we are more modern than you'd think," Helen said.

"Not that modern," Skeet added and chuckled. "It's just an old barn out in the country. But it's fun, and the music is good for dancing. You'll see."

"Oh god, I could use a drink. Let's go."

"Not tonight, dummy. Tomorrow night when you don't have to work on Sunday. I'll drive us out there. We'll see if I can't introduce you to someone who is at least actual facts gay and not a member of the AARP."

"Skeet, I already told your Nonnie, I'm not really looking for anything—"

"Oh, shut up, Marcus. You act as if the world will come to end if you accidentally have a good time. I'm just talking about gay therapy. You know? Dancing? No arguing."

"Fine. You'll have to drive."

"I know. Trust me. You're going to love it."

"HOW FAR AWAY IS THIS place?" Marcus asked as he stared out the window at the tilled rows of tobacco fields that whizzed by as they sped along the highway in Skeet's huge, black Mercury Montego.

Forty-five minutes earlier, when Skeet had pulled into the driveway of his grandmother's house to pick Marcus up, Marcus had been shocked at the sheer size of the boat-like car. The car swayed gently along the bumps in the road and the murmuring sound of the tires on the pavement had nearly lulled Marcus into sleep. His shift at the Tammy had started way too early that morning, and he regretted not working in a disco nap between getting home and Skeet picking him up at nine. An afternoon rain shower should have been the perfect inducement to sleep, but he'd laid down and closed his eyes only to toss and turn on the sofa for an hour before giving up and getting in the shower.

He couldn't decide why he was nervous. He had been to dance clubs hundreds of times, but had not stepped into a gay bar in over two years since he met Robert. Skeet had told him so little about The Woodshed, he was unsure what would be appropriate to wear. A nagging voice in the back of his head kept telling him, "You're going to look foolish." Hoping to look as though he hadn't put much effort into his appearance, he had changed into three different dress shirts before settling on a simple green T-shirt and blue jeans. Around the eighth time he paced from checking out the front window for Skeet to glancing in the mirror to debate his choice of shirt, he realized that the voice in his head was Robert's. The realization sent a wave of rebellion through his bones. *Screw you. I'm going to wear this shirt because it is comfortable. I'm going to have a good time. I'll look foolish if I want.* To prove his point, he crossed his eyes and stuck out his tongue at his reflection in the mirror. With a sudden desire to dance himself silly, he fussed with his hair until Skeet honked from the driveway.

Now the only things keeping him awake were the loud dance music thumping from the speakers, Skeet's endless prattle about the high school production of *Guys and Dolls* that he and Frankie had starred in the past spring, and the knot of nerves sitting in his stomach.

"We're almost there," Skeet said as he turned down the stereo. Skeet wore a tight black T-shirt with the sleeves rolled up over his biceps. His faded, baggy jeans were cuffed over black boots and he wore a leather belt with silver studs along the back.

"Anyway," Skeet continued, "I told Miss Henderson that even though Adelaide and Nathan aren't officially the leads of the play, that Frankie and I still clearly deserved the awards for best actor and actress because… shoot!" Marcus braced himself against the dashboard as Skeet stomped on the brakes and the car squealed to a stop in the middle of the road. "Almost passed it. I told you to help me look for mile marker seventeen! You know, Sarge should really put a sign out here."

Skeet flipped his turn signal and steered the car to the left, off the highway and onto a dirt driveway that led through a gap in a ramshackle wooden fence. The path twisted through row upon row of pine trees before it stretched out between two large but empty fields. A half a mile down, it emptied into the yard of an old, white farmhouse with a large porch wrapping from the front door around the side of the house. Though it had clearly been built at least a hundred years ago, the home was well maintained and clean. The full moon reflected off the bright white paint of its siding. A porch swing swayed gently in the evening breeze next to two wooden rocking chairs. Despite an overwhelming urge to jump from the car and run and plop into the swing, Marcus shifted in his seat and waited for Skeet to stop the car and hop out.

Marcus turned and mumbled, "Doesn't look like any gay bar I've ever seen."

Skeet glanced over at Marcus and chuckled. "No, silly. That's Sarge's house, not the bar. Why on earth would anyone put a bar in an old farmhouse? For somebody from the city, you sure don't know much about how things work."

"How things work?"

"Honey," Skeet drawled as he turned the steering wheel to the right and drove around the side of the house, "any good southern boy knows the real party is always in the back yard."

Behind the farmhouse, a big red barn came into view. The two massive main doors were thrown open and bright light spilled out onto the ground in front of the building. Through the windows on either side of the doors, Marcus could see flashing lights in red and blue and the silhouettes of a few people dancing. Some figures just inside the door sat at a picnic bench, clapping, laughing, and raising their beer bottles in a toast. Over the doors, a solitary, bare light bulb hung swinging in the breeze above a hand-painted sign that read: Welcome to the Woodshed. As Skeet pulled the car into an open spot between two trucks, Marcus noticed two men standing beside one of the trucks; one was leaning against the truck bed with the other standing in front of him with his arms draped lazily over the leaning man's shoulders. Their heads were close together; the wide brim of one of their cowboy hats hid their faces from Marcus's view. The men looked over and shielded their eyes from the bright light of Skeet's headlights. After Skeet turned off the lights, one of the men leaned over to say something to the other before they both turned and waved to the car with big smiles.

"Well, here we are! Welcome to the gayest little spot in South Georgia." Skeet turned off the car, flung open his door and looked back over his shoulder at Marcus. He grinned and wiggled his eyebrows. "Let's go look at some men!"

"Don't mind if I do," Marcus said as he opened the door and stepped onto the grass. He stretched his arms above his head and took in a deep breath, smelling the dirt of the nearby fields and the lingering damp of the afternoon rain. Strands of white twinkle lights stretched from the corners of the building toward the pecan trees along its perimeter. Through the open door of the second-story hayloft, a mirrored ball twirled lazily, sending glimmers of light dancing across the hoods of the twenty or so pickup trucks parked all around the yard. Marcus followed Skeet toward the doors and heard the familiar twang of older country music blaring out into the dark night. As they passed the two men beside the pickup truck, Marcus nodded a hello.

"Clint. Seth," Skeet said with a careless wave of his hand. "What's on the menu tonight?"

"Hey, Skeet," the taller man responded. "Low country boil. And Toona and Pattie are doing their Judds tribute."

"Ugh. Again?"

"Who's your friend?" the other man asked, turning his head to look Marcus up and down.

"His name is Notfa."

"Notfa?" the first man said and twisted his face.

"Notfa you to worry yourself with, you two old perverts." Skeet blew a kiss toward the men and sashayed to the barn.

As Marcus hurried to follow Skeet toward the door, Clint and Seth laughed before one said something about "that sassy little shit."

Marcus grabbed Skeet's wrist and slowed him down. "That was rude."

Skeet stopped and looked at Marcus. He rolled his eyes and giggled. "Oh, they know I'm kidding. Clint and Seth live over in Wellerton. One of them is a photographer or something for the newspaper there, and the other is a farm animal vet. They've been a couple for like a hundred years. Everybody gives them a hard time about being on the prowl for a houseboy or something, but it's not true. I think everyone does it because most of these guys are just jealous they both found someone. They're just here to have a good time like everyone else."

"Oh. Okay." Marcus glanced back to see the shorter man kiss the other on the cheek. "So they're regulars?"

"Hell, Marcus. Everyone's a regular here. Not a lot of choices of places to go. Now, can we go inside while I'm still young and fetching?"

"How much is the cover charge?" Marcus asked as he pulled his wallet out of his back pocket.

"The what?"

"The cover." Marcus gestured with his wallet.

"Money to get in?" Skeet laughed as he pushed Marcus's arm down. "It's not a *real* bar. That wouldn't be legal at all. No, this is a house party that has just been going on every weekend for about five years." Skeet walked into the barn. "Come on. I'll introduce you to Sarge, and he can explain it."

As Marcus stepped into the barn, the sound of people laughing and talking mingled with the loud country music from speakers mounted in the corners of the old barn. At the far end of the room was a small raised platform in front of a large open area. White twinkle lights were strung all around the room, and from the hayloft above, a multicolored spotlight flickered and flashed across the open area in front of the stage.

Two elderly men in poorly fitting dresses, bad makeup, and ratty red wigs danced and lip-synced to the Judds song playing over the speakers. A few men stood at the edge of the platform and offered dollar bills to the performers, who would wink and smile before shoving the money into their fake cleavage. Skeet stopped and nodded toward the stage.

"That's Toona Melt and Pattie Melt."

Marcus raised his eyebrows and nodded. "Tonight's entertainment?"

"Yeah. It ain't Ru-Paul, but they're kind of funny. Somebody said they're two old army buddies of Sarge's and he asked them to move down here with him when they all retired. Sarge calls them 'the twins' but I don't think they're really related." Skeet shrugged and then gestured toward the stage. "They all dressed up as country singers for Halloween one year. Everyone thought it was so funny that they just started doing shows for a lark. Everyone gets a kick out of it. I also heard they both are stinking rich from never having any wife or kids to pay for. All that combat pay stuffed away or something. Anyway, when they're done, we'll be able to go out on the floor and dance if you want to. I think they're almost done."

As the music began to die down, Marcus's attention was pulled back to the stage as a squeal of feedback shot from the speakers. "Ooh! Hot mic! Hot mic!" one of the men in drag said as he shook the microphone in his hand. "Sorry about that everybody. Whew, I'm getting too old for those upbeat numbers." The man fanned himself with his free hand and then patted his chest. "All right, Pattie and I are going to take a little break and let you kids dance for a bit."

One of the men standing at the edge of the stage booed and yelled out, "We want more!"

"Oh, honey, calm down," the other man on stage drawled. "We'll be back. You're just a little worked up because you're confused. It ain't often you meet someone whose stacked like your mama and hung like your daddy." The crowd in the room laughed, and a few men hooted and whistled. The man threw his head back and laughed loudly toward the rafters. The man yanked the wig off his head, revealing a bald head. "Damn, these things are hot. Well, glamor is pain. All right, Toona, put something peppy on the record player." The other man tottered in his high heels to the edge of the stage and began messing around with a record player. The opening chords of a dance song thumped through the room.

"So," Skeet said as Marcus turned away from the stage, "you want to dance?"

"Not yet." Marcus shrugged. "We just got here. But that food smells really good. I just realized; I never ate tonight."

Skeet tugged Marcus to a long table covered with old newspapers on which a mix of seafood, sausage, and corn on the cob had been dumped out. Beside the table sat three galvanized washtubs filled with ice, bottles of beer, and cans of soda.

"Just a Coke for me, but if you want a beer I don't mind. I'm driving you, after all." Skeet stuck his hand into the ice and pulled out a can of soda. "It's free. Sort of."

"What do you mean, sort of?"

"Well—"

"Skeet Warner, you little stinker!" a booming voice interrupted him. "If I've told you once, I've told you a million times, this here place is a barn, not a chicken coop. We don't need no little chicken like you strutting around. If Helen Warner knew I was exposing her grandson to all of these old perverts, she'd wring my neck."

A burly man in his late fifties walked through a side door of the barn with bright pink oven mitts on his hands and carrying a large silver stockpot with steam rising from the top. Atop his head was a platinum blond wig that had been teased to a height of nearly a foot. He wore an ill-fitting, pink-sequined dress that barely covered his muscular, tattooed and hairy arms, and his beefy, unshaven legs tumbled out of the absurdly high hem to land in dark black combat boots.

"Sarge, you old fart," Skeet shot back at the man, "you shut up. If it weren't for me coming in here, you'd have to call this place an old folks' home."

"First of all, missy, I'm in the dress, so it's Polly, not Sarge. Lord knows you can't miss these bazooms." The blue and red stripes of two beach balls shoved into the bust of the dress bulged out of the low neckline. Sarge shoved his chest out and gestured at the beach balls with his chin. "Secondly, screw you."

"Sorry, *Polly*," Skeet said and chuckled. "You better watch it or that hot pot is going to bust your boobs."

"You got that right!" Sarge nodded. "Honestly, I don't know how women stand them. At least I can deflate mine before I go to bed. Women have to maneuver around these things all night. Let me dump this pot before I cause permanent damage, and then come give me a hug." Sarge tilted the pot toward the table and poured the steaming seafood onto the newspaper. "All righty, kids. Fresh shrimp and crawfish are ready to eat!" As he set the pot on the ground beside the table, the man jerked his bewigged head toward Marcus. "It appears I'm not the only one bringing in something fresh. Has our little chicken found himself a rooster?"

"No, sir… um… ma'am… um…" Marcus stammered as he stuck out his hand. "Your little chicken is still a bit too close to being an egg for me. We're just friends. My name is Marcus Sumter."

"Yes, he's an egg, but he's a good egg." Sarge's eyes sparkled as he laughed. "This vision of loveliness standing before you is Miss Polly Darton. The Hostess with the Mostess. But you can just call me Sarge. So, Marcus, what brings you to my little barn? Wait, did you say Sumter? Are you kin to Eloise Sumter?"

"She was my grandmother. I'm here to settle her estate."

"Son, I was so sad to hear about her passing. Your granny was a fine, fine woman. When the twins and I would go into town to stock up on supplies, we'd always go in the Tammy to get some lunch. Your granny and the rest of those hens she flocked with would be in there all the time. But she was always a darling to us. You know, to Miss Eloise, all geese were swans."

"What?" Marcus said and cocked his head.

The steam from the simmering pot had caused the thick layer of makeup Sarge wore to sweat and run down his cheeks, giving his eyes the look of a horny yet confused raccoon. "She saw the best in everyone. When the twins and I first showed up here, well, people didn't take kindly to three old bachelor gentlemen living out here by ourselves. But your granny was always so kind to us. As a matter of fact, you see that blouse Toona is wearing? Well, don't tell anyone but it just might have been a donation from your granny. Toona once told your granny that with her red hair and wearing that blouse she was the spitting image of Naomi Judd. Well, that tickled your granny pink. So when Toona told her she wanted to be Naomi for Halloween, your Granny drove all the way out to the house the next day to give it to us. Yes, she was a mighty fine woman. I tell you what, you reach in that tub over there and snag us both a beer, and let's drink a toast to her memory. You're old enough to drink, right?"

"Yes, I'm twenty-two, but I don't have much money with me."

"Look, Private, tonight's on the house. Anyway, I can't really sell you a beer. That requires a license and a bunch of nonsense paperwork I ain't going to bother with. I gave up paperwork when I left the army. No, see, we got a little understanding around here. Everybody pays me some money to park on my lawn. Then I give them the food and beer for free. That keeps that old sheriff off my back and lets us have our fun out here without anybody bothering us."

"That reminds me," Skeet said as he dug into his pocket, pulled out a twenty-dollar bill, and handed it to Sarge. "Most expensive damn coke I ever had."

"Need I remind you that you're getting some first-rate live entertainment for that money as well? Which reminds me, I need to go freshen up before the next set. Standing over that steaming pot has made my face melt down closer to my chest than Mother Nature has already dropped it. But first," he shoved his hands into the nearest washtub, pulled out two beers, and handed one to Marcus. "Let's drink a toast. As classy a dame as Miss Eloise was, we ought to use champagne, but beer will have to do. To Miss Eloise Sumter. She could've taught the queen of England a thing or two about being a real lady."

"To Miss Eloise," Skeet said as he lifted his can of soda.

"To Miss Eloise," Marcus joined in and took a large swig of the cold beer.

"Now, I best get back there and change into my coat of many colors." Sarge winked at the boys and started out of the barn. He stopped, turned around, and said, "Marcus, you help yourself to some food and beer. And welcome to our little place. Any kin of Eloise is kin of mine."

"Thanks, Sarge. And that food smells delicious. Come on Skeet, let's grab a plate." Marcus took a paper plate from the edge of the table and began shoveling food onto it.

"Well, looky what just waltzed in here. If it ain't Cowboy." Sarge wiggled his eyebrows at the boys and nodded toward the door. "Must be spring chicken night in here after all. Got to say it makes me happy to see the young'uns coming in. Easy there," Sarge said as he placed his hand on Marcus's arm to stop him from adding more food to the plate. "Don't want to look like a pig while that one is here. Have fun, boys." Sarge tipped his beer toward the boys and walked out of the barn, leaving a few pink sequins on the ground behind him.

"Who?" Marcus asked as he turned around. He fumbled with the plate in his hands and nearly dropped it when he saw Hank Hudson walking across the barn straight toward him. "Oh, hell. What is he doing here?"

"Hank?" Skeet asked and scrunched his shoulders up. "He comes here every now and then."

"He's gay?"

"Gayer than Mardi Gras," Skeet whispered and then turned toward Hank with a broad smile. "Hey, Cowboy!"

"Skeet, I have asked you not to call me that."

"Sorry, I guess Sarge just got me in the habit."

"Hello," Hank said as he nodded at Marcus.

"Hey." Marcus darted his eyes around the room looking for somewhere to hide from the mechanic. When he noticed Hank watching him, he looked at the ground and tried not to blush.

Skeet shifted his eyes back and forth between the two men before stretching his arms above his head and taking a deep breath. "Oh, look. There's Darchelle Peterson. I've been meaning to ask her about… um… yeah. Excuse me." He scampered over toward the people sitting at the tables scattered along the far wall.

"Skeet!" Marcus hissed before turning back to face Hank.

"So."

"So." Marcus fumbled with the plate. "Um, do you mind if I sit this plate down? I'm about to spill it all over the place."

"Tell you what. You find us a table, and I'm going to get a plate too. I'm slap starving and I never pass up Sarge's low country boil."

Marcus stepped over to the closest table and put down his beer and plate. He pulled the chair out and sat where he could watch Hank at the buffet table. His muscled arms flexed under the tight sleeves of his blue shirt as he scooped several helpings of the stew onto his plate. The flashing red and blue lights of the dance floor swished across his brown hair and down his back, leading Marcus's eyes toward his narrow waist. A wide leather belt with a pattern stamped on it held up his snug, faded jeans. *God, that man can wear a pair of pants.*

Marcus dropped his eyes to his plate as Hank turned to face him. Marcus picked up his fork and shoved the shrimp on his plate around until the other man's shadow fell across the table. He looked up to see

Hank smiling at him with a plate in one hand and a can of soda in the other.

"Mind if I sit?"

"Free country." Marcus tried to sound nonchalant and nodded toward a chair.

Hank dropped into the chair and placed the plate on the table. He leaned over and inhaled deeply over the steaming food. "God, Sarge makes one ugly-ass woman, but he sure can cook. Isn't that the best thing you ever tasted?"

"I haven't had a chance to try it yet," Marcus said. "So, you come here a lot?"

"No. Not really. I mean, the garage is open every day but Sunday, and I have to be there so early. It doesn't really lend itself to late nights in a barn. Plus, it's always the same old people here. Nothing really of interest to me, you know."

"I was shocked to see you walk in tonight."

"Why?" Hank raised his eyebrows in a confused look.

"I mean, I didn't think you were gay."

"Ha! Well, yeah, I like guys. Just not anyone here in particular. But the food is good, and I do find the twins to be funny."

Behind Hank, the dance floor began to fill as the music grew louder and switched from a country ballad to a two-step. Marcus slid his chair closer to Hank so he could hear him over the raucous tune. He leaned closer and asked, "So why did you come tonight? For the shrimp?"

"Well. The garage is closed tomorrow, so I figured why not. Plus," Hank gestured to the other tables with his fork, "a little bird told me you were going to be here. Well, more of a little mosquito."

Marcus followed Hank's point to see Skeet at a table surrounded by people laughing along as he gesticulated wildly. "You asked Skeet about me?"

"You gave me a bit of a scare that day in my garage, Fiat. I wasn't sure what happened to you. I went to get the water and poof. You were gone. Been in the diner a few times to check on you, but you were never around. Also, I need to know what to do with that hunk of metal you got at my shop." Hank stabbed a shrimp with his fork and stuffed it into his mouth. "Anyway, Skeet's supposed to work for me, you know. He actually showed up to work today and told me he was bringing you here. I figured, I just wanted to make sure you were all right."

"Oh. Yeah." Marcus blushed and looked at the food on his plate. "Look, I'm sorry about skipping out. I just got overwhelmed by everything when I saw how bad the car is. Plus, I hadn't eaten anything in a while and I just… you saw." Marcus raised his head and gave Hank weak smile. "To be honest, I'm a little embarrassed that happened."

"Hey, don't worry about it. I have to say, I was pretty shocked you weren't in worse shape than that. I was also worried maybe it was something from the wreck that the doctors in that glorified first-aid stand might've missed."

"No. Just me being an idiot." Marcus scooped some of the food into his mouth. "Oh, my god, this is so good!" He took a few more bites of food then said, "I was better once I got to the Tammy and got some food."

"And a job, too. So, you decide to stick around for a while?"

"Nah. I agreed to help Miss Francine out until my grandmother's inheritance money comes through and I can get out of town. I figure between the money I make there and the inheritance, I can pay you to fix up the car for me. I really want to get that taken care of and hit the road as soon as I can."

Hank took a swallow of his soda. "Well, I hate to tell you, Fiat, but you'll be working there a while if you want me to fix up that car."

"You can't fix it?" Marcus dropped the fork onto the table and his shoulders sank.

"You saw that hunk of metal. That's way above my skill level."

Marcus slapped his hand to his forehead. "Well, shit. What am I supposed to do now?"

"Hold on, now. Don't go getting all worked up." He reached across and pulled Marcus's hand back to the table. "We can figure something out. I've got a couple of old cars there at the garage that I fixed up. I can sell you one of those."

"Well, I don't really have any money yet. Like I said, I'm waiting on my inheritance…"

"Hold your horses, all right? We can work out a little deal." Hank shifted his eyes upward. "I know, you can give what's left of your car as a down payment, and we will figure out a payment plan for the rest."

"Why would you want that hunk of junk?"

"Damaged doesn't mean useless." Hank shrugged. "Look, I can take a few parts off it. True, I don't really need much. Not a lot of call for those fancy little imports down here. But I can haul the rest to the scrap yard over in Eganville and get some cash."

"Hank, I appreciate that."

"No problem, Fiat." Hank winked at him.

"Why do you keep calling me that? My name is Marcus."

"It's just something I do. I'm not too good with names. But I always remember what people drive."

"Well, I guess you'll be calling me something new soon. What do you think? Am I a Jeep? A Chevy?"

"Nah. Fiat suits you."

"Oh, really?"

"Yeah. Sporty little body. Built for the road. And a nice little bubble back-end." Hank ticked up the corner of his mouth in a half-grin and then took a giant swig from his soda can.

Marcus's chin dropped. With the loud music thumping in his ears, he wasn't sure he had heard correctly what the other man said. "Did you just say I have—"

"Hey, Cowboy," a deep voice interrupted Marcus. One of the twins stood by the table with his large, vividly manicured right hand resting on the hip he cocked out to one side. The silvery threads in the blouse that was apparently a gift from Grandmother Eloise sparkled as the lights from the dance floor flashed around his shoulders. The bangles on his other wrist clanged as he adjusted the deep red wig on his head. "Welcome back. Long time no see."

"Toona." Hank nodded his head at the drag queen and turned back to Marcus with a frown. "And you know my name is Hank."

"Whatever, darling. Who's your friend?"

"I'm Marcus. And I'm not here with… I mean I came with Skeet."

The drag queen dropped his manicured hand on Marcus's shoulder. "I wondered what type of magic you had to finally catch Cowboy in a web."

"Toona, don't you have a show to do?"

"Oh, shit. I do. You boys have fun! And don't be such a stranger, Cowboy."

"It's Hank!"

"Okay, darling." The drag queen waved his fingers over his shoulder as he flounced away toward the other tables.

"Why do they call you that? Cowboy? You're a mechanic and work-shirts and blue Dickies aren't exactly western wear."

"Sarge started it. Let's just say that I've a bit of a reputation around here." Hank waved away the question. "It's stupid, really. I'd rather you just call me Hank."

"Aw. Come on. Tell me."

"Fine." Hank took a deep breath before explaining, "Sarge calls me Cowboy because he says I'm really good at keeping my calves together."

Marcus threw his head back and laughed. "Oh, my god! *That* is hysterical."

"Maybe to you. Look, I just don't feel the need to hook up with random people. I prefer to have my sex life mean something."

"Well, I guess that is one approach."

"Hey, forgive me for not seeing my being discriminate as a character flaw."

"No. I get it. I've never really been one for sleeping around either. The good southern boy in me just can't do it."

"What, because of Jesus or something?"

"No. I mean, who has the time to write that many thank-you notes?"

Hank stared thoughtfully at Marcus before busting out laughing. His laugh was deep, loud, and seemed to rise from his toes. As his laugh ebbed, he cocked his head and said, "You're pretty funny."

Marcus blushed. "Thanks."

"And cute too."

Though he didn't think he could do it, Marcus blushed harder. "Okay..."

"So, are you any good behind that grill at the diner?"

"Yeah. I am."

"Okay, I'm coming in there for lunch on Monday to see for myself."

"Wait. I've got an idea. Why don't you come in after we close on Monday? I'm sure Miss Francine won't mind if I use the diner after she closes. I'll make a special meal just for you. It'll be my way of saying thanks for your help with this car mess. And to say I'm sorry for sneaking out that first day I came in."

"You got yourself a deal." Hank stuck out his hand for Marcus to shake. "Monday at the Tammy. It's a date."

"Let's call it a thank-you."

"Okay. A thank-you."

The country dance song that had been playing abruptly changed to a thumping disco beat. Marcus pushed his empty plate away from himself. "So, Hank, you want to dance?"

Hank shook his head. "Oh, no. I don't dance. I'm good with my hands, not my feet."

"Good with your hands?" Marcus raised his eyebrows and smirked at Hank.

"Oh, my god, Marcus!" Skeet came rushing to the table and latched on to Marcus's shoulder. "Come on. We've got to dance to this song!"

"I'm coming!" Marcus stood and pushed his chair back under the table. "I was just convincing Hank to come join us."

"Actually, you weren't," Hank said and laughed. "But you boys go have fun. I'll be here when you're finished. I'll get you another beer."

"Suit yourself," Skeet said as he tugged Marcus toward the dance floor. "We might be a while. Now let's dance!"

Marcus worked his way through the crowd on the dance floor and found a clear spot. He closed his eyes and swayed his hips to the music. The thumping bassline vibrated in his ribcage and chased out any lingering feelings of exhaustion from his long day. As he found the rhythm of the song, he shuffled his feet and began shaking his shoulders. The tempo increased. Marcus danced faster and harder; sweat began to form on his brow. The music built in speed and volume until it rose in a thunderous crescendo of drumbeats and whistles. Marcus surrendered to the absolute joy of the music and his dancing, threw his hands in the air, and let out a whoop. As he spun around, he opened his eyes. Through a gap in the crowd, he could see Hank grinning as he watched him dance. Marcus smiled back and waved. He began to laugh as he recalled the way Inez had once described the mechanic.

Damn. That is a sexy young man.

"WHAT YOU MAKING THERE, SUGAR?" Francine walked behind Marcus and bumped her hip into his backside. She placed her hands on his hips as she peeked over his shoulder at the eggs sizzling on the griddle and let out a low whistle. "Scrambled eggs? Nothing but the fancy stuff to impress a certain fella, huh?"

Marcus picked up the spatula and scooped the eggs off the grill and onto a toasted slice of wheat bread sitting on a plate. He looked over at Francine and stuck out his tongue. "It's not just scrambled eggs, it's a full-on sandwich."

"You going to put some cheese on that?"

"It's already cooked into the eggs. That's my secret weapon."

"Secret weapon or not, it's still just an egg sandwich." Francine turned up her nose and sniffed.

"It's what he said he wanted and, again, I'm not trying to impress anyone. This is simply a way to say thank you for all the help he is giving me with my car."

"I see," Francine replied and then smirked. "Just a thank-you." She looked up and nodded toward the counter. "There is absolutely nothing about that *very* good-looking man sitting at the counter that interests you in any way whatsoever."

Marcus looked from the bacon sizzling on the griddle to stare at Hank sitting at the counter. Hank's head was lowered as he played with several packs of sugar he had spread out in front of him in a seemingly random pattern. Occasionally, he nodded his head politely as Paulette chattered away at him across the counter, though he never looked up from his hands. He said something to her out of the corner of his mouth, and Paulette threw her head back and laughed.

"What is she doing?" Marcus asked as Paulette leaned closer to the counter top, exposing more of her cleavage through the neckline of her pink uniform top.

Francine stood on her tiptoes to look out into the diner at her daughter. "Oh, don't worry about her. She can't help herself." Francine laughed and swatted Marcus with the dishrag she held. "And look at him. Who could blame her? It's harmless."

"And a waste of her time," Marcus said and grunted.

"Hmm. A little jealous for someone who is just saying thank you, don't you think?"

Marcus made a sour face at Francine before turning to look out at Hank. He could see the corners of Hank's brown eyes wrinkle as he smiled at something Paulette was saying to him. "Okay. Yes. He is good-looking, but I already told y'all that I'm not looking for anything right now. We just had a really good time talking at the bar the other night. Skeet finally had to tell me to shut up and drag me out of there."

Hank shrugged and shook his head at Paulette, keeping his attention on the packets he shuffled around on the counter. Marcus could tell that Hank was bored with the conversation and was merely being polite. Hank glanced up and made eye contact with him through the opening. Hank's face brightened as he smiled at Marcus and gave a quick wink. Marcus dropped his head to the grill and tried to focus on the food he was preparing, but was unable to stop the grin that crept across his face.

"Uh huh," Francine drawled as she walked to the sink and dropped some dirty plates into the soapy water. "Whatever you say. But between you, me, and the fencepost," she said as she pointed at the grill, "that man makes my bacon sizzle, too."

Marcus slid the spatula under the bacon slices and flipped them onto the eggs on the sandwich. He placed the other slice of toast on top and cut the sandwich in half with the edge of his spatula. Unhappy with the placement of the food, he nudged the sandwich a little closer to the pile of hash browns on the plate. He grabbed two pickle slices from the prep table and dropped them beside the sandwich. He twisted the plate around once, surveying the food from each side as he spun and wiping away a stray crumb. After giving the sandwich another slight nudge, he nodded his head. He slid the plate onto the counter of the pass-through and slapped the bell to call Paulette over. "Order up!"

When Paulette stepped to the opening to take the plate, a hand slipped past him and caught the woman's wrist. "Paulette, honey," Francine said to her, "why don't you come into the kitchen and help me clean up. I think we can let Marcus deliver his creation. Don't you agree?"

Paulette pursed her lips and stared at her mother before rolling her eyes. "Fine." She glanced back over her shoulder toward Hank. "He's shit at conversation, and his fingernails are filthy, anyway."

"Go get him, tiger," Francine said as she smacked Marcus on his backside and turned back to her dishes.

"Francine, cut it out," Marcus said, then chuckled. He screwed up his mouth and then threw his hands up in surrender. "Fine. I know when I'm beat."

He untied his apron and tossed it onto the metal table in the middle of the kitchen. He moved toward the swinging door, barely stepping out of the way as it swung in when Paulette stormed into the kitchen. She glared at him, then broke out into a giggle.

"I'm just messing with you," she said as she slipped past him. "Go get him, Romeo. But you might want to take that hairnet off first."

Marcus spun to look at himself in the mirror that hung next to the kitchen door. The hairnet he wore had smashed his red hair into an awkward-looking lump, and he had a streak of sauce across his cheek. "Oh, crap. I forgot I had this on. He saw me like this, didn't he?" Marcus yanked the net off his head and tried to neaten his hair.

Francine wiped his cheek with the dish rag. She patted his cheek and smiled lovingly. "You look fine, sweetie. And no man can resist someone who feeds him well." She winked and pushed him toward the door.

"Thanks for letting him come in after we closed. I didn't want a bunch of people in here when we—"

"Oh, Marcus," Paulette called out from behind him, "you won't be alone out there."

"What?"

"Those busybodies are still in the corner. Couldn't get them to leave. Never seen four old women make a club sandwich last so long in my life."

"Great. An audience." Marcus pushed the door open and stepped out behind the counter. As he sauntered past the pass-through, he snagged Hank's plate and twisted it onto his palm to carry it over his shoulder. He yanked the coffee pot from under the machine with his other hand and walked to the counter.

"Here you go," Marcus said as he lowered his arm and slid the plate onto the counter in front of Hank. "Adam and Eve on a raft. Wrecked, pickled, and high and dry. Hash browns scattered and topped. Can I freshen up that joe for you?" Marcus raised the coffee pot, gestured toward Hank's mug with his elbow and pretended to smack chewing gum.

"Ooh, I love it when you talk diner." Hank grinned at Marcus and wiggled his eyebrows. "It sounds dirty. Hit me," he said and nodded at the mug. He took a deep breath over the plate. He raised his head and opened his eyes wide at Marcus. "Oh, my god, that smells delicious."

"You know," Marcus said as he poured coffee into the mug then turned around to fling the pot back into the brewer, "you could've ordered anything you wanted. Steak. Chicken. Even if it wasn't something on the menu. I told you it was on me. I was hoping you'd at least give me something more challenging than a scrambled egg sandwich."

"Are you kidding? Getting scrambled eggs right is one of the most challenging things in the kitchen. Not too dry. Not too wet. Not overcooked. Everyone thinks they can do it but, yeah, not so much." Hank picked the sandwich up and took a large bite. He chewed a bit with his eyes closed before he swallowed and broke into a broad smile. "That, dude, is a good damned sandwich."

"Thanks." Marcus beamed. "Eggs are kind of my thing, so I guess it's good you picked that."

"I'm a man of simple tastes, Fiat." He took another large bite of the sandwich and made an audible "mmm" while he chewed. He picked up his fork and pushed the hash browns around a bit. "These look perfect, too."

Marcus raised his arm, blew on his nails, and then buffed them on his shirt. "Well, I don't like to brag."

"So, where'd you learn to do this?" Hank asked as he scooped a forkful of the potatoes into his mouth. "Oh, god, that's good."

"Oh," Marcus said with a shrug, "I grew up in it. I guess it was a family legacy. My mama worked in diners for years and I just picked things up." Marcus looked over Hank's shoulder to see the Do-Nothings sitting in their usual booth and watching his every move. He squinted his eyes at the women. He backed away from the counter and began to turn toward the kitchen. "You know what? I better get back in the kitchen and help with the—"

Hank touched Marcus's forearm to stop him from leaving. "Hold on there. Paulette already told me she was taking over for you. Stay here and talk to me like you did after you danced with Skeet the other night. I hate to eat alone."

Marcus's immediate reaction was to yank his arm away but as he looked at Hank's hand wrapped around his forearm, at the calloused fingers and slightly dirty fingernails that seemed so rough compared to Marcus's pale and freckled complexion, his skin tingled at the warmth of the man's hand, and the hairs on his arms stood. He looked from Hank's hand to his face and saw the other man's eyes imploring him to stay.

"Well, I guess I can stay for a minute," Marcus said. Hank took his hand away and Marcus's arm followed it, as if seeking the warmth. Marcus tried to hide the movement by dropping his elbows on the counter and leaning forward to rest his chin in his hands. "I'm in no hurry to get home anyway."

"Good. So…"

"You want me to play something on the jukebox?" Marcus started to walk to the jukebox.

"No. Let's just talk."

Marcus stopped and rested against on the counter. "About what?"

"Fiat," Hank said and sighed with his fork paused in mid-air, "it doesn't matter. Just ask me anything."

Marcus thought before asking, "Okay. I forgot to ask you at the bar the other night. You from around here?"

"Clichéd question, but okay." Hank put the fork on the counter and took a swallow of coffee before answering. "No. I grew up about an hour south of here. Valdosta. It's near the Florida line."

"I know of it. It's a lot bigger than here, isn't it? Why the hell would you move to this podunk town?"

"Hey now. Don't be insulting Marathon. It may be tiny, but it's my home now. It's a nice place to live."

119

"I'll have to take your word for that. But I'd never heard of this place before the lawyer contacted me. How on earth did you end up here?"

"There's a vocational school a couple of towns over. I went there to learn about cars, and there was a sign on a billboard at school about a mechanic here looking for some help. I figured what the hell and came over. I worked for Mr. Murphy for a couple of years and then I bought the place from him."

"So that was your dream? To be a small-town mechanic?"

Hank looked from the plate to Marcus and knitted his brows. "Something wrong with being a mechanic?"

"Oh, god, no. I didn't mean... I just... I'm sorry. Hell, I'm a fry cook, so who would I be to judge? Not like I'm curing cancer back there." Marcus jerked his thumb over his shoulder toward the kitchen.

Hank's face softened, and he shrugged as he pushed his empty plate away. "You may not be curing cancer but, dear god, that might have healed my soul. Damn, that was good." He wiped his mouth with his napkin and dropped it onto the empty plate. "And you're right. Being a mechanic wasn't really my plan."

"Oh? What was?"

"Mainly I just wanted to get out of my mother's house. My mama's a bit of a flake."

"So you ran away with the circus?" Marcus said with a smile.

"No. Long story." He paused and shook his head. "Actually, it's not. She kicked me out over the whole gay thing."

"Ouch."

"It is what it is." Hank took a large swallow of coffee. "Anyway, college was too expensive for me, and I always liked messing around with mechanical things so I just got a part-time job and went the vo-tech school route. I guess life showed me a path and I took it. It's worked for me so far."

"No, I get that. I grew up that way, just waiting on a path to show itself. But sometimes you can get a little lost doing that."

"Wait, did you say you'd never been here before the attorney got ahold of you?" Hank asked as he continued to eat.

"No."

"But I thought you were here because your grandmother died."

"Yeah, but I never met her. We didn't come around here when I was growing up. It's complicated. My mama was a flake, too." Marcus looked at the sugar packs Hank had arranged in a pattern on the edge of the counter, trying to figure out a way to move the conversation in a different direction. "We moved around a lot when I was a kid. And we got lost a lot. But Mama was good at avoiding this place. As a matter of fact, I'd never been here before the day Miss Richards slammed into me."

"Oh, shoot. I almost forgot," Hank slapped his hands on the counter, making Marcus jump in surprise. "Miss Richards. Her sister called me this morning about her car. I can't believe I didn't tell you this sooner."

"What?"

"Well, thanks to you, they took away Miss Delores's keys."

"Ugh. Yes. Everyone keeps reminding me."

"Well, her sister called and asked me to help her figure out a good sales price for the car since Miss Delores can't drive it anymore."

"Okay. And?"

"I convinced her to sell it to you at a real good price."

"Oh." Marcus stepped back from the counter a bit, his face falling. "Well, thank you, but I really don't have much money until I sell my grandmother's house..."

A big grin spread across Hank's face. "The price is zero. I mean her sister almost killed you, right?"

"But the accident was my fault. I swerved into her lane. I can't just—"

"Fiat, shut up and take the damned car."

Marcus looked at the floor. *It's a car. But it's another man giving me a car. What does he want in return? It's a way out of here. Do it. DO IT.*

"Fiat?" Hank snapped his fingers to get Marcus's attention. "You there?"

"It's kind of big."

"It's also kind of free. And you won't find a smaller car here. The men all want their trucks and the women won't drive little cars. Their hair won't fit inside."

"Right. Right." Marcus looked at Hank. "Okay."

"Great. So, it's settled. Come by the shop and pick it up later in the week. I can get the title work from Miss Richards and bam!"

"Ironic choice of words for her."

"Heh. Yeah. Speaking of the shop, I better get on back. I've been away too long as it is."

"But you just got here."

"Well, time and carburetors wait for no man. And I left Skeet watching the counter. He's probably so wrapped up in the television or texting with Frankie that someone walked away with the whole inventory." Hank jumped off the stool and brushed a few crumbs from the front of his shirt. "Thanks so much for the lunch. It was absolutely perfect. Damn fine eggs. Damn fine."

"Well, it was to thank you for helping me with the car." Marcus walked to the end of the counter and stood beside Hank. He crossed his arms and rocked on his heels. "Now that you've found me a new car I'm going to have to thank you again."

"So you are saying every time I do something nice for you, you will cook me a meal?"

Marcus laughed. "I guess that is a plan I can work with."

"Well, clearly," Hank said as he patted his belly, "I've got to be more of an asshole or I'm going to be as big as a house."

"No, seriously. Why don't you come over to the house Thursday night and I will make you dinner? And not just eggs. I'll do something nicer."

"That sounds like a plan. You live over by Skeet's grandmother, right?"

"Yes."

"All right. Well, then, Thursday night it is. And I'm serious about the car. Come get it whenever." Hank nodded a quick farewell, shook Marcus's hand, and walked out of the diner.

Marcus, a slight smile at the corner of his mouth, watched Hank go. He exhaled deeply and spun on his heels to go back into the kitchen and ran directly into the two women who were standing behind him. Marcus startled at the women's closeness and inquisitive stares. "Helen. Inez. Good grief. Don't sneak up on a guy."

"Well, that seemed to go well," Helen said, a satisfied smirk on her face. "I do believe I heard you making a second date. Why don't you come join us with Priss over here and tell us all about it?"

"Francine?" Inez yelled over Marcus's shoulder into the kitchen. "Girl, get out here! He's about to tell us all the horny details!"

"Inez, there are no horny details, it was just an egg sandwich," Marcus said as he walked away from the women. When he reached the kitchen, he was struck hard in the side by the door swinging open as Francine rushed into the diner.

"Oh, sorry, sweetie. You shouldn't stand in front of the door. Did I miss anything? I hope not. I love this part. The early dating when everything is still new and exciting, and you wonder if he is going to kiss you and—"

"It wasn't a date!" Marcus raised his voice and threw his hands in the air. "It was a thank-you!"

"A thank-you? For what? For being one hot little piece of mechanic ass?" Inez said and roared with laughter.

"Inez, language!" Priss yelled from the booth.

"Darling," Francine said and grinned, "you can call that whatever you want, but in my day when a man bought you dinner, it was considered a date. And if you made a man dinner at your house, that was most definitely a date."

"Were you all eavesdropping on our whole conversation?"

"It's a public place." Inez dragged him over to the corner booth. She plopped onto the bench seat and scooted over beside Priscilla. "We can't help it if we just happened to overhear a few things."

"Well, I can tell you one thing," Helen said as she sat, "there were sparks flying all over this diner between you two. I can't believe none of us thought to invite him to the diner that first night."

"Hell, I never knew Hank's gate swung to that side of the pasture." Francine giggled and leaned toward Marcus with her eyes opened wide. "Thank goodness I never tried to hit on him."

"You're old enough to be his mother, Francine," Priss mumbled as she shifted uncomfortably in place.

"All that matters is, our boy here has found something to occupy his fancy." Helen patted Marcus on the hand. "And maybe something that will convince him to stick around here after all. Don't you think so, Priss?"

Priss shook her head in a non-committal manner and picked at the edges of a napkin.

"Priss, I would like to say 'thank you' for staying out of this. Look, y'all, I appreciate what you are trying to do for my grandmother's wishes but it was just a lunch. You don't need to be planning a wedding. I keep telling y'all, I plan on getting out of here as soon as I can. And Hank actually just made that a little easier for me. He found me a car. So as soon as the house sells, I will be packing up and moving on, okay?"

"And going where?" Inez groused.

"I don't know. Somewhere bigger with a little more to offer me than this."

"Back to Atlanta?" Helen asked.

"You know, when I was leaving Atlanta, it was rush hour. But everyone was going the opposite way of me. I looked across the median and thought, 'what do they know that I don't? What's back there that they are all in such a hurry to get to? What am I missing out on? None of them are headed this way.' I swear I almost turned the car around and headed back. But no, I think I'm done with Atlanta. I need somewhere with new things to do. Places to go. Opportunities, you know? I mean no offense, but Marathon isn't—"

"Fabulous?" Inez interrupted him. "Isn't that the word you gay men like to use? You think life here can't be fabulous? Mister, you've barely been here two months. Let me tell you something, buddy boy, you keep thinking you are going to go somewhere and find a life that is fabulous. Well I say, you make fabulous wherever you are."

"You don't know just how fabulous life can be here," Francine added. "Just wait until you see the Hoedown for Health. You'll see. It will be *the* social event of the season."

"Which reminds me," Helen added, "you're still cooking for us so you can't leave town until the dance is over at least. Okay?"

"And I really need you around here a little longer. I can't seem to find anyone to hire."

"I'm not going until the house sells, okay? So, just chill out." Marcus jumped as his phone vibrated in his pocket. He fished it out and glanced at the screen, which notified him he had a text message. "Hopefully, this is Katie Nell about someone finally wanting to look at the house. So if y'all are done planning my future, will you…" Marcus read the text on his phone.

ROBERT: Where the hell are you? This is no longer cute or funny. Come home. NOW!

Marcus stood staring at the message. His heartbeat began to race and his knees wobbled.

"Sweetie? You look a little green. You okay?" Francine asked.

Marcus grabbed the edge of the table and steadied himself. He took a few deep breaths. *You've got a car now. You can leave. You are fine.* Marcus looked at the women and sighed. "It's nothing. I'm really tired. I need to go home and get some rest."

"And plan what you are cooking for that man," Helen added in a sing-song voice. "I can give you some wonderful casserole recipes if you—"

"Helen," Inez interrupted her, "he wants to woo the man in, not do the man in."

Marcus forced a smile at the women's banter. "Miss Helen, I'm good. I've got plenty of my own ideas of things to cook. And I'll call y'all later in the week to discuss the menu for the Hoedown. Could you ask Katie Nell to call me about the house? I don't know why I haven't had anyone come look at it yet." As he walked out of the diner, Marcus started tapping a reply to Robert on his phone. "See you in the morning Francine. I'm going to find Skeet for a ride home." When the diner's door had swung shut behind him, Marcus reread the text and then hit send.

MARCUS: Fuck off.

"DEAR LORD IN HEAVEN," HANK groaned as he rubbed his belly and leaned back in his chair. He dropped his fork on the table and pushed his mostly empty plate away. He stretched his arms above his head and let his head loll over the back of the chair. "If I eat another bite of this, I swear I'll just explode all over the place."

"That's a lovely image," Marcus drawled and scrunched up his face before breaking out in a smile. He dropped his own fork beside his plate and plucked his napkin out of his lap, then dragged it across his lips and discarded it on his empty plate. "Trust me, killing you was not my goal tonight. And we haven't tried my chocolate chip pound cake yet."

Marcus scooted his chair back from the table and stood. He crossed to the kitchen, grabbed the oven handle, and yanked the door open. The sugary, warm smell of the cake baking in the oven wafted out into the kitchen and spread throughout the small house. Marcus took a wooden spoon from the counter and hooked it through the gaps in the oven rack to pull it out. He pulled a toothpick from the small cloisonné vase on the back of the stove. He stuck the toothpick into the cake, pulled it out, and inspected it for any clinging pieces of cake. Satisfied that the cake was done, Marcus used two dishcloths from the counter to protect his hands as he picked up the cake pan. Marcus lifted the pan to his nose and took a deep breath.

He turned to face Hank and waved the pan around in front of him, swiveling his hips in a poor imitation of some Latin dance he had once seen on television. "But it smells so good," he taunted Hank in a sing-song voice.

Hank groaned again and slouched forward onto his elbows on the table. "Fiat, you've got to be kidding me. I don't know where I would put it." Hank laughed, picked up his fork, and pushed the last bits of mashed potato around his plate. "I swear I haven't eaten cooking like that since—"

"If you say since your mama's cooking, I will toss you right out of here."

"Oh, hell no. My mama couldn't make a peanut butter sandwich. No, I was going to say since I don't know when. But your mama must've been a hell of a cook to teach you to make food that way. Fried chicken, collard greens, and mashed potatoes—"

"Real mashed potatoes," Marcus interrupted him and gestured at him with the cake pan, "that weren't from a box."

"Right," Hank said and nodded his head. "Well, that ain't exactly Waffle Barn fare, you know. You didn't learn to make that food in a greasy spoon diner."

"No, I learned some of it from my mama; the rest I just taught myself when I was cooking for..." Marcus looked around the kitchen for somewhere to set the hot cake pan. "Will you be a sweetheart and help me for a second."

"I don't know if I can stand up." Hank rubbed his belly again, before grunting his way out of his chair onto his feet. "All righty, what can I do?"

"I still don't know where everything is in this house. Look in some of these drawers and see if you see a pot holder or something for me to put this on."

"You mean a trivet?" Hank asked as he opened a drawer on the kitchen island and looked inside. "Nope, just silverware here."

"Ooh," Marcus said and raised his eyebrows. "A trivet. Well, listen to mister fancy pants."

"Shut up," Hank said with a laugh as he pushed the drawer closed and moved on to the next one. He looked inside and said, "Nothing but foil and wax paper and… um… what must be about five hundred garbage bag ties and a bunch of artificial sweetener packs."

"Try the one over by the stove," Marcus pointed with his elbow and juggled the pan gingerly between his hands. "Hurry, this thing is really hot."

As Hank slid behind Marcus to move to the other side of the cramped kitchen space, his hands dragged across Marcus's waist, and he paused at Marcus's ear to growl, "not the hottest thing in this kitchen."

"I'm serious," Marcus said as he pushed his hips back to nudge Hank away. "It's really hot."

Hank slipped around Marcus and pulled open a drawer by the stove. "Bingo!" he yelled before pulling out a ceramic trivet with cherries painted on it and setting it on the counter.

"Ow! Ow! Ow!" Marcus said as he set the pan onto the trivet. "I wish I had a wire cooling rack. It'd cool faster so you could eat some sooner."

"Fiat, I already told you I'm going to need a little recovery time before I eat anything else."

Marcus turned to face Hank and leaned back against the counter, letting the dishrags hang beside his hips. "However will we pass the time?"

Hank stepped closer to Marcus, placed his arms on either side of him on the counter and stared into Marcus's eyes. "I might have an idea or two."

"Such as?" Marcus held his breath in anticipation as Hank moved closer to his face.

"Well…" Hank whispered and leaned closer. "We could…" Just as his beard was tickling at Marcus's cheek, Hank suddenly jerked back, lifted his hand in front of his mouth and tried his best to stifle a loud belch. "Oh, my god," Hank muttered, his cheeks growing red. "Well, that was real sexy, wasn't it?" He closed his eyes and splayed his hand over his face.

Marcus began laughing and pushed himself off the counter with his elbows. "Very." He stepped forward and swatted at Hank with the dishrag.

"I told you, I ate too much." Hank dropped his hands from his face and shot an impish grin at Marcus. "I swear, I may have to take off my belt and unbutton my pants."

"Well, my intention with cooking wasn't to get you out of your pants, but if you insist." Marcus cocked an eyebrow and smirked.

"I'm serious." Hank shook his head and let another small burp escape. "I may not fit in my truck to go home."

Marcus stepped closer to Hank and purred into his ear, "Then just stay here."

Hank's grin faded, and he took a few steps back from Marcus. "Um… look. I need to tell you something."

"Shit," Marcus said and slipped farther away from Hank. "I'm sorry. I thought you were… I mean when you said… I was just… You know what? I'm just going to start cleaning up these dishes." Marcus hurried over to the kitchen table and began gathering the silverware and plates, trying his best to keep his blushing face turned away from Hank.

"No, Marcus, it's not that I don't want to stay here with you."

Marcus dropped the silverware back on the table and turned back around. "So I'm Marcus now?"

"I'm trying to be serious here."

"It's fine." Marcus turned sharply back to the table, scooped up the silverware, stalked to the sink, and dropped the pieces in with a loud clatter. "I clearly misunderstood. You've had a nice meal and now you can go home."

Marcus hurried back to the table and grabbed the plates. He crossed to the sink and let the dishes fall. He muttered, "It's okay if you're not attracted to me, if you don't want to sleep with me."

Marcus stood staring at the water swirling over the dirty plates and tried to compose himself. Hank wrapped his hands around his hips and slowly turned him around. Marcus kept his head lowered until Hank touched his chin and lifted his face.

"I *do* want to sleep with you." Hank placed his lips against Marcus's before pulling away and adding, "A lot." He kissed Marcus again, harder.

Hank's beard tickled against Marcus's cheeks, and Marcus relaxed against the sink, feeling the warmth of Hank's body close to his. The hairs on the back of his neck stood as Hank's lips touched his lightly in several small nips of kisses. He placed his hands on Hank's shoulders and pushed him away slightly. "You do?"

"God, yes," Hank answered, his eyes wide and his eyebrows raised. He kissed Marcus again before adding, "Just… not tonight."

Marcus shifted his upper body, leaving his hands resting on Hank's chest, and stared. "What?"

"Fiat, we hardly know each other." Hank shrugged and took a step away from Marcus, causing Marcus's arms to drop to his sides. "I know it sounds old-fashioned, but I just prefer to get to know someone before we… you know. That's what I was trying to tell you. That's why I have my rule."

"Your rule?"

"Three dates." Hank held up three fingers and nodded toward his hand. "I never sleep with someone until the third date."

Marcus glanced back and forth between Hank's raised fingers and his face, trying to determine if the other man was joking. "Okay. But why three?"

Hank dropped his hand and shoved it into his pocket. His shoulders hunched up from the posture, and he shifted from foot to foot. He sighed and then explained, "Look, you know my favorite part about spending the night with someone?"

"Well, duh?"

"No. Not that." Hank chuckled. "I mean, yeah, I love that part. God, I love that part. But it's the talking afterward. You know, lying there and talking about life, dreams, how your day was, or whatever. And I just prefer that if I wake up next to someone, it's someone I actually want to hear what they have to say. Somebody who cares what I have to say. And well, that's not something you can usually tell after one or two nights. So..."

"So three dates."

"Three dates. And your water is still running." Hank pointed over Marcus's shoulder at the faucet.

Marcus turned his back to the man and banged the faucet handle down to stop the water. Marcus looked at the suds and dishes in the sink and considered the man's words. He quickly spun around and broke out into a broad smile. "But this is our third date."

"No. Second."

"Third." Marcus lifted his hand and ticked the numbers off on his fingers. "One. The Woodshed. Two. The Tammy. Tonight. That's three." He held the three fingers up and gestured them proudly toward Hank." Plus you've been in the Tammy every day this week. We've been talking a lot."

"The Woodshed wasn't a date. We just ran into each other there." Hank folded one of Marcus's fingers back down. "So this is date number two. Maybe one and a half, because the Tammy was a thank-you lunch, as you kept telling me." Hank pushed another of Marcus's fingers down. "Down to one."

"Well, Francine Jones told me if you cook for someone it counts as a date, so," Marcus popped the second finger back up, "The Tammy was definitely a date. So that's two." Marcus thought about the numbers and then glanced at Hank with a grin. "You could leave, circle the block, come back, and we could call it the third date." Marcus flicked the third finger back up.

Hank began to laugh and shake his head. He took Marcus's hand and moved it back to his waist. He held Marcus's fingers loosely in his fist. "No, Fiat. Look, if this is a problem for you, I can just leave now, and no harm no foul."

Marcus looked into Hank's eyes and let the man's words sink in. "You know what? I hate doing dishes with no one to talk to. Why don't you hang out and talk to me while I clean up?"

"I think I can do that." Hank cracked a crooked grin and stepped to the sink. "How about you wash and I rinse?"

"No," Marcus shook his head and pushed Hank away from the sink. "I'm the host. I clean. And there isn't a whole lot to wash. Just talk to me while I do it."

"Are you sure? I really don't mind." Hank turned the faucet back on, picked a plate out of the sink, and began to run it under the water.

"Just hush." Marcus took a butter knife out of the sink and aimed it at Hank. "Step away from the dishes, and no one gets hurt."

"Fine! Fine!" Hank threw his hands up in surrender and walked to the other side of the island. "You want me to turn on the television? We could watch a movie or maybe put on some music?"

"If you want." Marcus scrubbed a plate with a sponge. "I haven't turned cable on here so there is nothing to watch on television. There are some CDs on the shelf by the television, but I haven't really looked at what music my grandmother had." Hank crossed the living room and ran his fingers along the row of CDs in a rack above a small silver stereo system. "According to Miss Helen, my grandmother was really into music from the fifties."

"Oh, yeah," Hank answered back. "Connie Francis. The Platters. Elvis. Johnny Mathis. What the hell is a Ferrante and Teicher?"

"No idea," Marcus said. "We don't have to listen—"

"Oh! This will do." Hank pulled a CD from the rack, opened the case and turned on the stereo. He dropped the CD into the player and hit a button on the front. "I think this might be right up your alley."

Marcus stopped washing the dish he was holding and waited to hear what music Hank had chosen. As the first few notes plinked out of the speakers, Marcus began to grin and hummed along with the song. "Patsy Cline. Classic. I didn't think you liked country music."

"Patsy isn't country." Hank turned away from the stereo and crossed back toward the kitchen. "Patsy is a legend." He stopped at the piano to look at the pictures scattered along the top, his hips swaying in time with the music as he moved slowly from picture to picture. "Really, she's more like air. Necessary for living."

"There hasn't been anyone like her since." Marcus pulled the last dish out of the sink. "Some of the new artists are okay. But, I mean—"

"Oh, my god, Fiat. Is this you?" Hank pointed at one of the pictures.

Marcus looked from the sink and tried to see which picture Hank was pointing at. "Maybe? What is it?"

"An adorable little redhead with a parrot on his arm."

"Oh, jeez. Yeah, that's me. Though, I honestly don't remember when it was taken." Hank placed the last dish on the drainer, picked up a dry towel, and wiped his hands. He walked around the island and over to the piano to stand behind Hank. "That's me sitting on the stool at a diner counter too."

"And that one?" Hank pointed at another photo.

"No. That's my father." Marcus picked up the picture of his grandmother and her friends and handed it to Hank. "The woman on the right was my grandmother."

"Wow, she was really pretty."

"Yeah." He took the picture from Hank and set it back on the piano. He pointed at another frame. "I think that's her and my grandfather in that one with the old car, too."

"Look at all that red hair." Hank looked closer at the picture. "And that is not 'an old car.' *That* is a Cadillac. Practically a boat, they were so big back then. And power. Man, back then the engines were practically strong enough to…" Hank's voice trailed off and he stepped away from the piano. "You don't want to get me started on old cars." Hank crossed to the sofa and dropped onto the cushions. He looked at Marcus, patted the empty spot beside him, and draped his arm across the back of the sofa.

Marcus sat carefully beside Hank before scooting over and tucking himself under his arm. He placed his ear against Hank's chest and listened to the soft thud of the man's heartbeat through his shirt. "You can talk about cars if you want."

"I'd rather do this." Hank shifted Marcus off his chest and into an upright position and kissed him.

Marcus closed his eyes and surrendered to the kiss. He hooked his arms over Hank's shoulders. As he tilted his head to the other side, Hank pulled away from the kiss.

"Wait," Hank mumbled, "I thought you said you didn't know your grandmother."

"Really? I'm kissing you and you're thinking about my grandmother? Not sure how I should take that."

"No. I'm sorry. My brain just keeps rolling, and, if we keep this up, it's going to be hard for me not to break my rule."

"Rules were made to be broken."

"Fiat."

"Fine. No. I didn't ever meet her in person."

"Then how did she get all of these pictures of you?"

"Apparently, my mother sent them." Marcus sighed and leaned back into the couch. "My family history is screwed up. So, like I said, I never met her. I wish I had, though. The stories people tell me make her sound like a dream."

"I never knew any of my grandparents either. My mom's parents were gone before my parent's married. My parents were older when they had me. And my dad's mother died on the day my mother found out she was pregnant with me. Which, thank god I don't believe in omens or signs, because…"

"Oh, man, that's crazy."

"Yeah. Literally the same day. My mother said it was the disappointment that my father was now tied to her forever by a child. My Nana Hudson didn't care for my mother. But it was really diabetes. Anyway, I'm named after her."

"Your grandmother was named Hank?"

"No, silly. She was Henrietta. That's where I got Henry. Which became Hank. It's funny, I've always called her Nana Hudson, though she was dead before I was born."

"I never had a name for mine, and yet she still left me all of this." Marcus waved his hand toward the room. "Mama never talked much about her or my dad unless she had too much to drink. I guess it was too painful or something."

"Painful?"

"Yeah, my dad died in a car wreck before I was born. He was driving back to campus in Athens after dropping my mama off at work at the diner. That's where they met. He and a bunch of the other football players went in there one night after practice to eat, and he started flirting with Mama. He asked her out, and they got married a month later."

"Holy shit. That's fast."

"Yeah. Though I think I'm the reason it happened. Mama said my grandmother Sumter was furious with them for it, so Mama never would come see her. Anyway, one night my father dropped Mama off for a late-night shift at the diner and…" Marcus glanced over at the family photos on the back of the piano and then sighed.

"Oh, man. I'm sorry."

"Yeah. I guess it should make me sad, but can you miss someone you never knew?" Marcus shrugged and leaned against Hank's shoulder. He fiddled with the buttons along the front of Hank's shirt. "Anyway. It was always just me and Mama. But I do think it made her a little crazy, missing my daddy and raising me by herself. She used to…" Marcus sat up and shifted away from Hank. "I should shut up before you think I come from a bunch of crazy people."

"Fiat, we're southern. We all come from crazy. I think it's the heat. Or the bugs. I mean, it's funny. They call this part of the country the land of family values, but, I swear, everyone I know has the most screwed-up families. Hell, my own mother threw me out."

"Ha. I win. Mine abandoned me at a roadside diner."

"What?" Hank's chin dropped.

"Okay, if I'm going to tell this story, we're going to need cake." He eased himself off the couch and wandered to the kitchen. "Yes, my dear old mother just left me on the side of the road."

"Marcus, that's terrible."

"I was an adult, and I guess she figured her job was done." Marcus tapped the side of the cake pan to test if it was cool enough. "I don't know. But one day we pulled into a place, I went to buy her cigarettes, and when I came back, no Mama."

"What did you do?"

Marcus looked over to see that Hank had stretched out on the sofa and placed his arms behind his head. He stared aimlessly at the ceiling, his head cocked to listen to Marcus speak. "Well, at first I had a small panic attack. Then I sat on the curb and cried for about ten minutes."

"Holy shit."

"Then I just thought to myself, 'screw it.'" Marcus took a knife from the drainer and slid it carefully around the edge of the cake pan. "Then I picked myself up and went into that diner and got a job. I had some cash for a hotel room for a few nights and then I found a cheap apartment near the diner. I just started living life, you know." He opened the cabinet to his left and pulled out the largest plate he could find.

"Man, that's amazing. And your mother?" Hank's voice grew softer, and his words came out slower.

"No idea. Don't really care." Marcus gave the cake pan a gentle shake, and the cake fell out onto the platter.

"And then you came down here?"

"Well, no. That was several years ago." Marcus picked up the knife and held it over the cake, contemplating his next words. *Just tell him.* "I got involved with someone." Marcus took a deep breath and then plunged the knife into the cake. "Someone I met at the diner." After cutting two slices, he chose two plates from the dish drainer. "We started dating, and eventually I moved in with him. He had a really nice house, and he made me feel as though I was the best thing in the world. It was nice to start with, finally having a home. But he was really jealous." Marcus lifted the first slice with the knife and dropped it onto the plate. "When we first met, we had lots of friends, but I don't know. Eventually, he stopped wanting to be around people, and then I stopped wanting to be around him." Marcus dropped the second slice onto the other plate and dropped the knife into the sink. "So, yeah. That didn't turn out so good." Marcus pushed his shoulders back and shook the story from his body. "Unlike this cake, which turned out…"

Marcus looked toward the couch to see that Hank's eyes were closed and that his chest rose and fell in a steady rhythm. "Hank?" Marcus walked around the kitchen island and to the couch. He watched as

Hank dozed peacefully, completely unaware of his surroundings. Marcus bent and shook him lightly.

Hank popped open his eyes and stared at Marcus. "I'm awake. I'm listening. You worked in a diner and… okay. Sorry. I kind of fell asleep."

Marcus laughed. "Kind of? You were practically snoring. Was my story that boring?"

"No. No. I just had to get up really early for work and with my belly full and—"

"It's okay."

"But I'm awake now. What were you saying? Something about cake?"

"Why don't you go on home and get some sleep?"

"But the cake. You worked so hard on the cake."

"Look, I'll bring you a slice tomorrow when I come to pick up Miss Richards's car." Marcus held out his hand. When the other man took his hand, he pulled back and lifted Hank off the couch. "Then I'll have two excuses to come by and see you."

"But I didn't get to ask you out for that third date."

"I think you just did."

"Huh? Oh. Yeah. I… god, I'm so sleepy."

"It's okay, Hank. I need to go to bed too. I've got to be up at the butt-crack of dawn to be at the Tammy tomorrow." Marcus steered Hank toward the front door. "And I accept."

"Accept what?"

"That third date."

"Oh, yeah. But what are we going to—"

"We'll figure it out tomorrow." Marcus pulled open the front door and guided Hank out. "Good night, Hank."

As the screen door slammed shut, Marcus leaned against the door frame and watched Hank stumble down the sidewalk. As he slowly began to shut the front door, he heard Hank snap his fingers.

"Marcus, wait."

Marcus pulled the door open to find Hank waiting for him on the other side of the screen. "Yeah?"

Hank pulled the screen door open and grabbed Marcus's hands, pulling him forward through the doorway onto the porch. "Dessert." He placed a soft, quick kiss on Marcus's lips. "Mmm. My compliments to the chef." With a wink and a smile, Hank turned and walked away, leaving Marcus standing on the porch grinning from ear to ear.

MARCUS SPENT THE NEXT DAY humming and singing along with the jukebox and shuffling around the kitchen. Though the songs customers played were the same old things that were played every day, he could've sworn that each song seemed to be more romantic and sweeter than he had ever noticed. Several times as he passed behind Francine or one of her daughters, he would wrap his arms around her and spin her about in a quick two-step of laughter and song. Ever-conscious of the clock over the pass-through, he whistled, scrambled, and sautéed his way through the day until Francine finally flipped the sign on the door over to *Closed*.

"Get on out of here," she said and chuckled as she swung her dishrag at him. "Clearly something more interesting that the Jones women has been kicking around your mind all day. Something that's made you rather happy. Couldn't involve a certain grease monkey, now could it?"

Marcus ducked the question and hurried into the kitchen to fling his apron onto a hook and his hair net into the trash. He pulled the tinfoil-wrapped cake out of the silver refrigerator and tossed it into a plastic sack from behind the cash register. He set off at a trot toward Hank's garage, each step in time with the lovesick words that Patsy,

Tammy, Loretta, and Dolly had crooned from the jukebox. Before he turned the last corner, however, he stopped to let his breathing and heart rate slow so he wouldn't appear too eager. As he stepped through the opening of the garage doors, he saw Hank, in his usual blue work-shirt and dark jeans, lounging against the enormous, red LTD parked in the right bay. He had one leg hiked up behind him to rest against the white-walled tire and his arms folded across his chest. On one hand, he spun a key ring around his extended finger.

"Hey there, Fiat." He glanced at his wristwatch. "Right on time, aren't you?"

"Hey," Marcus said, his voice sounding breathy and faint despite his momentary rest.

"Someone's out of breath. In that big of a hurry to get this car?"

Marcus walked over to Hank and grabbed at the keys spinning on his finger. "Or something."

"Hold on," Hank said as he pulled the keys back from Marcus's grasp. "I need payment first."

"Payment?" Marcus asked. He cocked one hip and placed his hand on it. "I thought you said it was taken care of."

"Well, Miss Richards has been taken care of, but I deserve a finder's fee, don't you think?"

Marcus gave a quick glance around the garage to make sure no customers were lurking in the corners before putting his hands on the car on either side of Hank's hips. With his lips close to Hank's face, he purred, "What did you have in mind?"

Marcus shifted his weight forward until their lips met. Hank's hands moved down his back onto his hips and pulled him closer. Marcus relaxed his body into Hank's and closed his eyes until Hank pulled away. He opened his eyes and stared his confusion at the other man.

Hank blinked a few times and shifted his eyes between Marcus's lips and his eyes. He leaned into Marcus's face, his lips nearly meeting

Marcus's again and said, "That was nice, but I believe I was promised cake."

Marcus pushed off the car with a grunt to shift his body away from Hank's. He lifted the sack and waved it in front of Hank's face. "Right here. But I was promised something, too."

"The keys are right here." Hank lifted his hand to show the key ring again.

"No." Marcus shook his head and pouted. "I mean date number three."

"Oh yeah. I vaguely remember there being some discussion about that. So when did you have in mind?"

"Well, there is the big dance the Do-Nothings are throwing tomorrow night in the town square." Marcus traced the outline of Hank's name patch and pressed his hips into Hank's pelvis. He bent his head and looked up through his lashes at the other man. "Sure would be nice to have an escort for that. You know, make all the girls jealous walking in with you on my arm."

"Hardly," Hank said and laughed. "But I got to say 'no can do' on that one."

Marcus jerked his hand away from Hank's chest and took a few steps back. "Oh. Um… I'm sorry. I thought you wanted another date."

"I do. But that society stuff isn't really for me. Bunch of people standing around talking about nothing. Giving money—money I don't have—to get their name on a plaque on a hospital wall. Nah. That's the same stuff I got away from when I left my mother's house."

"Oh, good grief, Hank. It's not a night at the Metropolitan Opera. It's a bunch of biddies dancing poorly to old music and eating some food. Food prepared by the hottest new chef in town, by the way. And you don't have to give any money or talk to anyone. God knows I don't have any money to give. And you can hang out by the food with me all night. Well, at least, until you take me out for a spin on the dance floor."

"I already told you at The Woodshed, I don't dance. Also, I don't really have any fancy clothes to wear."

"I don't have anything fancy either. We can be the hobos in the corner together."

"Fiat," Hank said and sighed, "just drop it. I said no."

"Fine. But I still want that third date."

"Tell you what. Why don't you come over here tonight and I'll cook for you for a change?"

"Ooh," Marcus replied and raised an eyebrow. "What you going to make for me?"

Hank squinted and looked toward the ceiling. "Well, you can choose between spaghetti and spaghetti."

Marcus chuckled and pretended to consider the options. "I guess I'll take the spaghetti."

"Excellent choice."

"No, wait," Marcus said and snapped his fingers. "I have to start prepping some of the food for the dance tomorrow night. Why don't I just whip up something for us out of that stuff? You can come over and eat at my place, since you won't get to try any of my food at the dance."

"I really wanted to show you my place, though." Hank pointed above his head toward the apartment above the garage.

"Okay. I'll go home, do my prep work, make us something, and come back here. After all," Marcus yanked the key ring out of Hank's hand, "I have wheels now!"

MARCUS SAT IN THE OLD, red car and stared at the lights in the windows above the garage. In the five minutes he had been sitting parked on the street in front of the building, he had counted at least thirty times that Hank's shadow had passed by the window shade. Marcus's nervous heartbeat in his ears nearly drowned out the barely audible country music that twanged out of the stereo speakers. Two foil-covered plates sat on the passenger's seat; the food hidden within was growing colder by the minute. *Just open the car door and go upstairs.*

When he had hopped into the car ten minutes earlier, he had been a bundle of excitement and energy, but the drive over had altered his mood. When he'd put the car into reverse and backed out of his grandmother's, well, his, driveway, he had looked at his reflection in the rear-view mirror. The black eye that had marred his face was gone, much as thoughts of Robert had faded to an occasional moment of anger or panic. Life was exciting again. The ease with which he had fit in at the diner and the rapport he had built with the regulars had brought back so much pleasure to his daily life. His time spent chatting with the Do-Nothings as they loitered about the booth in the corner for their "meetings" had become the highlight of his day. He and Skeet had found an easy camaraderie, and a day without the banjo twang of the boy's excited voice seemed incomplete. Now he had an incredibly sexy man waiting for him. He had winked at his reflection and said aloud, "Let's go on that third date."

As the words hung in the air, Marcus remembered what Hank had said the previous night. *Won't sleep with someone until the third date.* Instantly he had begun to sweat and his heart began to race as he realized exactly what *could* happen at Hank's apartment that night. While he had been ready to climb Hank like a fireman's ladder last night, the seed Hank had planted about the importance of a night spent together had grown into a blossom of pressure in Marcus's mind. He had to be not only good in bed, but good at staying in bed. *Oh, for crying out loud.* He had pushed the thought down and begun the drive into downtown Marathon. As he'd stopped at the exit of the subdivision, he had glanced over to see the sign the Do-Nothings had hung below the stop sign—Be Safe! *Thank you, ladies.*

A few miles away from the neighborhood, he'd entered a sharp curve that he was sure existed solely because some farmer had refused to give up a piece of his land and the developers had just curved around it. As he'd turned the steering wheel to follow the curve, he'd noticed the traffic sign to his right: Slow. Dangerous curves ahead.

Well, yeah, I guess. Another mile down the road he had been greeted with several stop signs and a Do not enter sign on top of a metal post that had been twisted and mangled by some reckless driver so it faced the wrong direction. *Really?*

By the time he had reached the streets of the downtown area, he had nearly convinced himself to turn around and go home. Soft Shoulder. *Can I be that?* No U-Turn. *No turning back.* As he had sat at the last traffic light before arriving at the garage, he'd read the black and white sign overhead that was swinging in the early summer breeze—Don't Block the Box.

What the hell am I supposed to do with that advice?

Marcus dropped his head onto the steering wheel and closed his eyes, considering the implicit promise of Hank's third-date rule and trying to mute the nervous thoughts that screamed in his ears. *You are over-thinking this. He may not want to have sex. But what if he does?* His thoughts were interrupted by the vibration of his phone on the seat beside him. He opened his eyes, picked up the phone, and looked at the screen.

Robert: Please answer your phone. Or call me. Very important we speak.

Marcus quickly tapped out the digits of Robert's number on the screen and let his finger hover over the green "call" button. He counted to ten in his head and began to lower his finger when a tapping on the window made him stop. Hank was bent over and looking at him through the glass. He wore a snug white polo shirt that accentuated his full chest and biceps and khaki shorts that accentuated everything below. His eyebrows were angled down in the center in a look of concern, and the corner of his mouth twitched.

"Fiat? You all right?"

Marcus nodded his head and dropped the phone back onto the seat beside the plates. *No U-turns now.* He opened the door. "Sorry about that. I was just reading some emails."

"Well, I saw you sitting down here for so long, I was worried you changed your mind about coming up tonight."

"No." Marcus grabbed the plates. He swung his feet out of the car and handed the plates to Hank. "Unless this garage doubles as a drive-in restaurant, I guess we better get these upstairs and eat." He turned his upper body back into the car, took the phone off the seat, and shoved it into his shirt pocket.

"You sure you're okay?"

"Yes. Totally." Marcus stepped out of the car and nodded toward the building. "Give me the grand tour?"

Hank bowed slightly and swung his arm toward the door of the garage. "Right this way. So what are we having tonight? Is it the chili you are serving at the dance?"

"No. After I got the car from you, I realized I had the freedom to come and go around town as I pleased. I ran back by the diner to pick up a few ingredients from Francine and then rushed into Dale Clifford's butcher shop to pick up the beef, chicken, and sausage I need for the menu for the dance. In that long glass display case at the front of the shop, I noticed two beautiful cuts of veal and decided that maybe veal piccata was a good choice. It was a little expensive, but I figured we should celebrate me having a car again."

Marcus followed Hank into the lobby of the garage and waited while Hank locked the door, drew large blinds over the windows, and turned off the lights. They continued on behind the counter and into the office that Marcus had noticed his first day in the garage. It was just as messy as it had been that day, with catalogs and invoices scattered all over the desk and a greasy mechanical thing that Marcus couldn't name sitting on a newspaper with smaller pieces scattered around it. "I think you need an assistant to help with all of this paperwork."

"Well, Skeet was supposed to do that between car washes, but he seems to spend most of his day on his phone texting with Frankie and posting on his blog. Hell, some days he doesn't even bother to come in. Just pretend you didn't see any of that." Hank jerked his head toward the stairs in the corner. "This is where we're headed. Nothing but business down here."

"And up there?" Marcus regretted the question as soon as the words fell out of his mouth.

Hank looked at Marcus with a half-grin and shook his head as he chuckled. "Well, dinner at least."

Marcus's phone vibrated in his pocket as he made his way up the stairs behind Hank, who bounded ahead of him two steps at a time. He ignored the phone and regretted not turning it off or leaving it in the car. At the top of the stairs, Marcus stepped into Hank's apartment and pulled the phone out of his pocket to turn it off. He glanced at the screen and saw another text from Robert. He shoved the phone back in his pocket without reading it.

"So, this is my humble home."

Marcus looked up at the sound of Hank's voice. The stairwell opened directly into Hank's apartment, which was one large room spanning the length of the business below. Directly in front of Marcus was a green metal door with several hooks holding baseball caps. To his right, he could see a blue sofa, a hideous green plaid recliner, and a coffee table tucked into the corner of the room closest to the stairs. The windows to the street were open, and a warm breeze filtered in under the half-closed blinds. Despite the sparse interior, the room seemed cozy, warm, and inviting.

Hank gestured toward the sofa. "Come on in and make yourself comfortable while I finish a few things over here. You can put on some music from the shelf over there if you want."

Marcus wandered past the sofa to an entertainment center and glanced at the books, DVDs, and CDs lined up neatly on the shelves. Out of the corner of his eye, he noticed Hank's bed tucked under a pair of windows. He quickly averted his gaze from the bed to two large art nouveau lithographs that hung between the windows advertising performances at the Paris Opera House.

"*La Bohème,*" Marcus said.

"What?"

"The poster," Marcus pointed across the room. "*La Bohème.* I don't recognize the other one."

"*Orfeo ed Euridice.* It's about Orpheus. You know the story. His true love, Eurydice, goes to Hades, so he goes down to rescue her. He literally goes through hell for love. He leads her out of hell."

"Lucky girl."

"Not really. I can't remember why, but Orpheus isn't supposed to turn around to look at her until they are completely out of Hades. But he blows it and turns around. So, yeah. I'm not a big fan of the opera itself, but I love the poster. I mean, look at those colors."

"It really is, um, colorful?"

"You know *La Bohème?*"

"A… um… friend took me to see it in Atlanta. I fell asleep."

"Ugh. Really? I'm afraid I may have to ask you to leave." Hank laughed as he stepped into the kitchenette along one wall. He sat the plates on the counter. "But at least you pronounced it right. There was this complete idiot at one of my parents' parties that kept pronouncing it 'La Boheem.' It made my skin crawl."

"Ew."

"Right? He was the same idiot that told my mother he had spent over a hundred dollars on a bottle of Dom Perrier. Can you believe that? Dom Perrier! That was some damn expensive water." Hank picked up one of the plates and lifted it in front of his chest. "So do I need to throw these in the microwave?"

"Yeah. For a minute or two. Take the foil off first. Are we going to eat here?" Marcus pointed at a card table in the middle of the room. "I can get drinks ready or whatever. Maybe pour us some Dom Perrier?"

"Oh, no. We aren't eating here." Hank removed the foil from one plate and placed it in the microwave on the counter. "Follow me." He walked over to the door at the top of the stairs and pulled it open to reveal another staircase. "Watch your step. It's a little rickety." Hank disappeared up the metal stairs and through the opening at the top.

Marcus grasped the cast iron handrails, peered up the steps, and noticed Hank's backside and hairy legs as he climbed and disappeared above. Marcus tested the first step with his foot and then tottered his way up the shaky stairs. When he poked his head through the opening in the roof, he gasped.

The stairs led to the roof. Around its perimeter sat large planters with pink and purple flowers spilling over the edges and small shrubs covered with white lights. A few containers held tomato and pepper plants. Long wooden window boxes filled with multi-colored pansies, bright red geraniums, and yellow marigolds lined the ledges on two sides of the building. Two long strings of dimly lit paper lanterns hung overhead between poles at the corners of the roof, meeting at a wooden arbor in the center of the space. Vines of confederate jasmine grew out of pots at the base of the arbor and wound their way in and out of the wooden structure. Marcus could smell the sweet fragrance of the tiny white flowers as the breeze carried it across the roof.

Hank held his hand out to Marcus. "Come on up, Fiat."

"Oh, my god, Hank. This is beautiful."

As he stepped onto the roof, Marcus could see a small wrought iron bistro table with two chairs centered under the arbor. A single votive candle burning inside a mason jar sat beside an old jelly jar full of daisies in the center of the table. Hank pulled Marcus toward the table, only dropping his hand to slide out a chair and gesture for Marcus to sit. Instead, Marcus stood looking at the arbor.

"I'll go get the food and bring it back up. Why don't you pour us both something to drink?"

Marcus looked at a carafe in a cooler beside the table. "Is that wine? How did you know what to open when you didn't know what I'd be bringing to eat?"

"It's sweet tea, Fiat. House wine of the South." Hank walked over to the stairs and started back into the apartment. When only his head was visible, he stopped and called to Marcus. "You should take in the view while you're up here." Hank's head disappeared into the room below.

Marcus walked to the front ledge of the building, placed his hands on the bricks, and tipped forward to take in the view. From this height, he could see several of the streets of Marathon spreading out around him. To his left, he could see two men working in the town square in preparation for the dance the next night. Though he couldn't see their features, he knew by the similarities of their builds and the trucker caps on their heads that they were the Dobbins twins. He watched while the men strung lights around the white gazebo in the center of the grassy square.

Looking back to his right, he could see the flashing red, yellow, and green neon of the old movie theater marquee scattering swaths of color across the pavement and reflecting off the silver siding of the Tammy. The Tammy's pink and blue sign winked back at the theater, as if brazenly flirting right there on a public street. "How scandalous," Marcus said aloud.

Marcus shifted his focus to the street below him, where his huge red car sat by the curb in front of the garage. From this angle, he could see what a terrible parking job he had done, leaving the rear end of the car jutting out into the street. His stomach flipped at the vertigo leaning over the edge of the building gave him. As he stood, the phone in his chest pocket vibrated again. He pulled the phone out, swiped his thumb across the screen and read the message there. Three missed calls and two texts from Robert. *It's like you know I'm on a date.* Marcus stretched his arm out in front of himself and dangled the phone over the edge of the roof, daring himself to drop the nuisance and let it shatter on the pavement below. *I'd be rid of the phone, but not the pain in the ass calling it.*

"What you doing over there?"

Hank's voice startled Marcus and he fumbled with the phone to keep from dropping it. He shoved the phone back into his pocket before turning around to face Hank with a sheepish grin. "Just taking some pictures. It really is beautiful up here."

"It's a pretty little town, ain't it? And this is a pretty plate of food. Let's dig in."

"WELL, THAT WAS MIGHTY FANCY," Hank said as he shoved the empty plate toward the center of the table.

"An empty plate means you liked it, right?" Marcus scooped up Hank's plate and stood to walk to the stairs.

"Hey." Hank stopped Marcus with a gentle touch on the arm. "I'll clean up. You've done all the work."

"Okay." Marcus sat down and stacked the plate on top of his own. He gathered the silverware and set it on the empty plates. "But you still didn't answer me. Did you like it?"

"Yeah," Hank said as he slid his chair back and removed the dirty plates from the table. "Couldn't pronounce all of it, but it was good, I guess." He walked toward the stairs.

"You guess?" Marcus asked as he took the empty glasses and followed Hank.

"Fiat, can I ask you something?"

"Sure."

Hank lifted the empty plates and showed them to Marcus. "Is this the stuff you really want to cook?"

Marcus shrugged. "It's what I wanted to go to school to learn how to do, but those cooking schools are really expensive."

"Well, once you sell the house and with the money from your grandmother you could—"

"*If* I ever sell it."

Hank tilted his head to one side and smiled. "You're thinking of not selling?"

"No. I'm selling it. I just meant I haven't had one person come look at it. Maybe I'm asking too much?"

Hank's smile faded as he turned and clomped down the stairs. "But you're getting some money otherwise, right? You could use that."

"Yeah." Marcus followed Hank into the apartment. "I guess. Maybe once I find a new town and settle in there I will... wait..." Marcus stopped walking. "You hated the food, didn't you?"

"No." Hank shook his head and dropped the dishes into the sink. "It was good. It's... well..."

"What?" Marcus pulled Hank's elbow to turn him away from the sink and look him in the eye. "What was wrong with it?"

"The food you made me at the diner? The home cooking food last night? That was *so* good. I mean, I could tell you really had your heart into cooking it. I could tell you had fun making it. This chateau-alfredo-pizicato-whatever fancy-pants stuff just seemed, I don't know, like a chore?"

"Ouch." Marcus slumped against the counter.

"Don't be mad. I don't mean it like that. Not a chore to eat. For you to make. I'm sorry. I shouldn't have said anything."

"Well, I'm still learning some of this stuff and I had to teach myself, so maybe I didn't get it right."

"Look, don't get upset. I told you I'm not really into that highfaluting stuff. That was my parent's world, not mine."

Marcus frowned as he pushed off the counter and crossed the room to the entertainment center. He scanned the rows of books, surprised at the multiple languages on the spines. He could tell a few were French or Italian, but some he couldn't guess. Most of the books appeared to be about music and theater with the occasional manual on car repair shoved in between. He glanced at the opera posters on the wall and said, "Hold on. That dog don't hunt. You don't like fancy stuff? It doesn't get much fancier than opera."

"That's the exception. It makes me feel close to my dad." Hank walked up behind Marcus and reached over his shoulder to point out a picture on the shelf of a man and woman in evening clothes. "Dad taught music at the college. He loved opera, and I grew up listening to it with him. Every fall, we would drive all the way up to Atlanta to see an opera, just the two of us. After it was over, we would drive all night to get back home. He kept himself awake on the highway by telling me all about the different operas. That's him and my mom at the big party the fine arts department had every spring."

Marcus studied the faces of the couple in the picture. The woman had jet-black hair pulled back from her face in a tight bun. She wore a forced smile and cut her eyes to the side toward the man, who pulled her into his side with an arm around her shoulders. The man had his mouth open in a boisterous laugh and held a glass of champagne toward the camera in a perpetual toast. He had the same crinkles beside his eyes as Hank and the same dimples in his cheeks. "You look like him."

"Yeah. We were a lot alike."

"Were?"

"Yeah, he died not long before my mom threw me out. Drunk driver."

"I'm sorry to hear that. You know, my father got hit by a drunk driver too."

"No. Mine *was* the drunk driver. My daddy loved to drink." Hank wrapped his arms around Marcus's chest from behind and rested his chin on his shoulder. "I didn't realize how much he drank until we started cleaning out his drawers and closets after he died. We found bottles stashed all over the place, but especially in the backs of drawers behind his clothes." Hank dropped his arms and stepped away from Marcus to sit on the couch.

Marcus sat beside Hank. As he stared at the other man, his phone vibrated again. He ignored it and placed his hand on Hank's leg. Unsure of what to say, he rubbed Hank's knee and waited for him to speak.

"Remember me saying my grandmother died from diabetes?" Hank placed his hand on top of Marcus's to stop him from rubbing. "Well, when she died, evidently they found all kinds of candy hidden in the back of her drawers, too. I only know this because one day I came home from school and my mother was standing in the kitchen with this blue notebook in her hands. As soon as I saw it I knew exactly what it was—my journal. I had written all kinds of things in there about boys at school that I had crushes on and some of my sexual fantasies and it was just gay, gay, gay. I had hidden it in the back of my sock drawer, which was a stupid place to hide it since she put my laundry away."

Hank dropped his head onto the back of the sofa and stared at the ceiling.

"So my mother starts ranting about the candy in Nana's dresser drawers and the alcohol in Dad's and then she slammed the book onto the kitchen table and glared at me. I had never seen her so angry in my life. And then she yelled at me. God, I can still hear her voice. She said, 'You Hudsons and the things you hide in your drawers. They will be the death of all of you.'"

Hank looked at Marcus with his lips pursed, clearly trying his best to hold back his sorrow. Marcus shifted forward and rested his head against Hank's temple. Hank said, "I don't know why in the hell I'm telling you all of this. This was supposed to be a romantic night."

"No," Marcus whispered. "I want to hear it."

"Anyway. Mother kicked me out and I never looked back. I guess I could've tried to argue with her, but I don't like drama, Marcus. I'm going to prove her wrong with my life. Just because she was miserable in life didn't mean I had to… I mean, her idea of family made both of us miserable, so I figured I'd just find my own family. I mean, that's what we do, right? When you don't fit in with the family god gave you, you go make your own. Don't you think?"

"You know what I think?" Marcus asked as he pulled away from Hank. "Your mother is a total bitch."

He looked at Hank to see if he had crossed a line. Hank just stared at him blankly until Marcus could see the beginnings of a grin at the corners of Hank's mouth. His smile grew broader and his shoulders began to shake as a laugh built in his chest. He threw his head back and roared with laughter.

"Fiat, I think you are right," Hank wheezed as he continued to laugh. "I think she was a bitch."

"Trust me. I know crazy mothers." Marcus began to laugh as well. "Hell, my mama left me on the side of the road, and yours shoved you out the door. We both really hit the jackpot when it came to mothers, huh?"

"Oh, my god." Hank groaned as he wiped tears from his eyes. "This is not funny at all." He dropped his hands into his lap and began to giggle again. "Oh, my sides hurt."

"Me too," Marcus said as he continued to laugh.

"Whooo." Hank exhaled deeply. He stood from the couch and added, "I better go get those dishes started. You want to put on some music?"

"Hang on." Marcus pulled him back to the sofa. He pushed Hank onto his back and crawled up his legs onto his chest until he was lying on top of him, face to face. "I think your mother threw away the best thing in her life." He kissed Hank. Marcus could feel Hank's heartbeat quicken through his shirt as his lips parted to accept Marcus's kiss. Hank's arms crossed over Marcus's lower back and pulled him tight against his body as he moaned. Marcus pulled back from the kiss and looked into Hank's eyes. "Don't you think?"

Hank blinked slowly and whispered, "And your mother abandoned the best thing in hers." He tightened his grip on Marcus's body and lifted his face for another kiss. He stopped short and added, "Why do people do that? Throw away the good things in their life?"

"Shh." Marcus shook his head and then moved in for another kiss. As their lips touched, the phone in his shirt pocket begin to vibrate again. Ignoring it, he placed light kisses on Hank's cheek and the tip of his nose.

"Fiat…"

"Shh."

"Your phone."

"Ignore it."

Marcus pressed another kiss to Hank's lips. The phone began vibrating again between their chests.

"It's not stopping."

"Not important," Marcus mumbled out of the side of his mouth as he pressed his lips harder against Hank's.

Hank pulled his arms from around Marcus's waist and pushed his hands against Marcus's shoulders to move him away from the kiss. "I can't concentrate with that thing buzzing between us."

"Fine," Marcus said with a huff, leaned over on one elbow, and yanked the phone out of his pocket without looking at the screen, and tossed it onto the coffee table. "Now, more kissing." He rolled back on to Hank's chest for another kiss. The phone began to rattle and skitter around the table as it vibrated again.

"Maybe you better get that."

"Oh, for the love of…" Marcus struggled his way off Hank's body and flung his feet onto the floor. He picked up the phone and looked at the flashing screen. "It's just Helen Warner. She's probably having last-minute jitters about the dance tomorrow night. I'm sorry. This won't take but a second."

"No. Go ahead."

Marcus swiped his finger across the phone and lifted it to his ear with an irritated groan. "Hello?"

"Marcus, darling? Oh, thank heavens you finally answered."

"Helen, I'm kind of busy." He glanced over at Hank and forced a half-hearted smile. "What is it?"

"Sweetheart, there was a strange man trying to get into your house."

"What?" Marcus said as the smile faded from his face. "Like a burglar?"

"He was banging on the door and yelling for you to open up. Oh, the language he was using. The whole neighborhood could hear him."

Marcus stood from the couch. "Helen, what does he look like?"

"Marcus, he said his name is Robert."

Muffled voices on the other end of the line raised in volume; people were clearly arguing in the background. "Helen, hang up and call the police."

"Marcus, I think you should come home." Helen's voice faded as she spoke to someone on the other end of the line. "You stay right there, mister. Yes, I've got him on the phone. Yes, I'm telling him to come home. Inez! Don't you dare—"

"Helen, I said to call the police. I'm on my way."

"Marcus, please hurry. Inez, stop pointing that gun at the man. Marcus, I don't think I can keep Inez from—"

Marcus pushed the disconnect button. Hank sat forward on the edge of the couch and met Marcus' gaze with a worried look.

"I'm sorry. I've got to go." Not waiting for a response, Marcus hurried across the room, down the stairs into the garage, and out into the street.

"MARCUS, PLEASE SLOW DOWN." HANK braced himself against the dashboard as Marcus zipped through an intersection without bothering to slow down or look for oncoming cars.

"She's going to shoot him. She's going to shoot him." Marcus gripped the steering wheel tight and hunched his shoulders toward the windshield with his eyes focused on the road ahead.

"She's not going to shoot anyone. And Helen already called the sheriff. Just slow down, please, before you get us both killed."

"I can't believe he showed up here. And I told you to stay at your apartment. Oh, jeez, she's going to shoot—"

"Marcus! Red light! Oh shit." Hank covered his eyes and curled into himself on the seat beside Marcus.

"No one was coming, and I know more than a stupid light bulb," Marcus spat back without taking his eyes from the road.

He barely slowed down as he neared the entrance to Crepe Myrtle Manor. Without flipping his signal and only slightly tapping the brakes, he cut the wheel sharply to the right. The heavy bulk of the LTD groaned and the tires squealed on the pavement as he careened into the subdivision, just missing the curb of the median island.

At the entrance to his cul-de-sac, Marcus yanked the steering wheel again and slid into his neighborhood. Mere feet before the entrance to his driveway, Marcus stomped on the brake pedal and slid to a screeching halt in front of the house, inches behind a familiar black sedan that sat halfway in the street and halfway over the curb in his front yard. Katie Nell's For Sale sign was mangled on the ground behind the flat back tire of the car. His mailbox lay on the hood of the car; its post was wrapped around the front bumper.

Marcus shoved the gearshift to put the car in park and flung the car door open. As he slid out of the car, he looked at Hank and said, "Stay in the car. I will handle this."

"The hell I will," Hank said as he whipped off his seat belt and opened the passenger side door.

Marcus scurried around the front of his car and past the rear end of the black car. He skidded to a stop in a pool of light from the street lamp when he saw the scene in front of him. Helen stood halfway up his driveway with her cell phone to her ear, gesticulating wildly toward his house with her free hand as she paced back and forth. Inez stood a few steps closer to the house with her eyes trained toward the front door. She rested one hand on her hip and the other sat on the butt of a shotgun that she had slung over her shoulder. She wriggled her fingers on the butt of the gun and patted her foot. Both women wore robes and slippers.

Marcus followed Inez's gaze to the front stoop of the house. Robert sat there with his elbows on his knees and his face buried in his hands. The porch light over Robert's head cast shadows around his feet and showed the bald spot on top of his head in the middle of his silvery hair. He wore his standard navy blue dress pants and white dress shirt, though they were wrinkled and crumpled. *Guess you haven't found a new boy to do your ironing.* Robert's shoulders shook and his head bobbed as he bounced his leg on the pavement.

Robert threw his head back, stared into the porch light, and yelled, "Marcus!" Robert's sudden movement made Inez shift the gun from her shoulder to her side. The dogs in Priscilla's backyard began barking and howling. *Oh, for god's sake, Robert.*

Hank stepped beside Marcus and touched his arm. "See, I told you she wouldn't shoot him. Who is this guy?"

Marcus jerked his arm away from Hank. "I asked you to stay in the car."

Marcus stalked away from Hank up the driveway toward Helen and Inez but kept his eyes focused on the huddled lump of Robert on the stoop. As he neared Helen, he could hear her arguing with someone on the phone.

"Jeanette, are Spud and Randall on their way or not?" Helen asked into the phone. "You already said 'five minutes' over ten minutes ago. No, he isn't hurting anyone one but he is definitely…" Helen glanced up, and her face brightened as she saw Marcus making his way up the driveway. "Marcus! Oh, thank heavens you're here. Jeanette, just tell Sheriff Stewart to please hurry up." Helen tapped the screen of her phone and shoved it into the pocket of her robe. "Nothing like that crack Marathon police force. If I go two miles over the speed limit there are ten of them on the scene, but when some screaming maniac is in my neighborhood—"

"Helen, how long has he been here?" Marcus interrupted her. "Has he said anything to either of you?"

"No. He just keeps demanding to see you. And he smells like a brewery." Helen grabbed Marcus by the upper arm and pulled him along the driveway toward Inez. "I was watching my shows and minding my own business when all of the sudden Priscilla's dogs started barking all crazy. I figured some stray cat must've wandered into her yard, but they wouldn't shut up. I got up to call her and tell her to control those mutts. That's when I heard the tires squealing and the crash when he ran into your mailbox. I looked out the window and saw the car sitting here in your front yard." Helen stopped walking when they reached Inez. "When I saw this man stagger out of the car and wander toward your door, I figured maybe he was going to ask to use the phone to call the police. So I got my cell phone, threw on my robe, and headed out here."

"I heard the crash and looked out my window, too. I saw Helen coming out of her house. Elbert didn't wake up. That man will sleep through the rapture."

"Marcus!" Robert yelled from the porch again.

"Good lord, could you please shut that man up? Or I am going to have to shoot him?" Inez raised the shotgun a bit.

Marcus pushed the barrel of the gun back toward the ground.

"When I got outside, he started pounding on your door and screaming your name at the top of his lungs. That's when I realized he wasn't just some random drunk." Helen pointed at Robert. "He hasn't stopped no matter how much we asked him to."

"When I heard that bellowing start, I knew this wasn't just an accident. So I pulled old Ethel here off the wall." Inez nodded her head at the shotgun. "By the time I got out here, half the neighborhood was awake and staring out of their doors. Helen was standing at the end of her driveway calling Sheriff Stewart. That moron was yelling like a maniac, so nobody else would come out, but I ain't scared of nobody when I got old Ethel. So I just walked my ass over here and asked him what the hell he wanted."

"What did he say?" Hank asked as he walked up to the women and placed his hand on the small of Marcus's back.

"Oh, hello, Hank. I didn't realize you—"

"Hank, I told you I would handle this," Marcus said.

"He just kept pounding on the door and calling out for you. I started yelling at him to shut up, and he turned around at me. He almost fell off the steps, he's so drunk. He just stood there wobbling all over the place and saying your name over and over. I told him you weren't here, and he started yelling at me to get you here right now. I tried to encourage him to shut up, but—"

"That's when I walked up, and Helen called you."

"This is ridiculous," Marcus said and started walking toward the steps.

Helen grabbed Marcus by the arm and held him back. "Sweetheart, the police are on their way. Maybe you better just let them handle this. We don't need you getting another… you know." Helen pointed at her eye and squinted it closed.

Hank looked back and forth between Helen and Marcus with a shocked look. "You mean that black eye came from—"

"He won't do it again," Marcus said as he pulled himself free from Helen's grasp. "Let me go talk to him."

"Hold on," Hank said, "I'm not letting you go over there with someone who has already hit you once. Let's let the police handle it or at least let me come over there with you."

"No. You stay over here. This is my mess." Marcus turned away from Hank and walked over to Robert. His heart pounded in his chest with each step and he could feel the hairs on the back of his neck standing on end. *Stay calm. Stay calm.* As he neared the ring of light coming from the porch, he smelled the alcohol. He stopped walking and stood staring down at him from a few feet away. His stomach began to knot, and his tongue grew thick in his mouth. When he opened his mouth to speak, nothing but a gargled gasp came out.

Robert raised his head from his hands in response to the sound. He looked at Marcus and swayed back and forth as he squinted one eye and tried to focus. "Baby!" he slurred as his face lit up with a smile.

"Don't call me that," Marcus finally choked out.

"Where you been? Was looking for you. I tried to call and—"

"Robert, what the hell are you doing here?"

"I said…" Robert paused to belch. "I said I was looking for you, baby." Robert fumbled at the porch railing and attempted to stand. He wobbled from side to side until he finally tumbled to his right and fell against the railing. "Whoo. Ground's a little slippery here."

"You're drunk."

"Am not. Just had a few beers on the ride down to make that long drive tolerable. Made it easier to get here and find you. Shit. Why does anybody want to live in all this boring nothing down here? What the hell is in this town? Just naughty boys playing hide and seek?" Robert giggled as he struggled to stand upright. He kept one hand clutching the railing and pouted at Marcus. "Somebody won't return my calls and texts. Luckily, you're terrible at hiding what you're really up to, so I figured it out." Robert attempted to tap his temple but missed and poked himself in the eye. "Ow. Son of a bitch. Now look what you made me do."

"Robert, you know how I feel about people drinking and driving. With my father and all."

"Oh, calm down. I ain't the one who ran over your daddy. I know how to drive. Hell, if I'd hit anyone, it would've been your fault anyway. Making me come all the way down here looking for you."

Marcus glared at Robert and folded his arms across his chest. "That's not funny."

"Aw, c'mon, baby." Robert shifted on his feet and began tottering forward. He lifted his arm to attempt to grab Marcus by the shoulder.

Instinctively, Marcus cowered and took three steps back from Robert. He lifted his arms in front of his face and turned his eyes away. The knot in his stomach tightened and his earlier meal rose in his throat. The familiar flashing of light at the corner of his eyes began to throb in time with his racing heartbeat. He took two more steps back and bent over at the waist to put his hands on his thighs and stare at the ground, willing the food to stay in his stomach and the breath to return to his lungs. As he closed his eyes and tried to steady himself, a hand landed softly on his back.

"Everything okay over here? Who the hell is this man?"

"Who the hell is *this* man?" Robert asked.

"That is none of your business," Marcus mumbled as he opened his eyes and stared at the worn leather toes of Hank's work boots standing by his own shoes. With his hand under Marcus's upper arm, Hank lifted him back into an upright position.

"I think I hear the police sirens." Hank placed his arm around Marcus's shoulder and started steering him back to the driveway. "Why don't we go back to my place and let them—"

"Your place?" Robert spat out his words and scoffed. "You little shit. You running around on me? I knew it. You were doing it in Atlanta too, weren't you? Probably some trash you found in that Waffle Barn." He tottered back on his heels while he smirked at Marcus. "No. Not enough money from those losers, is there? I bet it was that Stephen guy from the cancer fundraiser. Couldn't keep your eyes off of him and his wallet, could you? Nothing gets that little ass in the air like a fat wallet."

Hank stopped and turned back to face Robert. "I think you should shut up."

"That's not very nice, Marcus." Robert tried to cluck his tongue in disapproval but only managed to spit on his chin. "Taking *my* gifts and giving *your* ass to someone else." Robert wagged his finger at Marcus and giggled before an angry cloud fell over his face. "Not nice at all." He staggered again and then took a few steps forward to poke Hank in the chest. "If you want this little slut, you better be prepared to pay him well. He likes a fancy house and all the expensive things that go with it. But don't let him talk. His roots start showing when he talks."

"Robert, please," Marcus mumbled as he collapsed into Hank's side. His head swam and his knees quivered.

"Well, lucky for you, I'm a forgiving man." Robert swung his arm around and clutched the collar of Marcus's shirt. "Come on, baby. I'm taking you home."

Marcus lifted his hands and pushed back against Robert's chest. As he pushed, he heard the sound of Inez cocking the shotgun behind him followed by the increasing volume of the police sirens. He looked back at Inez and pleaded, "Please, don't."

Inez lowered the gun and frowned at him. The flashing lights of the police cars pulling into the driveway behind Helen and Inez sent red and blue streaks of light bouncing around the tree limbs and the fronts of the houses. Marcus squinted his eyes against the swirling brightness, feeling dizzier and unable to focus his eyes as he looked back at the fuming Robert. His collar pulled against his neck as Robert jerked him forward. Hank's grip tightened on his arm and pulled him in the other direction.

"Oh really, you old bitch? Like you would shoot me?" Robert shifted his arm and pulled Marcus forward.

Marcus tried to yank himself away and slipped from Hank's grasp in the process. He tripped over his feet and toppled backward to the ground, landing hard on the sidewalk and scraping his elbow on the pavement. He rolled onto his side and looked back to see Helen and Inez rushing to help him.

"That's where you belong, you trash," Robert ranted from behind him as the women helped Marcus to his knees. "On your knees."

"Okay. That's enough," Hank said behind him.

Marcus spun back around in time to see Hank ball his hand into a fist, draw back his arm, and land a punch square in Robert's face. As Robert staggered back and fell to the ground, he let out a loud yelp. He landed in a pile on the ground at the base of the steps just as two policemen bustled between Hank and Robert with their guns drawn.

Robert rose on one elbow, shook his head, and looked at the two policemen. "Jesus. Does everyone in this Podunk town have guns?"

Marcus took the hand Helen offered to him and let her help him back to his feet. "Officers," she said, "there's no need for guns. Please put them away."

"Miss Inez," the younger policeman, Randall, said, "I know you have a permit for that gun, but it'd make my job a whole lot easier if you would just take that on back into your house."

"Shit. Someone has to protect us when you take forever to—"

"Inez, go," Helen demanded as she pointed back toward Inez's house. Inez stomped off as Helen lifted Marcus to his feet, wrapped her arm around his shoulder, and walked him over to Hank and the sheriff. "Spud, that man on the ground is the one you need to arrest. He's been here disturbing the peace and he's drunk as Cooter Brown. Look what he did to poor Marcus's mailbox."

"I'm not disturbing the peace!" Robert yelled as he tried to stand from where he had fallen. He lost his balance and crumbled back to the ground twice before successfully making it to his feet with the deputy's help. "I'm trying to get some peace back. It's that redneck with the beard you need to be arresting. He's the troublemaker. You saw him assault me!"

"Robert, shut up," Marcus mumbled as he lifted his arm and looked at the raw skin on his forearm that was beginning to bleed.

"Spud, I didn't assault this jackass," Hank explained. "He came at Marcus and I had to stop him."

"He's lying!" Robert yelled, losing his balance and staggering into Deputy Randall's side. "Don't just stand there, you yokel. Haul this man away. Look what he did to my face!" Robert pointed at the red mark on his face.

The sheriff glanced back and forth between the two men with a confused look. "I did see him hit you."

"Spud, don't listen to this drunk fool." Helen stamped her foot. "Inez and I saw the whole thing. He's a drunk driver! And he started it. Hank had to hit him, just to shut him up."

"You see! He did hit me." Robert flung his arms out to his sides. "But don't listen to this old biddy. I was just sitting on the porch and trying to find my friend Marcus. It was completely unprovoked."

"Mister, you're pretty drunk. I think I better take you down to the station to dry out. Drunk driving is not tolerated here." Sheriff Stewart pointed at the mangled mailbox on the hood of the car. "Also, there's the property damage."

As the deputy pushed him toward the police car, Robert lifted his head and shot Marcus an evil grin. "Property. Yes, property. I'm just here trying to get my property back." Robert yanked his shoulder away from the deputy and wavered on his feet.

"Property!" Hank spun around and gawked at Robert. "Marcus is not property."

"No, you idiot. My car. It's worth more than that boy." Robert looked at the deputy and gave a half smile. "It's a yellow Fiat that this boy over here took without my permission. So, if you're going to arrest me, you need to arrest that little thief, too. Of course, if he and the car will just come on back to Atlanta, we can forget all of this nonsense. I just want my car and…" Robert suddenly staggered and dropped to the ground.

"See, Spud," Helen said, "he's drunk. You can't believe anything he says."

"Hold on. If I remember correctly, this young man did come into town in a little yellow car." Sheriff Stewart looked around at the assembled group, adjusted his hat, and knitted his brows while he thought. "Well, I don't rightly know exactly what is going on here. That man is clearly drunk and disorderly. Maybe we better all go down to the station and straighten this out. Randall, put that drunk in your car and take him downtown."

"Oh, come on, Spud," Helen said and threw up her hands in frustration. "You're being ridiculous. Just haul this drunk away and let me get poor Marcus into his house. Look at him. He's so upset that he's shaking. Plus, we're keeping the whole neighborhood up."

"Marcus, did you steal that car?" Hank asked, his face a mix of fear and confusion. "Tell him the car is yours."

"Yes, Mr. Sumter, you can clear all of this up now or we can go down to the station. Do you have any proof that the car is yours?"

Marcus looked around at all of the faces staring at him in expectation. He saw Robert stand behind Randall and glare at him over the officer's shoulder. He opened his mouth to speak but could only produce a loud sob. He shook his head as he dropped to his knees and vomited.

"Marcus?" Hank said, his voice full of disappointment. "Please tell him… you didn't really… did you?"

Marcus looked at Hank with a guilty frown. Hank's face shifted from shock to irritation.

"I see." Hank sighed and crossed his arms as he turned away from Marcus. "Spud, can you give me a ride home after I give you my statement? I think I'm done here."

"Hank, let me explain," Marcus said from the ground, his voice barely a whisper.

Hank put up a hand to silence him. "It's late. I've had enough drama for one night." He turned back to the sheriff. "Can we go?"

"All right," Spud said and slapped Hank on the shoulder, "let's head down to the station. Helen, you go get Miss Inez and bring Marcus down with you, please. I'll need statements from all of you."

Marcus sat up and wiped the tears from his eyes. Hank stormed over to the patrol car and opened the back door. He paused with one foot in the car and gave Marcus a look of dismay, then he shook his head and ducked into the car.

With a voice growing hoarse from the burn of vomit, Marcus croaked out, "Wait. It's not like that." He recoiled from the weak kick Robert made at his leg as the deputy led him to the other patrol car.

"Should've left you where I found you," Robert yelled back at Marcus as the deputy opened the back door of the car and tucked him inside. The yard grew darker as the flashing lights shut off and the cars cranked.

Marcus sobbed as the two police cars back out of the driveway. "Hank, wait."

Helen knelt beside Marcus and tucked him under her arm. "Sweetie, you need to get up. We need to call Raff and have him meet us at the station. I'm sure he can get this all straightened out."

Marcus looked at Helen with his lip quivering. "Oh, Helen, what have I done?" He bucked forward and vomited again.

MARCUS SQUINTED AT HIS REFLECTION in the glass of the Tammy's door and sighed. No amount of cold water splashed on his face or hot coffee poured down his throat would hide the fact that he had slept a grand total of fifteen minutes.

After the embarrassing and terrifying encounter with Robert and watching Hank storm off, he had spent the ride to the police station flipping between attempting to calm Helen and Inez and crying while Helen and Inez tried to calm him. By the time he had given his statement to Sheriff Stewart, shown the title to the Fiat in his name, and been released to go home, he only had four possible hours of sleep ahead of him. He had asked to see Hank before he left the station, but had been refused. He tried arguing with Deputy Randall for ten minutes, but finally gave up and allowed Helen and Inez to drive him home.

After he had convinced both women that he did not need either of them to stay with him, he had fumbled into the house and collapsed on his bed fully clothed. A mere five minutes of lying in bed had revealed that instead of sleeping, he would spend those four hours worrying about Hank, fearing Robert, and planning his getaway. When the first drops of sunlight crept under the blinds in the bedroom, he had made up his mind. He packed his clothes and a few photos from the back of the piano into his duffel, thrown it into the trunk of the car, and practiced his resignation speech to Francine at least thirty times in front of the mirror.

Marcus pushed at the bags under his eyes and groaned into the morning light. He pulled the glass door open and slipped into the diner as quietly as he could, hoping to avoid any conversation with the sisters. He ignored their now-familiar calls of "mornin' sugar," "hey there, sweet cheeks," and "oh my God, Marcus, it's too early." Lowering his head, he made a beeline past the empty tables, around the counter and into the kitchen to look for Francine. His head pounded from the night spent tossing and turning between fits of anger and tears. He had tried to call Hank twice, hoping he had already been released and would be up early to go to the garage, but had only reached his voicemail. For all he knew, Hank could be sitting at the jail or just ignoring his calls completely.

"Francine? You back here?" Marcus poked his head through the swinging door.

"Hey there, punkin'," Francine said through the matchstick she held clenched between her teeth. She looked up from the pile of onions she was cutting on the prep table and gave Marcus a kind smile. "Trying not to cry my eyes out while cutting these things."

"I know the feeling."

Francine glanced quickly at Marcus before shifting her eyes back to the pile of onions. "I figured you might be a little late this morning, what with all the drama at your house last night."

"You heard."

"Georgette told me. Spud Stewart told her. Honey, I'm sorry you had to go through that."

"Well, that's the reason I'm here." Marcus shuffled from one foot to the other and fidgeted with the hem of his shirt. "I hate to do it to you, but I need to quit. I've got to get out of here."

"Oh, now, hold on, honey." Francine dropped the knife on the table and picked up a rag to wipe her hands. "There's no need to go skittering off like a spooked squirrel just because some jackass made a scene at your house last night. No one ever has to know that all went down. I mean, it'll kill Inez not to be able to blab all over town, but she knows when something needs to be kept just between us girls. No one that comes in here ever has to know. Shoot, if you just stay back in the kitchen all day, no one has to know that you're here. No need to be embarrassed."

"Francine, it's not that I'm embarrassed," Marcus shot back at her and leaned back against the prep table. He blew out a long breath in frustration as he shoved his bangs away from his face. "I've got to get away from Robert."

Francine stood looking at the onions before saying, "Well, I won't stand in your way. But you're going to need some money to get on the road. Why don't you finish out your shift here today, and I can pay you for that? After we close, we can work on the food for the party tonight." She picked up the knife and pushed the onion pieces around on the cutting board.

Marcus smacked his hand against his forehead. "Crap, I forgot all about that party."

"The girls are really counting on you, and I can't make that stuff you planned all by myself." Francine pointed with the knife toward Marcus's hand-written menu for the party that was stuck to one of the freezers with a magnet.

"You don't need me. It's all easy to make."

"Not by myself while I'm still cooking for customers. And the girls will pay you tonight. One more night in town won't make much difference. You can hit the road tomorrow with some gas money in your pocket at least."

"I guess." Marcus flipped his apron off a hook and slipped it over his neck. He tied it around his waist and slid beside Francine at the prep table.

"Trust Francine, sweetie." She shifted his head back and forth by the chin as she inspected his skin. "Did he hit you again?"

"No. Didn't give him the chance. That's the one good thing my mama taught me. She used to tell me, 'A man gets the chance to hit you once and never again. Cause you don't stick around for that. If you stay, he'll do it again.' God, how sad is it that it happened so often she had to have a rule about it. You know, when I met Robert, I thought he would be so different from all those losers my mother would date just because he had money."

"Assholes come in all shapes, sizes, and income brackets." She banged the knife against the cutting board to knock some lingering chunks of onion off the blade. "Grab those peppers and start cutting them for the crudités platters."

Marcus opened the refrigerator and took the bag of bell peppers from a shelf. He dumped some out on the table and pulled a knife from the rack over the sink. He began slicing the peppers into petite slivers. As he finished the last pepper, he realized Francine was watching him work.

"You've got wonderful knife skills. You ever think about trying to cook something fancier than this hash?"

"I like cooking this hash." Marcus shrugged and turned around to look at his menu to decide what to work on next. He opened the fridge and chose three heads of broccoli. "Being a fancy chef was Robert's idea. Fancy is important to him."

"Wash that broccoli first," Francine suggested. "So he wanted you to be a chef? Didn't he know you were a fry cook when he met you?"

"Yeah. He used to come into the Waffle Barn I was working at almost every morning. He was such a distinguished-looking man with his gray temples and his business suits. I learned his order and would have it started the minute he walked in the door." Marcus tossed the broccoli into a colander and shoved it into the sink. "The first time I did that, he called me over and we started talking. I was used to customers flirting with me all the time, but he had something that... there was an authority or a, I don't know; he just made me feel as if he was really interested in what I said. One thing led to another and the next thing I knew I was agreeing to a date."

"I'm going to start the potatoes for the hash browns." Francine slipped past Marcus and pulled a bag of potatoes out of a drawer. "Keep talking. I can listen and work."

"He took me all kinds of fancy places. Opera. Ballet. Art museums. We went to all these fancy-schmancy fundraisers where I met all of his rich friends. He never told anyone that I was just some short-order cook at a greasy spoon. And he didn't want me telling people that either. He didn't let me talk much to people at all, really. Told me it was better if I just listened and learned. He kept telling people I was studying to be a chef, which, I guess I wanted to do but I couldn't really afford it. When I told him that, he suggested I move in with him, and he would help pay for school." Marcus pulled the colander out of the sink and moved back to the cutting board.

"How much does that cost?"

"For the school? A lot. For living with him? More." Marcus began chopping florets off the broccoli, grunting with each push of the knife. "I didn't realize it at the time, but the price was... well... me. I lost me. It was wonderful to start with. A beautiful house. Clothes and shoes and a car. He would throw these big parties and invite people over, and I would cook the food for them. The whole time he kept telling them how one day I will be a world-class chef with my own restaurant. I kept working at the diner, but I really didn't need the money. Robert handled everything." Marcus looked from his work to Francine. "Can you hand me that big bowl?"

"Here." She handed him the silver bowl and returned to her task.

"Anyway," Marcus continued, "one night, a guy came to one of our parties and he would not stop hitting on me. Practically chased me around the kitchen. Telling me he'd like to butter my waffle and junk like that."

"Ew."

"Right? He was some jerk we met at a cancer fundraiser. Robert was so jealous, he caused a bit of a scene. Called the other guy out on it right there in front of everyone. Well, the other guy fired back that he didn't know why Robert was being so snooty about a guy who worked at a Waffle Barn."

"What an asshole."

"After everyone left, Robert suggested I stop working at the diner and just take care of the house. So I did, and things were almost fine again. But I think a seed was planted. Robert was terrified someone would steal me or recognize me from the Waffle Barn. Before I knew it, the opera stopped. And the ballet. And the parties. Soon we were just staying home all of the time." Marcus dumped the vegetables he had cut into the bowl.

"I got bored, so I went back to work. But I didn't tell Robert. I knew he wouldn't like it or understand. I would just take shifts while he was at work. And it felt so good to be back there cooking and talking to people. I didn't have to pretend that I understood what people were talking about. I could just be me." Marcus covered the top of the bowl with plastic wrap and tossed it into the refrigerator. When he closed the door, he ran his finger along the menu to decide what task to work on next. "Except I screwed up one day and got home late. Robert could smell the diner on me. And he hit me." Marcus turned back around to find Francine standing with a potato in one hand and the peeler in the other and listening to him intently.

"And that is when you left?"

"Well, sort of. I couldn't very well go to work the next day with the black eye. So I stayed home, and I was there when the mail came. You know, it never struck me as odd that I never got any mail. I didn't have any bills, and who was going to be writing me? Robert always went through the mail. But that day I was home, so I had to sign for the letter from Raffield. I opened it and found out about my grandmother. Suddenly, it was all clear. I packed the car and, well, here I am."

"Oh, sweetie, that was the smartest thing you ever did."

"I'm not so sure. Look at the mess it's made."

"Can I be honest? I'm proud of you for leaving." Francine took a potato and began forcefully rubbing it against a metal grater. "My second husband, Paul, liked to hit, too. I knew the first day that I saw you what was going on. That's why I hired you. I mean your cooking is fine and all, but I could see it. And I wanted you to give you the chance I never had."

"Chance?" Marcus asked.

"A chance to get away." She picked another potato and sighed. "I never left Paul. He died of a heart attack. It still pisses me off that the sorry sonofabitch died before I finally got the nerve to leave him." She began grating again, punctuating her words with a harsh push against the potato. "I mean, I was glad he was gone, but I'm a strong woman. I honestly don't know why I put up with it. And I let my girls be around it. That messed me up for the longest time. I didn't think I could ever be with a man again. How could I trust myself? How could I ever be sure I wasn't picking another one that would just go bad?"

Francine stopped and looked at the kitchen door as it swung open. Georgette and Paulette walked in giggling with each other, but stopped abruptly at the glare from their mother.

"Mama?"

"Get out of here and let us work."

"Sorry." The girls scurried back out into the dining room.

"I could've holed away in my house and just waited to die." She gestured toward the kitchen door, still swinging behind the girls. "I had two little mouths to feed. Paul never could keep a job, and my first husband, George… Let's just say waiting on child support from him was like waiting for a donkey to shit diamonds. So I came up here to this diner and got me a job. And I met Frank. And he was a good man."

"Well, that's you. Tomorrow morning, I'm out of here. You know, I think I'm just built to be on the road. It's all I ever knew growing up."

"But, honey, that's no kind of life. You need family. You need roots. You need a home."

"The road can be home, and it's a beautiful place. When I was little and we'd be driving in the middle of the night so the landlord wouldn't catch us sneaking out, Mama would point out the white headlights and the red taillights on the highway. 'Who needs gold, baby? Look at the riches all around us. Diamonds going one way. Rubies going the other.' And I need to get back out there and try again. Find someplace new. Follow those rubies and diamonds until I find…" Marcus trailed off and shrugged. "I need to get busy on this chili."

Ten minutes passed in silence as Marcus and Francine continued preparing the food for the diner and the party. Marcus let her words roll around his mind as he filled pots, measured ingredients, and listened to the girls working in the main room. Francine finally interrupted the sounds of chopping and stirring and asked, "What about Hank?"

"He won't answer my calls. And now that he knows about Robert, he probably won't give me the time of day. And who could blame him? He thinks I'm a liar and a thief. I don't deserve someone as good as Hank."

"Foot. That type of thinking almost screwed up my life. I resisted Frank for the longest time. I just assumed that because of my past…" She crossed the kitchen and stood facing Marcus. "Then I remembered what my mama always told me. Just because you burn your biscuits once don't mean you never eat them again." Francine stroked Marcus's arm. "You didn't ask to get hit. You didn't try to find an asshole. Shit happens. And a good man will understand that."

"I don't know. There's still Robert to—"

"Stop it." Francine took him by the shoulders and looked him in the eye. "When you first came in here, that man had given you a black eye. What is a black eye? A bruise. It's not a scar. Bruises fade. Scars don't. If you let that man steal the rest of your life away, you're letting him be a scar, not a bruise." She patted his cheek and turned to leave the kitchen. "Don't let him scar you, Shoe Button. Don't.

14

"Marc? You here?" Marcus heard Skeet's voice call through the screen followed by the bang of the screen door slamming behind him. "I come bearing gifts!"

Marcus stepped out of the bathroom wearing only his boxer shorts and rubbed a towel over his damp hair. "Hey, Skeet. Come on in. I'll be ready in a little bit."

Skeet stood in the doorway holding a garment bag over his shoulder. He wore snug black leather pants and a form-fitting black dress shirt. His floral-patterned necktie hung untied around his neck. His usual upward swoop of hair had been gelled into a severe part. Skeet eyed Marcus up and down and let out a wolf whistle. "Marcus, you have a wonderful body, but I'd suggest something a little less revealing for the dance. There are standards to be met and you might give some poor old woman a heart attack."

"What kind of girl do you think I am?" Marcus laughed and flung the wet towel toward Skeet. "No, I'm just running a little behind. The Tammy was a madhouse today and I spent all afternoon with Francine getting the food ready for tonight. I really wanted a nap, but that didn't happen."

"Yeah, I heard you had a late night." Skeet stepped to Marcus and inspected his face. "Ooh, you shouldn't have skipped the nap. Those bags under your eyes practically say Samsonite. Got any cucumbers? Or put a spoon in the freezer and stick it on your eyes. No, wait, that's to get rid of a hickey, I think. At least he didn't give you another black eye this time. I heard Hank walloped the other guy real good, though."

"Jesus, can't those women keep anything to themselves?" Marcus bent and picked up the discarded towel.

"Why should they start now?"

"Yeah, but still."

"Anyway, it was Frankie that told me, not one of the Do-Nothings. Georgette heard about it from the Spud and told Frankie. Evidently, Spud had to cut out on his date with her to come out here and handle it. Deputy Randall isn't very good at handling calls by himself. He's got a cute ass in that uniform, but that's about all he has going for him. At least you saved Georgette from having to turn down Spud's marriage proposal again."

"God, it's so embarrassing." Marcus closed his eyes. At Skeet's touch on his bare shoulder, he raised his head and looked at the other boy.

Skeet shook his head and patted Marcus on the shoulder. "I guess, but how dashing of Hank to step in and protect you." Skeet tossed the garment bag onto the back of the sofa. "Your own white knight! You must've been all over him after such a heroic move."

"No." Marcus turned to look in the mirror over the piano and rubbed the towel on his damp hair. "Hank won't answer my calls. I just want to talk to him to explain, but every time I call it goes straight to voicemail."

"Did you try going by the garage?"

"I didn't have time and I don't think I could've done it face to face. I still don't know if he's in trouble for hitting Robert."

"He's not. Frankie said the sheriff didn't keep him. Apparently, my daddy convinced that ex of yours to drop the assault charges."

Marcus looked at Skeet's reflection in the mirror and frowned. "Well, then that means he really is ignoring my calls. He told me he hated drama and, boy, did I deliver the drama last night. I shouldn't have kept the truth from everyone." Marcus studied Skeet's face for any reaction. The other boy broke eye contact and shrugged.

"Look, I don't care about some dumb-ass you used to date. Especially one who was stupid enough to show up drunk and think that would make you want him back. Ugh."

"Skeet, when you make it to New York, you be careful who you get mixed up with, okay?"

"You don't have to worry about me." Skeet jabbed at the air with his right hand. "I've got a mean right hook."

Marcus spun around and placed his hands on Skeet's shoulders, holding him at arm's length and locking him in an earnest stare. "Skeet, I'm serious."

Skeet broke the stare before shaking Marcus's hands off his shoulders. "Anyway, Mama asked me to put a new sign out front since that asshole ran over the other one."

"Thanks. Did she say if she's had anyone interested in looking at the house? I really need to sell this thing as soon as I can."

Skeet shrugged and looked away. "Something in here smells dee-lish."

"I took the food over to the town square hours ago, but that chili smell lingers. Robert used to get so mad when I would…" Marcus stopped and grunted. "You know what? Screw Robert."

"Isn't that what got you into this mess?"

Marcus shot a disgusted look at Skeet. "Well, not exactly." Marcus shook his head to clear his thoughts. "I'm sick of thinking about him anyway. So, what you got there?"

"This?" Skeet lifted the garment bag off the sofa and wiggled his eyebrows. "This is a little gift from the dear old dames of the Do-Nothing club." Skeet carefully laid the bag on the back of the sofa and slid the zipper down. With a flourish, he pulled a dark suit out of the bag. "The girls said they knew you wouldn't have anything to wear to the dance tonight. So…" He motioned his hand up and down in front of the suit. "Voila! Well, nothing lifts a fella's spirits like a new outfit, right?"

"Um, most fellas don't think that way." Marcus walked over and ran his hand over the lapel of the suit. "Holy cow, that is beautiful. But I can't take it."

Skeet laughed. "I'd like to see you try showing up in something else."

Marcus read the price on the tag on the sleeve of the jacket. "But it's too expensive."

"Oh, please. If there is one thing Nonnie and Miss Inez enjoy more than being busybodies, it's shopping."

"But how could they know what size to—"

Skeet grinned. "You really should lock your doors. Miss Annie isn't the only one who can just wander in."

Marcus looked over at the front door standing wide open. "But who?"

"Obviously someone snuck in here and wrote down your sizes while you were at work." Skeet pursed his lips and batted his eyelashes in what Marcus could only assume was an attempt to look as innocent as possible.

"You sneaky little—"

"If Cinderella taught us anything, it's that fairy godmothers need a little mouse to help them sometimes."

"Or a mosquito."

Skeet smirked and handed the suit to Marcus. "Guilty. Now, quit being stupid and put it on. We need to get to the square before people start arriving. Nonnie will murder us if we're late."

"I don't know." Marcus ran his hand down the smooth fabric of the suit. "It'll just get messed up while I am serving the food."

"So you wear an apron. I'm sure Nonnie has something at her house to use if you can't find one here."

"Fine." Marcus hooked a finger under the hanger and slung the suit over his shoulder. Nodding toward the hallway, he said, "I'll be out in just a second."

"All right, but I got to run over to Nonnie's house and pick up something for her. I'll get you an apron, too. I'll come back after that."

"Okay."

After Skeet scooted out, letting the screen door slap shut behind him, Marcus carried the suit into the bedroom and spread it out on the bed. He slid the gray coat from the hanger and carefully pulled the matching pants off the hanger bar. Behind the coat, he noticed a plain white dress shirt and a deep purple tie. He ran his finger along the tie; the silky fabric was cool to the touch. He stepped into the pants and hiked them onto his hips. He pulled the freshly ironed shirt off the other hanger, slipped it on, and buttoned it. After tucking the shirt into the pants, he picked up the coat.

"Too hot to put that on right now," he said as he tossed it back onto the bed and turned to look at himself in the mirror. *Hey there, Mr. Fancy.* Marcus turned to his left and then his right to check himself from each angle. He caught himself smiling in the mirror at the way the pants draped perfectly off his backside. *Wow. These pants give me an ass.* Marcus heard the screen door slam shut. He picked up the tie off the bed, draped it around his neck, and said, "Well, that was fast. Did you find the apron?"

When no one answered, Marcus turned and stepped back into the living room with his head down and his attention focused on his attempt to tie the necktie. "Can you help me with this?" He took a few steps toward the front door.

"Well, someone found a new person to buy him fancy things."

Marcus stopped and slowly raised his head to look at the person speaking. "Robert."

"Hello, Marcus," Robert said as he stood blocking the front door with his arms folded across his chest and his legs spread widely. He still wore the same clothes. His silver hair stood out at odd angles over his ears, and it appeared he had not had a shower. His right eye was swollen and beginning to show the first signs of a bruise.

Marcus began slowly backing away from him until he hit the piano bench, making his knees bend and his body drop clumsily onto the bench. "Robert, what are you doing here again? Why aren't you—" Marcus's heart began to race, and he clasped the edge of the bench to steady himself.

"Still in jail?" Robert raised his eyebrow and shook his head. "Marcus, I paid that stupid, hick sheriff his little fine, and he let me out. That lawyer friend of yours and I made a deal with the police. They'd drop the drunk-driving charges if I didn't press charges against you or that man you were with that hit me. Disorderly conduct, my hind leg. I'm less than happy *that* will be on my record. But you can make that up to me when we get home."

"Well, you have no one to blame but yourself." Marcus temples throbbed with the beat of his heart. "What in the hell were you thinking showing up here?"

"I was thinking that you clearly needed me to come down here and get your head out of your ass. You know you scared me to death just disappearing like that."

"Really?" Marcus closed his eyes and took a deep breath to calm his racing pulse. He rose slowly from the bench. "Is that why it took you over two months to actually try to find me?"

"I tried calling you and texting you. Then I remembered those certified letters from that attorney. Once I found where I had stuck them, it was pretty easy to put two and two together. I found this address online. Marcus, let's just go home and put all this silliness behind us."

Marcus's mouth fell agape, and he stared at Robert. "You honestly expect me to go anywhere with you?"

"Come on, you're being a drama queen." Robert put out his hand to Marcus. "Just throw your stuff in a bag and we'll head out. Once I get my car out of impound, we can head home. It's at some place called Murphy's garage. If you need to come back down here to settle your grandmother's estate, I'll drive you back." Robert took a step toward Marcus.

Marcus bumped into the piano bench again as he tried to back away. "Robert, you hit me. Why would I ever get in a car with you again?"

"And I'm sorry about that." Robert took another step forward. "I had a bad day at work. You caught me off-guard. And, need I remind you, you were the one lying about working at the diner again. I thought I had made it perfectly clear that I didn't want—"

"*You* didn't want." Marcus stepped toward Robert and put his hands on his hips. The throbbing in his temples began to fade. "That's all that matters, isn't it, Robert? What you want. But what about what I want?"

"What do you want, Marcus?" Robert threw up his hands in frustration. "I gave you everything anyone could ever ask for."

"Well, I *didn't want* to get hit! I didn't ask for that."

"I told you I was sorry. I promise you it will never happen again."

"You're damn right it won't, because I'm not going anywhere with you." Marcus turned his back on Robert and looked at the pictures scattered along the back of the piano. He straightened one of the frames that had shifted when he backed into the piano bench. In the picture, his grandmother and the Do-Nothings stood with their arms around each other. "It isn't just that you hit me. You were killing me daily in that house. I had no friends. I had no job. I had nothing except trying to make you happy and trying to become who you told people I was. You keep saying let's go home." Marcus laughed. "Home? You don't know the meaning of the word. Robert, you promised me a home and you gave me a prison."

"You didn't seem to mind as long as I kept buying you things. Baby, I—"

Marcus whipped around and glared at Robert. "Do not call me baby."

"Oh, come on—"

"Fine. I'll admit it. I was blinded by the gifts and the fabulous life you offered. But I began to see that those gifts weren't free. They came with a very heavy price—my soul." Marcus sighed. "I am done, Robert. Just go away."

The room was silent as the two men stared at each other. Robert put his hands on his hips and broke the silence. "What am I supposed to tell people back in Atlanta? That you've decided to run off to this hick town and play house with a bunch of gun-toting old ladies and that little twink I saw coming out of here earlier? Or is it that redneck who hit me last night? Is that the kind of people you want to be around? Should I tell people that?"

"Frankly, I don't give two shits what you tell them. Tell them I died. Tell them I ran away with the circus. Tell them the truth, for once in your life. How do you think your society dames will react knowing that you hauled off and punched me?" Marcus rolled his head back onto his shoulders and tried to release the tension in his neck. "Or just keep spinning the same lies you always lived under. I *do not* care. And they won't either. Those people don't care about me. You don't either, really. All you want is someone to look pretty on your arm. Well, that ain't me. And I won't stand here and let you say anything about those old ladies."

"And the twink?"

"Not that it is any of your damn business, but that boy I *am not* involved with is Skeet. He's just a friend. You know. Friends are those things you wouldn't let me have out of some stupid fear that I might want one of them more than you."

"And the hick that hit me? Look what he did to my face." Robert pointed at his eye.

"It's a bruise. Bruises fade."

"I thought you said you didn't want a man that hits."

"He hit to protect me, not to frighten me. Though, thanks to your little performance last night, he'll probably never speak to me again."

"Then I did you a favor. He's a small-town boy with a small-town brain. What can he, or for that matter, any of these people, offer you?"

"They're friends. No, not just friends. They're family. They want me to be happy. They want me to be safe. They want me to actually enjoy my life. You know, those things people want you to have when they really love you? You see this house?" Marcus gestured at the room. "You know why my grandmother left it to me?"

"God only knows."

"With her dying breath, she said she wanted me to be happy." Marcus stepped to Robert and glowered close to his face. "She wanted me to have a home. And she never met me, Robert. You claim to love me and you don't want me to have the things a woman who never met me wanted me to have."

Robert narrowed his eyes. "I want the car."

"The car?" Marcus walked away from Robert and then turned back to add, "Ha! You can have it. Or what's left of it. Take it and go."

"What did you do to the car?" Robert began storming across the room toward Marcus. Marcus stood firmly in place with his hands on his hips and his chest out. Over Robert's shoulder, he noticed a figure standing in the doorway with something slung over its shoulder. Marcus put out his hand onto Robert's chest and stopped his advance. "Do not take another step." Marcus twisted to one side and called out around Robert's body. "Hey, Miss Annie. Are you here to play me a song? That would be just wonderful. My guest here is just leaving."

Robert's eyes grew wide with fear as he turned around to see the old woman standing in the doorway with a garden hoe raised over her head ready to strike. He turned back to Marcus with his mouth agape. "What is with you and these murderous old women? You know what? Fine. I'll go. You really are the same trash I found in that diner. No matter how much anyone tries, that is all you will ever be. Trash."

"Fine. You think of me as trash. And you can tell everyone you threw me away." Marcus pointed toward the front door, his hand trembling slightly. "Now go."

Robert spun on his heels and stormed toward the door. When he came face to face with Annie, he stopped and turned back to Marcus. "The car?"

"It was totaled. I'm selling it for scrap. I'll send you the money. And don't bother coming back down here looking for me. I'll be moving on very soon."

Annie dropped the hoe onto her shoulder and stepped to one side of the doorway. She swung her arm out across her body to gesture Robert out of the door toward a taxi sitting there. Marcus waved at Robert as he walked quickly out and down the sidewalk. Once he could see that Robert had reached the taxi, Marcus dropped back onto the piano bench and let out a long sigh. He held his hands in front of him and tried his best to calm their shaking. As the flashing in the corners of his eyes began to ebb, he looked at the old woman still standing in the doorway.

"Miss Annie, it would sure make me feel a lot better if you would come play me a song." He patted the piano bench beside him.

Annie swung the hoe from her shoulder and propped it against the door frame before tottering over and sitting beside Marcus. She looked him in the eye and then gave him a wink and a smile. After she patted him softly on the knee, she placed her hands on the keys and turned her eyes upward in thought. With a firm nod of her head, she began playing a jaunty tune.

"What hymn is that?" Marcus asked.

She grinned and shook her shoulders in time with the music.

Marcus closed his eyes and listened to the tune Annie cranked out. When the song she was playing dawned on him, Marcus popped his eyes open and began to laugh aloud. "Is that 'Hit the Road Jack?' Oh, Miss Annie, that is the perfect hymn." Marcus threw his arms out to the side and sang the words at the top of his lungs. As she pounded the keys harder, he began to spin and sway around the room behind her as his words tumbled into an unstoppable peal of laughter.

"WELL, WOULD YOU LOOK AT that," Skeet said and let out a long, slow whistle. "These old broads have really outdone themselves this year. Jeez Louise, they must have used every string of Christmas lights they had between the four of them."

Marcus opened the car door and stepped out into the parking lot of the Ginsburg Pharmacy. He slammed the car door and then leaned on the roof of the car with his arms crossed under his chin as he took in the dazzling array in the town square. Scattered around the empty streets were bales of hay, wooden hitching posts, and an old watering trough. In the center of the square was a small park with an octagonal white gazebo covered in small twinkling lights. Strands of larger bulbs extended from each of the eight corners of the structure out across the park and across the surrounding streets to wrap around the streetlight poles along the sidewalks. The usual rows of cars parked along the edges of the square had been cleared away, and the parking spots were filled with folding tables and chairs.

"Yeah. It looks amazing. I still can't believe they just threw all of this together in a few weeks." Marcus pushed himself off the car and walked around to join Skeet on the other side.

"Hell, these women could outfit an army in a weekend if it gave them an excuse to buy a new dress and drink a cocktail."

Marcus laughed and nudged Skeet. "Yeah, I don't think real cowboys would particularly approve of suits and dresses."

"Or vodka cranberries, even if they are served in a jelly jar."

"Or your pants. Can you breathe in those things?"

"Tight pants have a long tradition in the world of the cowboy, I'll have you know."

"Well, at least my menu is reasonably Old West. If nothing else, I can impress the hell out of this town with my cooking before I ride off into the sunset." Marcus hooked his hand around Skeet's upper arm and tugged him off the car. They walked around the orange and white barricade the police had set up to block each of the streets that lead into the square and down the sidewalk toward the sounds of music and laughter. The dogwood trees planted in small square openings in the sidewalks were each swathed in strings of lights, turning the whole square into an oversized jelly jar filled with shimmering lightning bugs. "Speaking of cooking, we better go help set everything up. I promised Francine I would handle everything so she could enjoy herself tonight."

"Wait, how did your making a promise turn into me helping all night? I'm here to have a good time as much as everyone else, and I don't do food service. Anyway, I promised Sarge I would help him and the twins with the music."

"They're here?" Marcus stopped and stared at Skeet in disbelief. "I mean, that's great, but are the people of Marathon really ready for that kind of performance?"

"Aw, come on Marcus. We thought we might convince you to slap on a wig and join us for a tribute to the Grand Old Opry. You'd make a fabulous Reba McEntire." Skeet looked at Marcus with an earnest and determined set of his chin before breaking into a fit of giggles. "Oh, my god, I wish you could see your face right now. No. No one is doing drag tonight, silly. I just asked Sarge to be the DJ. Usually Martin Prescott handles the music, but apparently after you didn't show any interest in him, he got very upset with Miss Inez and refused to do it."

"Okay, you're not going to make this my fault." Marcus glanced over at the gazebo to see Sarge standing behind a turntable with headphones on his ears. He wore a blue suit that barely buttoned over his belly and a pink bowtie so bright that Marcus would've sworn it required batteries. He looked up from the record player and, when he noticed Marcus and Skeet, he lifted his hand and threw a salute to the boys followed by a kiss thrown with his other hand.

The twins, who looked absolutely nothing alike when they were in men's clothes, sat on the steps of the gazebo flipping through crates of albums, occasionally pulling one out and showing it to each other. They wore matching blue and white seersucker suits and straw boater hats. One of the men pulled a cover out of the box and screamed in delight as he hopped up and handed it to Sarge. Sarge said something to the man and he turned around to tip his hat at Marcus, revealing his bald pate. Marcus waved back and chuckled.

"Look at their little matching suits!" Skeet squealed. "Trust me. I'm glad it happened. Sarge and the twins will play much better music than that old fart would've. Frankie and I might get to show off some of the moves we learned from that bootleg copy of *Best Little You-know-what House in Texas* that we found online. Wait until you see my hitch kick."

"Well, if I can get out from behind the food tables, I might be persuaded to spin you around the square once."

Skeet placed his head on Marcus's shoulder, stared up at him, and batted his eyes. "But Mr. Sumter, oh my! How the townsfolk will talk!"

Marcus shrugged Skeet off his shoulder and laughed. "You're such an idiot."

"Marcus, sweetheart! Over here!" a voice beckoned across the square. "Get your bony little butt over here!" Marcus looked over the tables, where a few early arrivals sat chatting and tapping their toes to the music that filled the air, toward the source of the voice. Inez stood behind a long table covered with chafing dishes, platters, and bowls. Much like the smaller tables in the square, the food tables were covered with red bandanna print tablecloths, and each held a centerpiece of vibrant flowers and mason jars filled with votive candles. Instead of her usual Braves T-shirt, Inez wore a green sleeveless dress and a tiny sequined cowboy hat pinned at a cockeyed angle.

Helen stood beside Inez, her usual bob twisted up in a loose bun, and her vibrant purple dress hidden behind a blue gingham apron. She was fussing with the arrangement of crackers and cheese cubes on a tray.

Marcus grimaced at Skeet. "Well, duty calls."

"And gossip as well. I'll hang out with you until Frankie shows up."

Marcus stepped quickly over to the table and surveyed the spread before him. Two of the chafing dishes held the chili that he and Francine had worked on all afternoon. He had made one vegetarian version, though Francine didn't think there was a person in town who wouldn't eat meat. Marcus still wasn't sure if chili was the right decision with the possibility of dribbles on fancy dresses and the heat of the late summer night, but he had gone with the original plan.

Beside the chili were trays of crudités, pigs in blankets, cheeses, and fruits. Other chafing dishes held small ears of corn and small white potatoes. Marcus had found the Do-Nothings cowboy theme a bit challenging to fulfill beyond beans, but the dessert tray at the far end of the table was his *pièce de résistance*—haystacks. The caramel-covered chow mein noodles weren't something a cowboy would ever have eaten, but their resemblance to hay stacks was too good to resist. He had filled in with cakes and pies donated by the women of Priscilla's Sunday school class.

"Darling," Helen purred as she looked at the trays on the table, "I hope we have everything laid out in a way that pleases you. Inez and I weren't sure you would make it tonight after all the, um, drama last night, so we started without you. You won't hurt my feelings at all if you want to shuffle things around a bit."

"No," Marcus replied. "I think it all looks absolutely perfect. But I thought we were going to put those palomino figurines of Inez's in the center of the cheese tray."

"Shit!" Inez spat out and snapped her fingers. "I completely forgot those durn things."

"They do look a little bare, don't they?" Helen said.

"I can call Priss and ask her to bring them over."

"No. I've got an idea." Helen turned to Skeet and asked him, "Baby boy, won't you be a darling and run over to Ginsburg's and pick up some toy pistols? I know they sell them in there because Cookie and I went around and around about the appropriateness of selling guns to children. She has those and some little sheriff badges and such."

"Is Miss Cookie just going to give them to me?" Skeet kicked at the ground. "I don't have any money on me."

"What about your car wash money?"

"Um, I sort of, didn't work much this week."

"Fine." Helen pointed to the coolers sitting behind the table. "Look in my purse over there and get some money."

"You know what, Inez," Marcus said as he picked up a tray off the table, "Let's swap these two trays here. I think it makes more sense to have the cheese closer to the crackers."

"Nonnie?" Skeet said as he rooted around in his grandmother's pocketbook. "Why do you have a bag of nails in here?" Skeet pulled a brown paper sack out of the purse and held it over his shoulder as he kept digging around in the purse with his other hand.

Helen blushed and stomped over to snatch the bag out of Skeet's hand. "I have those in case we needed to hang any decorations with them. And quit snooping around in there. Just take my wallet out of the side pocket where you know it always is."

"Got it!" Skeet handed the fat red leather wallet to Helen. She opened it and pulled out a twenty-dollar bill.

"I'll be right back."

"And I expect change!" Helen called after the boy as he rushed toward the pharmacy. "I swear, that boy has been raised to think that money just grows in a cotton field. I blame his mother for that. Lord knows I didn't raise his father to—"

"Girls," Priscilla's voice interrupted her as she waddled to the table, "everything looks absolutely lovely. I'm so sorry I couldn't be here earlier to help with decorating. You know I have that women's prayer group on Saturdays that I just can't miss."

"I think you could have skipped just this once," Inez muttered. "After all, Jesus forgives. I don't."

Priscilla ignored her and asked, "So has anybody seen him yet? Did our plan work? I took the Reverend's suit over—"

"Priss, shh." Helen chastised.

"I'm right here, Priss." Marcus leaned out from behind Inez and waved.

"Oh! Marcus, sugar, there you are. I'm so glad you didn't go running off before this party." Priscilla tugged at the collar of her ill-fitting fuchsia dress. "Lord, this heat. I don't think we could've raised a dime tonight if people thought your food wasn't going to be served. You've made a lot of happy eaters in your few weeks here."

"I doubt that's the reason people are here." Marcus waved the compliment away.

"No, you've made a lot of fans in this little town," Priscilla said.

"Well, one man isn't a fan now."

"Oh, come on now," Helen said, "it can't be that bad."

"Yeah. It can. Usually, if you get a man into a fist fight and get him hauled off to jail, he doesn't tend to come back for more. It's for the best, really. Ladies, you should know that I told Francine I'm leaving tomorrow morning. I only stuck around to finish this party. Once you pay me, I'm back on the road."

"Sweetheart, you think we don't know that?" Priscilla asked. "You know by now how this works. You tell one Do-Nothing, you've told all the Do-Nothings."

"And you aren't going to try to stop me?" Marcus asked, not quite believing the women's passive acceptance.

Helen waved her hands in defeat. "You're a grown man, Marcus. What are we supposed to do? Chain you to the diner stove? No. We've tried. But what about the house?"

"Katie Nell has my number. If I get an offer, I can come back to take care of it. I mean, clearly, it's going to take a while. I don't think she's had a single person interested in buying it."

Marcus noticed the women all cutting sideways glances at each other. "Is there something you ladies aren't telling me?"

"No," Helen said. "You just have to be patient. We don't have a lot of people coming in and out of this town. It might just take a while for it to sell. But without the house selling, what are you going to do for money?"

"I've got what I earned at the diner. And I'll just find another diner to work at on the way."

"And what about that man?" Inez asked.

"Hank?" Marcus shrugged. "Like I said, he wouldn't return my calls so—"

"Not him," Inez said. "That idiot I nearly had to shoot last night."

"Oh. That's been handled."

"Handled?" Inez's eyes opened wide and she gasped. "Oh, dear lord, child, you didn't go and kill the man, did you? I mean, if you did you should have called us first. You don't know this town well enough to know where to put the body. I mean, things like this can't just be done willy-nilly. You've got to—"

197

"Inez Coffee! I know you are not advocating this boy committing murder! That's right there in God's big ten no-no's."

"Priscilla, don't be such a hard-ass. I was just suggesting that if he needed a little help with—"

Marcus laughed. "Priss, it's okay. Calm down. No one is dead. Let's just say between Miss Inez's shotgun and Miss Annie's hoe, Robert may think it's safer just to give me a wide berth from now on."

"Annie's hoe?" Helen wrinkled her brow in confusion.

"Not important." Marcus stood and walked around to the front of the table. He adjusted a tray of cookies while talking to the women on the other side of the table. "I finally stood up to him. I don't know if he understands at all why I left. Hell, I don't care if he understands. That can be the next boy's problem. He knows to leave me alone, and I think this time he really will."

"Girls," Francine said as she walked to the group, stopping to kiss each woman on her cheek. Francine stood next to Marcus and draped her arm over his shoulder.

"Francine!" Marcus said as he stepped back to appraise her dress. Her sequined top sparkled under the white lights around the square and her skirt flared out as she gave a quick spin. "I don't think I have ever seen you not in uniform. Your dress is beautiful."

"Thanks, sugar." Francine nodded at Helen and said, "I'm here with the delivery."

"Well, it's about time." Inez turned around and clapped her hands. "The square is starting to fill up."

"What delivery?" Marcus asked. "I think all of the food containers are here. Did we forget the—"

Francine winked at Marcus. "Shoe Button, this is a special delivery."

"Just for a certain VIP," Helen said and winked at the other women.

"Who? The mayor?"

"Well, as I live and breathe, would you look at that?" Inez let out a slow whistle. "My lord, he does clean up nice."

"Ooh, he's headed this way," Helen said, breaking into girlish giggles.

Marcus turned around to see what the women were looking at. Across the town square, Hank stood looking through the crowd. Marcus's breath caught in his throat. Hank wore a simple dark suit, a white dress shirt, and a bright paisley tie. His hair glistened under the twinkling lights from a heavy layer of pomade that sculpted his usually unruly hair into a slicked-back sweep above his face. His beard was trimmed, and his usual work boots were replaced by shiny black and white oxfords.

"Hank?" Marcus spun to face the women. "Oh, my god, what have you ladies done?"

"I know I said we'd given up but…well… God forgive me, I lied." Priscilla held her hands in front of her chest as if praying.

"Sweetheart, we may be called the Do-Nothings but, frankly, it's just not in our nature to do nothing. Sometimes things need a little push."

Hank made eye contact with Marcus and began to work his way through the crowd. As he neared, the women began chattering over each other behind Marcus.

"Here he comes."

"You know, I thought he was fun to watch go away, but he looks even better coming toward you."

"Lord, do you know how long it's been since a man crossed a crowded room for me? Isn't it romantic?"

Marcus clenched his teeth in a fake smile and hissed at the women, "Would you ladies hush?"

Hank walked to Marcus and stood in front of him with his hands crossed behind his back. He rocked back and forth on his heels and looked at Marcus with a bashful smile.

"Good evening, Hank," Helen purred over Marcus's shoulder.

"Ladies." Hank nodded at the women.

"Whoo, boy!" Inez hooted. "I didn't know you had it in you to look this sexy!"

Priscilla stepped to Hank and brushed some lint off the collar of his jacket. "See Hank, I told you that suit would fit you perfectly. I know y'all think I'm an old prude, but I can judge a man's body from a hundred paces." She plucked a daisy out of one of the flower arrangements on the table, broke the stem, and stuck it in the buttonhole on Hank's lapel. She beamed with satisfaction as she patted his chest.

Hanks blushed and ducked his head. "Yes, ma'am it does fit well. Tell the reverend thank you for me, will you?"

"Francine, why don't you run over to the gazebo and ask that Sarge fellow to play something nice for dancing?" Helen pushed Inez and Priscilla away from the men. "Inez. Priss. Come help me with these chafing dishes."

"Hold on," Inez said as she yanked her arm out of Helen's grip. "I want to see what happens."

Priscilla clutched Inez's arm and yanked her backward. "Inez, don't be a pain in the ass."

"Priscilla! Language."

Marcus waited for the women to walk away before turning to face Hank.

"Good evening, Fiat." Hank bowed slightly.

"Good evening."

"Wonderful weather tonight."

"Yeah."

"Want to dance?"

"You don't dance."

Hank held out his hand to Marcus. "Just shut up and come on."

Marcus noticed that every speck of grease and grunge had been scrubbed away, and his nails appeared to have been freshly manicured. He took Hank's outstretched hand. "Okay. But you have to lead."

"Lead? You expecting Fred Astaire? I'm afraid, Fiat, you're going to have to settle for the old grab and waddle."

Hank looked at Marcus's hand and squeezed it. He led Marcus out in the center of the street in front of the square into a small crowd of people dancing. Hank turned to face him and wrapped his arms around his waist. As Marcus tucked himself closer into Hank's arms and draped his arms over Hank's shoulders, the first notes of a Judds song floated across the town square from the speakers on the gazebo. Hank began to gently rock their bodies back and forth in time with the song. The twins stepped up to the microphone and began to sing the words of the song in a tight, soothing harmony.

"Did you pick this?" Marcus craned his head back and wrinkled his brow at Hank.

"No. I have no idea what it is."

"It's called 'Mama, He's Crazy.'" Marcus chuckled and shook his head. "Probably Francine's choice. It's oddly perfect."

The couple swayed back and forth to the music. Marcus closed his eyes and surrendered himself to the gentle rocking motion, letting the tension of the previous day slowly slide out of his muscles. He tipped his head forward and rested it on Hank's shoulder. "So does this mean you aren't mad at me?"

"No. Not mad," Hank mumbled in his ear. "Not anymore."

"What changed your mind?" Marcus said as he opened his eyes to look at the other couples dancing around them. He could see the Do-Nothings standing in a line along the sidewalk watching him with smiles on their faces. As Hank spun them slowly around, the reflections of the lights swirled on the pavement below their feet.

"It was the strangest thing," Hank answered. "This morning, I got to the garage late. Was up last night at the police station, you know."

"I'm sorry about—"

"Shh. Let me finish." Hank cleared his throat. "Anyway, Miss Helen was there waiting on me. Seems she had a nail in her tire. I told her she could sit in the waiting room while I fixed it, but she followed me into the garage and talked to me while I worked on it. Told me some

201

interesting stories. She wanted to encourage me to come to this dance tonight. Then around lunch time, Miss Inez had a nail. She was chatty, too. By the time Miss Priscilla showed up, I was on to their game. Either they were up to something, or someone really needs to check the streets in your neighborhood for nails."

Marcus looked over Hank's shoulder at the women. "Busybodies. Wait, Priss was involved? I thought she didn't approve of—"

"Yep." Hank nodded his head. "Miss Priscilla brought me these clothes. I found a note she stuck in the pocket."

Marcus took his arm from Hank's neck and pulled an index card out of the breast pocket of Hank's jacket. In a childish scrawl were written the words, 1 Corinthians 13:13. "What is that?"

"I had to look it up. 'The greatest of these is love.'"

"Subtle." Marcus stuck the card back in Hank's pocket.

"Don't be mad at them. They were trying to help. Francine was the last to show. She told me... about the eye." Hank stopped dancing and stepped back to look Marcus in the eyes. "I know the truth. The whole story."

Marcus's face grew flush. "And?"

"And… I wish I had hit him harder than I did."

Marcus dropped his head against Hank's chest and sighed. Hank touched Marcus's chin and lifted his face.

"I know you didn't steal the car. Sheriff Stewart told me you had the title in your name. And I know what that jerk—"

"I'm sorry I didn't tell you all of it before. I tried that night I made you dinner but…I was just embarrassed and—"

"Shh. I understand."

Hank wrapped his arms around Marcus's waist and began dancing again.

"Hank?"

"Hmm?"

"I know you said you don't like casual flings. You know I'm probably still leaving?"

"Fiat, I said I don't like meaningless. Casual and meaningless are not the same thing. I can do casual."

Hank lowered his hand down Marcus's back and pulled him closer.

"Hank?"

"Yes?"

"The music stopped."

"Don't care."

The men continued spinning silently around on the concrete as all the other couples wandered off to the tables at the sides.

"Hank," Marcus whispered, "you're Orpheus."

"What?"

"Helping to lead me out of hell."

"No, Fiat, you got yourself out of hell. I'm just a guy who wants to dance with you."

"Well, you want to lead me out of here back to my place?"

"Yes. I do."

Marcus dropped his arms from Hank's shoulders and took his hand. As they walked past the grinning Do-Nothings toward Hank's truck, Marcus looked at Hank and whispered, "No looking back."

MARCUS SHIFTED ACROSS THE COOL sheets until Hank's chest and pelvis rested along his spine and hips, his chest hair tickled at his shoulder blades, and his warm breath tiptoed around the fine hairs at the back of his head. Hank grunted lightly and grabbed Marcus's hips to pull him closer before draping his arm across Marcus's waist. Marcus lay awake and listened to the steady rhythm of Hank's breathing and the low murmur of the ceiling fan slowly twirling overhead.

The night spent together after leaving the dance had been nothing Marcus had previously imagined or experienced. With his few one-night stands, the point had been to get in, get off, and get out with as little connection, communication, or concern as possible. With Robert, lovemaking had grown from a mildly pleasant way to spend half an hour, to an occasional chore as tedious as dusting louvered blinds.

His night spent with Hank had run the gamut from sweaty and passionate to quiet moments of fingers and eyes exploring each other's skin. Stretches of time punctuated only by the sounds of kisses and sighs and low rumbles of pleasure interspersed with long tumbles of laughter and drowsy conversations about topics Marcus couldn't remember in the amber-colored haziness of half-sleep. In the dim light, Marcus could see from the longing in Hank's eyes before and after sex that this was a man who craved his words and thoughts as much, if not more than, his body.

Marcus kept his eyes closed and enjoyed the warmth of Hank's body curled around him countered by the cool trails of air from the ceiling fan that spilled across the points of bare skin where his arms, legs, and face poked out of the cotton sheet. Just as the darkness of sleep began to envelop him again, Hank's body suddenly tensed.

"Marcus," Hank hissed into his ear.

"Hmm?"

"Marcus." Hank shook his shoulder gently. "Are you awake?"

"Uh-uh. Sleeping."

"Wake up."

"Are you that horny?" Marcus mumbled as he rolled over to face the other man, one eye barely open. "I need a little more sleep before we…well, if you insist." Marcus nuzzled his nose into Hank's chest, only to have Hank push him away.

"I'm serious." Hank rose on one elbow and stared at the door over Marcus's hip. "I think I heard someone come in the house."

"What?" Marcus's eyes popped open wide. He searched the other man's face for any sign this was one of his silly jokes.

"I swear I heard the front door open and shut."

Marcus rolled onto his back, shifted onto his elbows, and listened for any sound coming from the other room. Hearing nothing but the whir of the icemaker in the kitchen refilling, he shook his head. "I think you're imagining it. Go back to sleep. Too early." He lay back down, curled onto his side and draped Hank's arm back over his waist.

"Sorry." Hank pecked the tip of Marcus's nose before easing back down beside him and looking into his eyes. "I must've been dreaming. Thought I heard—"

"Shh," Marcus hissed and abruptly pushed his upper body away from Hank. He sat up in the bed and looked over at the bedroom door. "Now, I heard something."

"It's probably just because I put it in your head." Hank pulled him back to the bed. "Come back and cuddle."

Marcus began to lower back down, but stopped and sat up as he heard the distinct sound of footsteps in the other room. "No," he whispered. "There is definitely someone in there."

"Didn't you lock the door?"

"I don't remember. I was rather preoccupied with getting you naked and other stuff."

Hank jumped naked from the bed and fumbled around on the floor for his clothes. He stepped into his boxer shorts and hiked them up on his waist. "Where is my damned shirt?" he asked in a whisper and he spun around in small, panicked circles. "Do you have something in here we can use for a weapon?"

"I don't know." Marcus clutched the sheet and pulled it under his chin, cowering his way toward the headboard. His heart beat began to race and the first flashes of light signaling a panic attack began beating at the corners of his eyes. "Like a gun? Why would I have—"

"A baseball bat. Anything." Hank tiptoed to the closet and slid open the folding doors. He jerked his head back and forth, searching for anything he could swing at the intruder. "Ah ha!" he said as he stuck his arm into the closet and grabbed something. As he spun back around, Marcus could see the shimmering shaft of a golf club.

"I didn't know my grandmother played—"

"Not the time," Hank hissed as he slipped over to the bedroom door. He placed a finger to his lips to signal Marcus to be quiet and then placed a hand on the door knob. He put his ear against the door. "Someone is definitely out there, but it doesn't sound like they're walking around."

"Are you really going to hit someone with that?"

"I don't want to but… it might be a burglar. Or that asshole."

"Robert? No, I don't think he—" A loud thud from the other room made Marcus jump. "Where is your phone? Call 911!"

"It's in the other room, I think. Where is yours?"

"I don't know," Marcus whined, his voice rising in pitch from his fear. "God, I thought I convinced him to leave town. Oh, shit. Oh, Shit." Marcus buried his face in the sheet crumpled in his fists. "I honestly thought—" Marcus stopped as a loud glissando from the piano cut through the quiet. "Oh, my god!" Marcus threw his head back and began to roar with laughter. "It's Miss Annie."

"Miss Annie?" Hank knitted his brows and pressed his ear against the door. "Is that 'When the Saints Go Marching In'?"

Marcus threw the sheet toward the foot of the bed and flung his legs over the edge of the mattress. "Wonderful Miss Annie!" Marcus hopped up and bounced over to the door, dancing to the rhythm of the rousing hymn banging through the closed door. "Come on. Let's go say good morning."

"Fiat, stop."

"It's okay."

"No, don't go out there—"

"It's fine. She'll play a song or two and be on her merry way." He turned to Hank and kissed him quickly on the cheek. "Then we can come back in here and maybe go for… what round were we on?" Marcus began to yank the door open.

"No." Hank placed his hand on the door and slammed it shut. "I don't think Miss Annie particularly needs to see this side of you." Hank lowered his head and ran his eyes down Marcus's body. "I mean, it's a beautiful sight, but let's not give the old woman a coronary."

Marcus glanced at his naked body. "Oh, my god." He looked at Hank and began to giggle. "Can you imagine?" He snatched his discarded underwear from the floor. As he stepped into it, he said, "You might want to find some pants too."

Hank propped the golf club against the wall beside the door and crossed to the far side of the bed. He turned from left to right searching for his clothes before dropping to his knees and crawling around on the floor, looking under the bed and the chair in the corner for any sign of has discarded clothes. He stopped when he found a solitary black sock and plopped onto his backside to slide it onto his foot. Marcus continued to giggle as Hank resumed scurrying back and forth on the carpet, one foot bare and his backside jiggling under the taught fabric of his boxer briefs. Hank stopped and rocked back to sit on his heels. "Where the hell is my shirt?"

"I think I threw it somewhere in that direction," Marcus gestured toward the far side of the room as he dropped to his hands and knees and began to search the floor for his clothes. When he felt a wad of fabric next to his hand, he scooped it up and let it unfurl in front of him. "I think this is yours," he said as he tossed a black sock across the room toward Hank. "At least your feet won't be naked."

"Crap, Fiat." Hank slid the sock onto his foot before hopping up and standing beside the bed with his hands on his hips and his head thrown back in frustration. "My pants."

"What?"

"I'm pretty sure you got those off me somewhere in the kitchen. Right after you tossed my shirt over the sofa."

"Yeah, we did have each other pretty much naked by the time we got in here." Marcus stopped scrounging around the floor and sat up to look at Hank across the bed. He rested his arms on the mattress and looked at the nearly naked man across the room. The sunlight streamed through the half-opened blinds and created an aura around Hank as it illuminated the dark hairs on his chest, arms, and legs. "Yep. Getting you naked was a good idea."

"But that means my clothes are out there." Hank pointed toward the door. "With her."

"So are mine."

"Yes, but you've got clothes in here."

"Then put on some of my clothes."

"As if I could get into your scrawny-butt jeans."

"Fine." Marcus stood and walked over to his duffel bag. He unzipped the top and began digging inside, choosing a pair of sweats and the first T-shirt he found. "I'll go out and get your clothes."

"Or you could ask her to leave."

"Oh, hell no. After Miss Annie's help yesterday, she can come in and play all the muzak she wants as long as this house is mine." He stepped into the sweat pants and pulled the T-shirt over his head. "You just hang out in here and I'll bring your clothes back. Or you can wait until she leaves. No one ever has to know you were here."

"Okay. Just go." Hank pulled the sheet off the bed and wrapped it around his shoulders.

Marcus crawled across the bed and squatted on his knees. He grabbed the edges of the sheet and pulled Hank in for a kiss. As he moved away, he winked and said, "I'll be right back." He swatted Hank on the backside before hopping off the bed and walking out of the room.

After closing the bedroom door behind him, Marcus stepped out of the small hallway and into the living room. He paused at the piano and said, "Good morning, Miss Annie."

The woman looked over at him and smiled broadly. She nodded a greeting as she continued to plunk out the notes of the song. She wore a periwinkle sundress over a rainbow-striped turtleneck and a wide headband covered with fake sunflowers. She looked at the piano keys and rocked from side to side in time with the music she played.

"Have a good time at the dance last night?" Marcus asked as he crossed over to the kitchen to flip the switch on the coffee maker. On the kitchen island, he noticed all of his and Hank's clothes folded into two neat piles side by side. "I see you straightened up for me."

Annie played the last few notes of the song and then swiveled around on the bench to face Marcus. She nodded again and sat looking at him. Not knowing what to say, Marcus turned to continue around the island into the kitchen. When his back was turned, he heard the woman clear her throat. Marcus looked back to see her jerk her head first toward the pile of clothes and then toward the bedroom door. She raised her eyebrows and hands in an inquisitive manner.

"Um, yes. He's back there."

Annie clapped her hands rapidly in front of her face and then spun back to the piano. Holding her hands above the keys, she closed her eyes before launching into another boisterous song.

Marcus shook his head and grinned as he flipped the switch on the coffee maker. As the water began to drip out of the basket into the carafe, he began to tap his foot and hum along with Annie's playing until he realized what the tune was. He turned on his heels and asked, "Miss Annie? Is that 'Oh Happy Day'?" She nodded her head and hunched forward to strike the keys harder and play louder. "Why, you old softy." As Marcus opened a cabinet over the coffee pot to look for two mugs, the doorbell rang. "Who the heck is that?"

"Yoo-hoo?" a voice called through the front door as someone opened it a crack. "Anyone home?"

"Yes, Helen. Come on in." Marcus hollered across the room, trying to be heard over Annie's loud song.

"It's not just me," Helen said as she pushed the door open and peeked around the edge. "Are you decent? We all wanted to catch you before you left town to say our goodbyes. We were worried if we came after church, you might be long gone."

"Y'all come on in. I'm just in here listening to Miss Annie play. And you know good and well I wouldn't skip out without saying goodbye to all the Do-Nothings."

"Annie! I told you to come over to my house for a ride to church. Not to come interrupting whatever Marcus might be up to." Helen craned her neck to peer around the room, clearly looking for anyone else who might be inside.

"Is he in there?" Marcus heard Inez half-whisper over Helen's shoulder.

Helen glanced back over her shoulder and said, "It appears, except for Annie, Marcus is alone." Helen stumbled through the door as Inez pushed her in from behind. "Inez, there is no need to shove."

"Well, quit lollygagging in the door." Inez burst into the room and strolled over to the island. She pulled out a barstool and hopped onto it. Placing her elbows on the counter, she dropped her head into her hands. "So, Marcus, how was the rest of your night?"

"Inez, that's none of your business." Priscilla stepped around Helen and into the living room, tugging Francine along behind her. She waddled to the counter and pulled out the other bar stool. She grunted as she rested one hand on the back of the stool and the other on Francine's shoulder so she could hop onto the stool; her chubby legs swung far above the floor as she landed with a heavy plop. "What he did when he *abandoned* us at the dance is none of our business."

"Even if I still didn't get to dance at our party because I had to cover the food tables, yet again." Francine shot a dirty look at Marcus. "We didn't interrupt something, did we?"

"No." Helen shrugged. "It appears Marcus was just listening to Annie play the piano."

"Well, with the way he and that Hudson boy tore out of the dance last night, I thought for sure—"

Helen swatted Francine on the arm and turned to walk into the kitchen and pinched Marcus on both cheeks. She patted him softly on the side of his face and then tapped the tip of his nose with her finger. "As Priss said, that is really none of our business. Even if he did run off and leave the party way before he was supposed to be finished serving the food."

"I'm so sorry! I totally didn't mean to leave all of that work for y'all," Marcus said and rested his hands on each of Helen's shoulders. "I got so caught up in… well… anyway." Marcus dropped his chin and tried his best not to blush.

"And before he got paid," Francine added as she stuck a hand into her blouse and pulled a white bank envelope out of her bra. She dropped it on the counter and slid it toward Marcus. "He's going to need that if he is skipping town today."

"Well, he can't leave before he hears the grand total for the night," Priscilla added.

"Oh, that's right!" Marcus said. "How'd we do?"

"We raised twice what we expected, and I think we can thank you for it."

"Oh, who cares about that shit," Inez said and banged her hands on the counter. "Spill it, boy. We want all the details and you aren't leaving town until we get them."

"Inez, you know a gentleman doesn't kiss and tell," Marcus said and shot her a crooked grin.

"So there was kissing!" Francine crowed as she leaned over the counter toward Marcus. "Come on, Shoe Button, we want all the—"

A loud banging on the front door interrupted her, and everyone turned to look at the door as it swung open.

"Marc? Are you… oh, good morning ladies," Skeet said as he swept into the room with a stack of papers in one hand and a tube of cookie dough in the other. He set the papers and dough on the island before folding his arms across his chest. "I swear; you old ladies need to pay Marc rent since you're over here so much."

"Perfect timing," Marcus said as he looked at the stack of papers, realizing it was a pile of mail. "And you know, since I can't seem to get anybody to come to look at this house to buy it, maybe I *could* rent it." He turned to the group of women gathered around the island and added, "I should rent it to you to use as the official clubhouse for the Do-Nothings."

"No," Francine said and smirked, "the Do-Nothings meet at the Tammy Dinette. That's our home."

"Actually," Skeet said, "that's why I'm here. My mama has been trying to call you all morning. She's got someone interested in looking at the house today." He looked at Helen and added softly, "Sorry, Nonnie. Mama says she can't steer people away any longer. Her boss is thinking she's lost her magic touch."

"Why are you apologizing to Helen?" Marcus glanced over to see Helen cowering into her shoulders and stepping behind Inez.

"Let me explain," Helen said and raised her hands in front of her chest in a defensive manner. "I just told Katie Nell not to be in any rush to show the house. I was thinking that if you stuck around here and actually got to know the town that maybe… well, I don't know. But there was no harm in it. And I wasn't the only one. Inez told that one couple—"

"You stool pigeon!" Inez said and turned to Helen with a shocked look. "I suwanee, Helen. You say I'm the gossip but you can't keep a damned thing—"

"Inez, what did you do?" Marcus asked and put his hands on his hips.

Inez squirmed and stared at her shoes. "Well… I might have told someone who was wandering around the yard that a woman died in here and it might be a little bit haunted."

"Inez!" Marcus said and rolled his eyes.

"Well, they were damned fools to believe it."

The room fell silent as the women each stared off into a different direction to avoid eye contact with Marcus. He pushed a few of the letters around on the counter top, surprised to see they were addressed to him at his former Atlanta address. Marcus noticed the return address on one of the envelopes—Atlanta School of Culinary Arts. He slid it out of the pile and opened it. "Skeet, where did this mail come from?"

"It was in a stack on the porch," Skeet replied and shrugged. "Anyway, there's someone who wants to see the house today. Mama wanted me to come over and make sure it was clean and to see if you could be out of the house this afternoon. She also wants me to bake these cookies in here for some reason."

"That's the oldest trick in the book," Helen noted and shoved the dough across the counter. "The least your mother could do is bake something from scratch."

"Oh, I have a recipe for an RC Cola cookie that smells heavenly when it's baking." Priscilla offered.

"You have to share that with me," Inez said.

Marcus tuned out the women's prattle as he unfolded the letter and read the opening lines.

Mr. Sumter: We are pleased to inform you of your acceptance...

Helen tapping on his shoulder pulled Marcus's attention away from the letter.

"What you got there, honey?" she asked. "You just went white as a sheet."

Marcus dropped the letter onto the counter and shrugged. "It's nothing. Looks like this all my mail from Atlanta. Guess Robert left it here."

"Oh. Let's not talk about that asshole," Inez said and made a sour face. "I still want to know about the Hudson fellow."

"Yeah," Skeet said, "I was wondering where you disappeared to last night. Frankie and I were looking for you to show you our dance routine, and you were gone."

"Girls—" Priscilla said, her head hung down as she stared at the counter.

"Come on, Shoe Button," Francine pleaded, "give some old women a few vicarious thrills."

"Girls—" Priscilla tried to interrupt again.

"Honey," Helen said as she rubbed Marcus on his upper arm, "you just ignore these busybody old hens and keep your business to—"

"Girls!" Priscilla said, her voice shrill. Marcus looked over to see her pointing at the piles of clothes on the kitchen counter. She looked at him with a bemused smile. "That right there is the suit I loaned Hank last night. It's the Reverend's. I'd recognize it anywhere."

"Oh, yeah," Marcus stammered as he hurried over and began to gather the clothes off the counter into his arms. "He asked me if I would return—"

"Return hell," Inez spat out and jumped off the barstool, "that boy is still here! Hank Hudson!" She yelled into the hallway toward the bedroom, "You get that sexy butt out here!"

"Inez!" Priscilla said and gasped.

"Ladies," Marcus said as he began to back down the hallway toward the bedroom, trying hard not to drop all of the clothes he had bunched in his arms, "Maybe y'all come back a little later and…" He stopped walking as he heard the bedroom door creak open behind him.

"Well, good lord in heaven!" Priscilla said as she peered over Marcus's shoulder.

Inez let out a wolf whistle and slapped her hand on the counter in delight.

"You know, Hank, I really don't think that pink is your color," Francine drawled and fell into a fit of giggles.

Marcus turned to see Hank standing in the hall wearing a sheepish grin, his black dress socks, and an ill-fitting pink chenille robe with butterflies appliqued on the front. Hank held one arm modestly across his chest, though the sleeve of the robe barely reached his elbow, and tried to cover the broad swath of his chest that the tight-fitting robe could not stretch across. The hem of the robe fell just above the hem of his boxer shorts and his thick legs looked twice as large poking out from the bottom of the tiny pink robe. He shifted from foot to foot and tugged at the belt as he said, "It was all I could find in there."

As the women's laughter faded, Helen said, "I think if Eloise had known a gentleman caller would wear that bathrobe, she might have put a little more fabric into it when she made it."

"And chose a different color," Francine added as she wiped tears from her eyes. "And maybe something other than butterflies. Hank, would you prefer tractors or maybe sparkplugs?"

'No, no!" Inez said and threw her head back to howl with laughter, "He needs those god-awful silver nudie girls you see on the big rig mud flaps!"

"If you must know, I happen to appreciate the butterflies," Hank said and sniffed. "And I think I look perfectly lovely in pink." He dropped his arm from his chest and pulled the hem away from his thighs as he gave a quick curtsy. "Now if you ladies are finished with the fashion critique, I think I'll get dressed." Hank took the wadded clothes from Marcus's arms and tucked them under his arm. As he turned to go back into the bedroom, he called out over his shoulder, "Oh, ladies?" Then he reached back and lifted the hem of the robe, flashing the seat of his boxer briefs at Marcus, Skeet, and the women.

"Oh, my lord." Priscilla groaned and ducked her eyes behind her hands. As the other women hooted and hollered, Annie began to play a bawdy bump and grind tune.

"Miss Annie," Skeet said as he sat beside her on the piano bench and swatted her shoulder, "cut that out. Don't encourage them."

Annie's shoulders shook as she giggled and pounded away on the keys.

Hank turned around in the hallway to face the women. "So that's what you old perverts want?" He shot an evil grin at Marcus and wiggled his eyebrows. He dropped the clothes, grabbed the ends of the robe's belt, and twirled them. He began walking back into the kitchen, bumping his hips in time with the tune Annie played. When he reached the women, he began to shimmy his shoulders and seductively untie the robe.

"Hank, cut that out," Marcus said through his laughter.

"Like what you see, ladies?" Hank asked as he slid one shoulder of the robe down to flash a bit of his skin at the women. "Well, there's more where that came from!" He turned his back to the women and swiveled his hips.

The women continued hooting and clapping. "Take it off, baby! Take it off!" Francine yelled as Inez whistled loudly. Helen leaned against the counter with tears rolling down her cheeks as she laughed. Priscilla slid her fingers apart just enough to peek through and watch Hank dance.

Marcus's sides began to ache from his laughter and he braced himself on the counter. He took in the scene before him.

Inez clapped along to the bawdy rhythm of the song.

You make fabulous wherever you are.

Francine pulled a dollar out of her bra and shook it at Hank.

Because you burn the biscuits once, that doesn't mean you don't eat them again.

Priscilla finally dropped her hands and joined in with the other women's laughter.

The greatest of these is love.

Helen opened her purse and fumbled around in the pockets until she pulled out her phone, quickly snapping pictures of Inez dancing beside the nearly naked Hank.

That boy needs love. He needs a home.

Marcus looked at the letter from the cooking school on the counter. He grabbed it and folded it back into thirds.

Is that what you want to cook? The diner food has more of your heart in it.

Marcus looked from the letter to Hank dancing across the room with the Do-Nothings gathered around him clapping, laughing, and dancing to the tune Annie cranked out of the piano. Skeet hopped up from the bench, took his grandmother in his arms and twirled her around as he roared with laughter.

When you don't fit in with the family God gave you, you go make your own.

Hank caught Marcus's attention as he spun around in the middle of the group of women. With a quick bump of his hips in Marcus's direction, he winked and smiled broadly. He motioned for Marcus to come join the dance and then blew him a kiss across the room. Marcus pretended to catch the kiss but shook his head to refuse the invitation to dance.

I'm just a guy who wants to dance with you.

Marcus's smile faded and he turned to slip out of the front door. He wandered into the yard and listened to the sounds of music and laughter pouring out of the front door. He raised his face to the sky, closed his eyes, and let the morning sun warm his face. The trees behind the house rustled as a summery breeze drifted through them. Marcus could hear his mother's voice in their whispers.

Read the signs, baby. Read the signs.

Marcus lowered his head and opened his eyes. In front of him was the For Sale sign Skeet had stuck into the ground the previous day; the golden garland around its edges sparkled in the warm breeze and sunshine. Marcus walked to the sign and read it again. "If you lived here, you'd be home!"

Marcus glanced at the letter from the cooking school before crumbling it and shoving it into the pocket of his sweat pants. He grabbed the edges of the sign and pulled it out of the ground. As he walked back to the house, he tossed the sign into the azalea bushes by the front door. He paused with his hand on the handle of the screen door to listen to the group singing along to a song Annie played.

Marcus took a deep breath and pulled the screen door open.

Baby, it's time to settle down.

SPECIAL TODAY

The End

Acknowledgments

THIS BOOK IS ABOUT FINDING family and would not exist without the members of my many families.

To them I give my eternal love and thanks.

My IP family: Candy, Annie, Choi, Nicki. Thanks for letting me do this a second time and guiding me all the way.

My IP Dames: Stoney, Heidi, and Knits. Thanks for listening to me talk and talk and talk about this book until it made sense and had an ending.

My IP sister: Carrie. Thanks for being my bestest reader, cheerleader and Nutter Butter eater. You never fail to remind me how to giggle.

My Brewer family: Daddy and Mama. Thanks for teaching me the joys of telling a story and the importance of home. My sister, my brother, and their families. Thanks for encouraging and supporting my dreams and for telling me so many stories.

My Georgia boys: Scott, Nalo, Scott. Thanks for keeping me grounded and getting me out of the damn house.

And most of all, my home and heart, Fabrice. Thank you for teaching me that a very happy family can be just two old farts and a dog. I love you.

About the Author

KILLIAN B. BREWER LIVES IN his life-long home of Georgia with his partner and their dog. He has written poetry and short fiction since he was knee-high to a grasshopper. Brewer earned a BA in English and does not use this degree in his job in the banking industry. He has a love of greasy diner food that borders on obsessive. *Lunch with the Do-Nothings at the Tammy Dinette* is his second novel. His first novel, *The Rules of Ever After*, is available from Duet Books, an imprint of Interlude Press.

One **story**
can change **everything.**

@interlude**press**

Twitter | Facebook | Instagram | Pinterest | Tumblr

For a reader's guide to **Lunch with the Do-Nothings at the**
Tammy Dinette *and book club prompts,*
please visit interludepress.com.

also from
interlude press™

The Rules of Ever After by Killian B. Brewer

Published by Duet, the young adult imprint of Interlude Press

The royal rules have governed the kingdoms of Clarameer for centuries, but princes Phillip and Daniel know that these rules don't apply to them. In a quest to find their own Happily Ever After, they encounter meddlesome fairies, an ambitious stepmother, disgruntled princesses and vengeful kings as they learn about life, love, friendship and family—and learn to write their own rules of ever after.

"The humorous, satirical tone is reminiscent of Jean Ferris and Gerald Morris." —*Kirkus Reviews*

ISBN (print) 978-1-941530-35-1 | (eBook) 978-1-941530-42-9

Idlewild by Jude Sierra

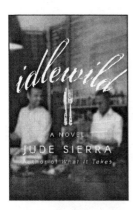

Set against the backdrop of Detroit's revival, Idlewild is a love story between Asher, a widower who tries to bring the gastro pub he started with his late husband back to life, and Tyler, the pre-med college graduate he hires to help him.

ISBN (print) 978-1-945053-07-8 | (eBook) 978-1-945053-08-5

Chef's Table by Lynn Charles

Chef Evan Stanford steadily climbed New York City's culinary ladder, earning himself the Rising Star James Beard award and an executive chef position at an acclaimed restaurant. Patrick Sullivan is contented keeping the memory of his grandmother's Irish cooking alive through the food he prepares in a Brooklyn diner. The two men begin a journey through their culinary histories, falling into an easy friendship. Can they tap into that secret recipe of great love, great food and transcendent joy?

ISBN (print) 978-1-941530-17-7 | (eBook) 978-1-941530-20-7

CPSIA information can be obtained
at www.ICGtesting.com
Printed in the USA
LVOW11s0410050917
547547LV00002B/159/P